LOBOTOMY

The drill was switched on and moved slowly forward on the track. He could hear its high whine like a mosquito trapped on his eardrum. The point of the bit was an inch, a half inch, a quarter inch from his temple. He could not bear to look. He shut his eyes, but compulsively opened them the next instant. He felt nothing but winced, seeing a spurt of blood when the bit punctured his skin.

From the sterilizer the nurse brought a long steel straw on a towel. It was more than a simple tube; within it were tiny knives. As the surgeon prepared to insert the dreadful device through the hole in his temple he began to strain against his bindings and to make strangled sounds in his throat, and his face became burstingly red.

Then the surgeon was inserting the device. The steel straw was deep into his brain. Still the surgeon thrust deeper and deeper. . . .

STUART FRIEDMAN

Maniac

LEISURE BOOKS ❧ NEW YORK CITY

A LEISURE BOOK

Published by

Dorchester Publishing Co., Inc.
6 East 39th Street
New York, NY 10016

Copyright©1987 by Stuart Friedman

Printed in the United States of America

As always . . .
For my wife, Jeanette

1

The view from the fourteenth floor was an undifferentiated gray gloom with no horizon, clouds blurring together with dim expanses of snow-covered fields. He turned away from the rain-streaked window and left the room. He sensed himself as following some obscure path through shadows, his step like air on air leaving no imprint, as if he did not exist. But the fantasy was fleeting. His grasp on the here-and-now reality was firm.

He knew where he was, in the creamily lighted little hall leading to the back of the apartment. He was walking on a gray carpet, the flocked wallpaper was silver and gray, he was wearing robe, pajamas, slippers, and he was alone. But at the same time he was dominated by the feeling that he was in another, longer, wider hall with green concrete walls, the floor covered with shiny dark green linoleum, the light a bloodless blue-white fluorescence, and he was barefoot in dirty white ducks, his arms were imprisoned in the tied sleeves of a rough canvas straitjacket, and he was flanked by two burly orderlies.

There was a sensation inside his upper abdomen like a suddenly clenched fist that interfered with his breathing when he reached the end of the hall. Beyond the closed door, he knew, was not a cell but a sanctuary, his wife's studio. He could not bring himself to open the door.

He knew what ailed him. She was leaving on the Spring Tour with the orchestra in the morning. He was letting himself get emotional about it, thinking of it as going away with her own world of music. At best he existed only at the periphery of that world.

He felt shaky. He was worn out, scraped raw with the accumulated fatigue of tax time and 12-hour days at the big accounting office where he worked. He'd got home late, spoiling their last evening together before the tour. Then he'd failed to pick up her lovemaking signal. He hadn't slept 15 minutes at a stretch since, in spite of sleeping pills.

He went back to the bedroom, sick with loneliness, and entered quietly.

For a while the darkness seemed absolute, a timeless void. But then the luminous dial of the bedside clock emerged, glowing, and the delicate scent of lotions and powders and perfumes and of Pam's sweet body filled the emptiness, and faint window light seeped in through the drapes and he saw himself, a grayish contour in her dresser mirror. He noticed a partially opened bureau drawer and had an image of her in a charmingly careless rush. He went to the drawer to close it properly. Instead he glided his hand in and fondled a voluptuous heap of what he knew was a rainbow assortment of panties. He smiled, imagining her putting them on, taking them off.

He gazed over at her lying there, so still, so beautiful, and wanted her passionately!

His smile froze. He saw in the mirror—he did not remember doing it—that his arms were crossed over his chest, his hands clasping his upper sides tightly. Immobolized in an imaginary straitjacket! He freed his arms. But he could see in the mirror that they remained in that straitjacketed position. There was a disconnection between the decision to free himself and the actuality. He could move his arms only in imagination. It was some sort of hysterical paralysis. It infuriated him. He was in a condition of fierce lust by then. The struggle to free himself built up such pressure that he thought his head would burst open.

Something worse happened: he saw the faces of four dead girls.

He got out of that dark bedroom. He stood in the bright kitchen trembling, his broad face ashen, his deep-set dark eyes staring, his head splitting.

He poured and drank a double shot of vodka, neat.

He lit a smoke. There was no remnant of lust in his cold groin. Fondling those panties and thinking about their many colors was what opened up horrors he'd thought were buried forever.

There had been white panties and lavender panties and yellow panties knotted around the throats of those tortured-raped-murdered girls out there in California. None of the panties had been pink, as the newspapers had reported. Knowingly or not, the papers and wire services had cooperated with the official version that the panties were pink. The trick had been meant to trap the innocent, to eliminate mentally unbalanced punishment seekers who would read about the sensational case and confess.

He had confessed.

It seemed incredible from this distance. Beyond his comprehension. As impossible for him to believe as . . . his thought line fragmented . . . as . . . it would be for Pam.

She'd probably never heard of that sensational case.

There was no way she could ever have come to love Paul Borland, whose name was inextricably linked to such sordidly brutal sex crimes.

Of course she had no idea she was married to Paul Borland.

And she *wasn't*. Paul Borland no longer *existed*.

My God, if he thought that creature was still alive in him down there under his new legal name and was even remotely a threat to Pam, he would . . . he would. . . . His eyes suddenly burned with tears.

He shook his head, frowning. He mustn't get emotional. He was already under too much stress.

He had to hold tight. And *think!* Beginning with plain facts.

It was true, a matter of official record, that Paul Borland had, of his own volition, turned himself in and confessed.

He had been unanchored; a San Francisco State College dropout. At that time he saw himself as a dedicated seeker and searcher for truth and justice and identity. For some weeks there had been wide publicity about the case. Whomever he talked to on the road or in Haight-Ashbury pads or in the communes where he often stopped off for enriching philosophical discussions and experimentation with heightened altered states of consciousness there was always talk about those dead girls, who, while not part of the counterculture itself, had aspired to lives of simplicity and honesty and wanted only peace and love. Their deaths were always deplored, and as some of the brothers and sisters were fond of saying, those deaths diminished their own lives.

But as often as not the true feeling of loss would become subordinated to the total experience of the drugs and become only a part of the trip, if it was LSD or psylocybin or mescal, or part of the kick of the speed if they were popping Meth.

He remembered one night around a campfire on Russian River when everyone was sipping wine and smoking marijuana. The torture-rape-murder deaths had come up. The mood had been relaxed and happy and filled with that universal sense of oneness they all tried to achieve.

"Sadism," Paul had said suddenly. "That's what this is. Sadism. Feeling high and happy and full of pleasure while we talk about that horror."

"Oh, no," one of the girls said in a dreamy, blissful voice. "You're uptight, Paul."

"We're not suffering but relishing it."

"Poor Paul. You acidheads all have bummers. And beauty turns ugly."

"I had Thorazine yesterday and no acid since. My head's straight. *This* is the bad trip, the whole sickening bunch of you getting a higher high out of what happened to those girls. Enjoying the pain they went through. Sadism, that's what it is for all the bullshit about love love love!"

"He's horny. Hasn't had any . . . Stell, why don't you get him off his uptight—"

"Yeah, yeah, Stell . . . he's uptight. Vietnam draft breathing down his neck and no college to save him now he's dropped out. He wants to make love, not war."

"Yeah! Yeah!"

There were giggles and guffaws and agreement that all he needed was love and Stell came and stood in front of him and swished her hips and laughed and got hold of his beard and pulled. He slapped her hand and held his nose.

"You stink."

She laughed and slid a filthy foot to his crotch and wriggled her toes. He got up and walked away, glowering. She followed him out to the edge of the firelight and skinned her jeans and gummy-crotched panties down from her naked ass and lay down and stretched her forked legs up and spanned his hips. He started to twist her ankle but instead shrugged and mounted her.

But immediately afterward he walked off without a word and kept going, brooding, alone. From then on he kept on the move all over the state, working when he had to, thinking long long thoughts about himself, about authenticity, rejecting the hypocrisies of pot-heads, acidheads, pill poppers, and love spouters as well as the fraudulence of straight society.

For months there was no development, no sign of finding the monster or monsters who had killed those girls. He became compulsive about the case. He couldn't get it off his mind. He began to wonder if he was titillating himself with it. If so he was little better than an accomplice after the fact of sadistic murders. If there was anything more than hypocrisy to his own aimless, nowhere-going life beyond the negative of dropping out, he must do something positive to prove his authenticity. Otherwise he was fully as callous and narrowly selfish in pursuing his own vague ends as the most unfeeling, inhuman of the Establishment types.

It gradually grew on him that guilt was as universal as love should be. He decided that it was a cop-out to assign specific guilt to any one person, who was only, after all, a creature conditioned since infancy and imprisoned in his identity and helpless to break free of society's prison. The selfish, heartless values of the society were the causes of all crime, and as a universalist, theoretically affected by every man's death, he had a duty to give meaning to those girls' deaths, not merely to mourn them and take pious pleasure in the feeling of mourning. No—he must do something authentic, something purposeful, to wipe out the ugly guilt of all, by sacrificing himself.

He could not imagine such emotional excess now. But at that time, at that time, in that state of mind, there had finally seemed to be no other possibility than confession.

He went to the front room. It was chilly. But he felt needling sensations like prickly heat and started sweating as if it were summer in his body.

It had been summer—Indian summer—in

that town in the Sierra foothills where he turned himself in.

There was a shoeless, braless girl in tight-assed jeans and a loose half-buttoned cotton shirt, showing breasts too full for her slight body. Her long dark hair looked too heavy, as if it was pulling her small head back so that her face tilted upward toward him. He didn't know if she was pretty or not but there was a passionate intensity about her young face that held his gaze. Her mouth was thrust out succulently, inviting, or more, *demanding* a kiss. She seemed to be in a trance of lust that finally overwhelmed her. When he was within a few paces of her, she came directly at him. What that kissable mouth did was spit in his face.

The officer on his right pushed her away. Too hard. She stumbled and would have fallen except hands from the crowd caught her. She began to spew out a rage of curses and obscenities in a knife-edged shriek that agitated the angry gathering of townspeople out there in the street. There had been some mutterings and guttural curses before, but no disorder; now the crowd became menacing.

Several officers, state, county, local, moved into a circle around him and a bullhorn voice warned everyone to stand back and a siren on one of the police cars started up full blast. One lanky wild-eyed drunk broke through and aimed a roundhouse swing at his head that missed. There had been no guns visible but men surged forward from the rear of the crowd with shotguns, rifles. A few men were shouting for order; others were bellowing threats and shoving and jostling. Word got around that he had kicked the girl and that the police had punched her.

A second loud siren was started, and all the while the spinning and blinking roof lights of official cars were adding a sense of nightmarish confusion.

The weekly paper had come out the day before with a splash-headlined front page editorial calling for a return to the forty-niner spirit of mining camp vigilante justice. All that day hell-for-leather young drunks raced up and down the main street in trucks and jalopies shouting threats at the city hall-jail building, some of them brandishing hang ropes. While the lynch-mob atmosphere built, the officials planned to spirit him out to a jail down in Stockton. It was carefully timed. The hysteria had begun to ebb and the town seemed to have calmed and gone to bed and there was nobody on the streets. But the timing of the plan had been leaked, and minutes before the state and county reinforcements arrived, a mob had gathered and packed around the front of the jail.

The police had trouble getting him to the car. He was thrust sprawling into the backseat of a state vehicle. He sat there frozen, arms handcuffed behind him, the spit on his cheek running into his beard. The officers, who despised him, were being forced to fight for him. It took a long time, a long, long time, before the threat of violence subsided. The shouting voices lowered and calmed. Citizens and officials and police spoke man to man about the mockery of laws that protected killers instead of their victims. Bottles were passed around and they looked in at him and came to a fundamental agreement that it was a sick society, an insane society, that did not kill its killers.

In his case there was no question of his guilt. He had confessed, in detail, to the rapes and murders of four lovely, decent young women.

One outraged voice declared loudly, "And goddamn if he won't get out of it on some fuckin' bleeding-heart civil rights technicality!"

"Yeah, Christ, or by playing crazy!"

"Shit! Crazy like a fox!"

He had been taken to Stockton that night, but transferred to Sacramento next day because the crimes had been committed on state property.

A week or so later the *Sacramento Bee* ran a feature story with two pictures of Paul Borland. One was captioned, *Crazy like a fox?* the other, *Crazy as a loon?* He looked frenzied in the "loon" picture, long-haired, bearded, and with white expanses of eyeballs showing because he'd been looking to one side. In the "fox" picture he was clean shaven, his hair was cut and neatly combed, and he not only looked composed but seemed to be grinning slyly.

When that second picture was taken, he had just come out of a court hearing with a bailiff, two jail guards, and his lawyer. The corridor ahead was blocked by a pack of local and out-of-town reporters and photographers. He stood mashing his lips together so hard that one corner of his mouth indented, giving that sly-grin look. Actually he'd been close to rage against his court-apponted lawyer, who had just told him, "Keep your mouth shut, Borland. Pearls don't drop from your lips. Every word you say is like a cyanide pellet plunking into that acid vat at Quentin. You figure they don't use that gas chamber these days? They could make an exception for you."

The lawyer, Charles De Groot, not much older than he was, had a radical activist background at Berkeley. He was abrasive and ambitious, and he and the reporters baited each other. The lawyer proceeded to turn the case into a political sideshow, calling the police sadistic pigs who had tortured a confession out of Paul, symbollically castrated him by cutting off his hair, terrorized and intimidated him into silence. And why? Because, De Groot speechified, Paul Borland was the voice of youth and of protest against the corruption of a murderous imperialist society. Not content with driving him out of college, the Establishment harassed him for seeking joy and a higher consciousness through drugs and because he preached love instead of hate. It was because Paul Borland wanted liberation instead of enslavement for mankind that they were making him a victim.

A woman reporter jeered, "He's the victim? Not the dead girls?"

"That's an inflammatory question, indicating the prejudiced approach of the press in this community."

"You'll seek a change of venue?"

"Obviously, a fair trial here in the bastion of repressive government would be impossible."

"Why did he turn himself in when they weren't even looking for him?"

"Why did Jesus Christ—the first hippie, gentlemen, remember that—why did Jesus Christ submit himself to his persecutors?"

"He's Jesus? You plan an insanity plea?"

"Our strategy can only be determined after psychiatric examination."

"Mr. De Groot, is it true that there were many discrepancies between his version of what happened and the known facts?"

"True. Which is sufficient to invalidate the confession, which, in any case, is inadmissible in court."

"Specifically, Counsellor, your client did not know that the panties found around the throats of three of the girls were not pink."

"He had nothing whatsoever to do with any of those deaths. As I have been telling you, it's a conspiracy, an attempt at a legal lynching, and the people will rise up against this monstrous injustice!"

"You going to whistle up a demonstration?

Start a riot here at the capital against the administration over this rape-murder case? Word's out that you'll be busing in some radicals from Berkeley."

"I know nothing of inflammatory rumors of that sort. You may quote me as saying I would deplore violence but would do nothing to stifle the voice of the people in any spontaneous uprising."

"Spontaneous? You'd call a timed, organized, orchestrated gathering spontaneous?"

"Next question. We haven't got all day."

"Wouldn't you think the combined conspiracy creators could come up with a less sloppy confession? Why didn't they 'torture and intimidate' him, as you put it, into confessing accurately? Getting the colors of the pairs of panties right, for instance."

"De Groot, how come his lie detector test results show he was telling the truth? In other words, even if he was wrong on facts, he himself believed what he was saying?"

"Please, one question at a time. Polygraph testing is inadmissible as evidence."

"Is that an answer? Anyway, from such testing they can follow leads he gives them. If it's confirmed that he actually did as he says, barring a few slipups and discrepancies, it would mean he confessed because he was guilty. Also if he's not guilty but the lie detector shows he's telling the truth as he believes it to be, he is either insane or a pathological liar. . . . Which are you, Borland? Are you muzzled? How about free speech for the client, De Groot?"

"Paul Borland's interests are best represented and protected by counsel. We've exhausted the time and patience of the guards. No more comments or questions at present."

"Or maybe he's not a loony or a pathological liar but crazy like a fox, eh, counselor? And he knew very well he was making errors in the confession and that those errors would ruin the case against him and he'd be acquitted. That would suggest a lot of cold-blooded planning by a murderer smart enough to outfox everybody. . . . His San Francisco State grades were in the top tenth percentile. He's got an IQ of one forty-six. He'd be smart enough to know that the state investigators *did* have some clues that would eventually have led to him. He could've anticipated that they'd nab him. Maybe he hoped he could put across an insanity plea, or else, if indicted and brought to trial, the case would fall apart because of mistakes in his so-called confession."

Another reporter, following them, called, "It's true, isn't it, that investigators from the Attorney General's office were dubious about his guilt. And after carefully reading his confession and interrogating him about discrepancies, they wanted to boot his tail out of jail, considering him just one more confession-prone kook, the type that shows up after all major crimes? Counselor, why didn't you let them boot his tail out of jail?"

The reporters, with two questioners in the lead, kept following them toward the elevator. De Groot spun around to face them, bristling indignantly.

"Why? Why would I prevent them from callously throwing a sick man out in the streets, penniless? Why? A man who needs psychiatric examination and possibly treatment?"

"Yeah, why? There are clinics. Hospitals. Maybe you want to use the courtroom as a soapbox for your own political ideas."

"I will not demean myself or jeopardize the interests of my client by responding to insinuations at that level. Guards, these people are harassing the prisoner!"

Before they could get on the elevator a belligerent reporter demanded, "Borland, it's true, isn't it, that you yourself made an official request, in writing, for a barber to shave your beard and trim your hair?"

"Yes."

"I didn't know that." De Groot glared at him, then at the reporter. "He was coerced into making that request."

"Were you?"

"No."

"What *could* he say? He has to go back into the custody of the very people who had him under the gun."

"If the hair cutting was a symbolic castration, it was by your own hand."

"I didn't think of it that way. I wanted to be rid of a wrong image, a hippie image, a drug-cult image. I want to look like what I am. Of sound mind. It would *not* be to the advantage of police and prosecution to cut my hair."

"You admit it wouldn't."

"Yes," Borland answered in a droning, toneless voice. "Bearded and long-haired, I'm the image of the counterculture, an avowed enemy of the Establishment, capable of any crime. Short-haired, I look more respectable and harmless."

"I told him," De Groot said, lifting both hands, palms up, "that every word he said was a cyanide pellet dropping into the sulphuric acid in the gas chamber. I told him!"

"You seem to have a good grasp of things, Borland."

"I have. I want to prove that I am competent. Sane."

"What he's proving is he's not," De Groot said.

"Obviously you and your lawyer don't see eye to eye. Why are you rejecting his efforts to help you? Back there in the court you got out of order and attempted to enter a guilty plea. Are you going to fire De Groot?"

"I didn't hire him. It's a judicial farce. Why should I be forced to accept help to get me out of the position I have, of my own will, assumed?"

"You mean you're guilty and want to pay for your crimes?"

"Yes."

"A guilty plea is almost never accepted in a capital case. You must have known that. And you know it now. So all this *mea culpa* stuff could be mere rhetoric."

"No. I'm sincere."

"Suicidal sincerity might well characterize my client," De Groot put in with a nasty laugh.

"Borland, you admit you're conscious of 'image'. You've cast off the loony-hippie image like a snake skin. Maybe right now, creating the new image, you're being very cute. Pretending you don't want to plead not guilty."

"Cute? Pretending?"

"Yes, cute and, yes, pretending. You know damned well they won't let you plead guilty. Meantime, the *mea culpa* stuff can soften up the public attitude toward you. Or even cuter, it can look like you *must* be crazy if you don't try to save your own skin."

Another reporter shouted, red-faced; "I've covered a lot of killers, Borland. They all try to save their own skins. Are you telling us that this conscientious image you're trying to sell, this practically Jesus-y idea of accepting suffering . . . are you trying to square all that with the character who committed rapes and murders? Not one, not two, not three, but four. And in at least one instance, the youngest, tenderest child deliberately and lengthily tortured. She was burned, she was cut, she was hacked. She was, over a period of *hours*, possibly *days*, subjected to unimaginable agony and not permitted to die. . . ."

"Get me away from them, De Groot," Borland pleaded hoarsely.

"What don't you want to hear? What can't you stand to hear, Borland? My voice? Or *her* voice. Sadism and masochism go together. Do you want to suffer now and get your masochistic kicks too? Is that it, eh? Is that it?"

He felt himself being roughed up, not by the reporters but by the guards, the bailiff, and De Groot, rushing him into the elevator.

The girl who'd spat in his face followed him like Nemesis to three different cities in California. She'd been at hearings and always looked at him with that same disturbing intensity, seeming to be lusting and demanding a kiss, but hating him. She'd have liked to spit in his face again if she got the chance. Once, just once, his last week in California, she almost got close enough to him and the lawyer then representing him. What she did was hiss venomously, "Crazy like a fox! You vicious—" He couldn't remember all the things she'd called him. Hearing her, a cynical reporter grinned at him lopsidedly.

"Hey, Borland. Do you agree with the young lady's feelings about you? To be consistent, you should."

"She is misguided in thinking I am 'crazy like a fox.' I did not cunningly plot to get out of punishment. But it is entirely just for her to revile me. Because I am guilty."

"You're consistent. Crazy as a loon."

The encounter had been just after it was settled that he would not stand trial.

But nobody had wanted to set him free. There had been surly accusations, even by a couple of psychiatrists that he was in some ways worse than the actual rapist-torturer-murderer. His trying to confess to something he hadn't done amounted to a protection of the actual killer. Paul Borland was unofficially accused of identifying with a monster like that, idealizing him, in a sense. To imagine committing such a crime meant he would like to commit it, and untreated, he remained a potential mass murderer.

His lawyer, a low-profile type who didn't make waves—not the noisy surface kind—knew that the prosecutor was doubtful he could get a conviction and didn't want to risk a big, splashy public failure in court. It was arranged for Paul Borland to enter a new federal mental rehabilitation program and he had been moved quietly to Shaunautaukee in this state.

"Spirited out of California" was how some people had seen it all. That girl, for one, had been bitter about his escaping punishment.

2

His first doctor at Shaunautaukee, Dr. J. Maurice Hillman, had been an authority on fantasy. He'd written his doctoral thesis, two learned books, and eleven papers for professional journals on the subject. With two other doctors he'd obtained a multimillion-dollar grant to establish a federal mental health rehabilitation program. The program had been set up within the existing facilities of Shaunautaukee State Hospital. The resident administrators and staff didn't want it, looking on the experimental program as alien and, although small, as deadly as cancer.

The three "hippie" doctors got only minimal professional courtesy and no cooperation. Their "zoo" of kinky patients were under constant suspicion, and routine privileges were granted only after nitpicking petty delays calculated to frustrate them and push them over the edge into a "disturbed state."

But the outside pressures made rapport between doctors and patients in the program easier. The outnumbered doctors needed successes. Paul Borland got the feel of the situation the first week he was there and expected to walk out a free man within two months. Especially since Dr. Hillman took a personal interest in him; he'd subscribed to a clipping service and had a bulging file of news and magazine articles concerning the California case.

Their first session had been upbeat.

"For the time, Paul, I want you simply to exist. Acclimate yourself to this pleasant environment. Do not flagellate yourself because your fantasy life led you into a wilderness. Together, Paul, we will return from that wilderness, strengthened, healthy, and you will be free, in every sense."

"I thank you, Dr. Hillman, but—"

"Maury. No titles, status symbols, or false labels such as schizophrenia, dementia praecox, manic depressive, psychosis. Agreed?"

"Yes. And I thank you, Maury, but it will not be possible for me to be free. As you know, I am a mur—"

"As I do *not* know, Paul." He stood up, offered his plump hand to shake and said warmly, "We'll talk again tomorrow."

Maury gave him one of his published articles

on fantasy to read the next day. And day after day he had him read a monograph or a chapter out of one of his books. Paul never commented, never admitted the possibility that he had fantasied those killings.

During the seventh week, Paul Borland decided the time had come to yield a little. He had gone to Maury's office, a high-ceilinged third-floor corner room overlooking a pleasantly contoured explanse of rolling lawns, with the background of a little woods in the distance, beyond the high iron pales of the fence. The place had been the country retreat of a railroad-banking-lumber tycoon, who'd made a gift of it in his senility when he could no longer enjoy his private Eden . . . and got a good tax break on the gift besides. Maury had told him that history in a buddy-buddy-we-the-oppressed-against-the-exploiters way. Maury also told him the happy news that the grant for the program had been renewed for two years.

"Good morning, Paul. Come breathe with me the sparkling wine of this summery sunlit morning."

"Good morning, D—Maury." He crossed, stood uncomfortably beside him.

"Ah, that quick recovery after you almost called me doctor." Maury laughed. "Tell me, Paul, where will you sit today? In the authority chair behind the desk?"

"No equality games today, thank you."

"Games, Paul? What's this somber cast? Aren't you happy? What more could we ask for? These landscaped grounds far from the maddening crowd. Comfortable living quarters. Excellent food, games, movies, TV, health spa!"

Maury patted his shoulder and gave him a kittenish look, his fat, bearded cheeks crowding his eyes. Paul averted his face and stepped away, remembering a session in the sauna. Maury had whacked his behind playfully and commented about his fine dong. Paul ignored it, but thought it over and knew it had to stop. That would be all he needed, to have a fairy, a girl hater, befriending a girl killer and working to set him free.

"When are we going to get down to business, Maury?"

"We're in *rapport*, Paul. Close, productive rapport. We have been moving forward at all times." He plumped down in the swivel chair behind his desk and turned and rocked and gave him an injured look. "I've let you read my works on fantasy."

Paul sat across from him, put a cigarette in his mouth. Patients weren't allowed matches. Maury's lighting it for him was routine, probably.

"This is fantasy. You and me, pretending we're equals."

"We are. If anything, it is I who serve you. That's my job. To serve your health needs. Cure your predilection to fantasy."

"We're equally free to drive out the gate any damned time we please."

"Patience. Once you have come to accept the

necessary reality about certain past events . . .

"Well, maybe it was fantasy."

"Killing those girls?" Maury alerted, sat forward, watched him. "You're ready to acknowledge that at least *maybe* it was?"

"Everybody has fantasies. Your books make that clear. Some get too big, and maybe—"

"*Not* maybe. I can *prove* it to you if you're ready."

"I'm ready to get out of this damned tranquilized jungle."

"This what? Tranquilized jungle?"

"Right from that window you can see that's what it is. The scrub growths and weeds and trees would jump the fence and take over the whole place if they didn't have a crew of gardeners always making it look pretty."

"Well, by God, Paul, that's perceptive. And by God, *true*. And you elaborate it, don't you, as an allegory, as a commentary on the human condition, these tamed grounds representing the civilized pretensions of mankind. And in reality, how flimsy, how flimsy. . . . The wilderness is always there, the greater natural primitive force . . . and just so the primitive unconscious id lies in wait to overpower the small, relatively weak conscious mind. Yes, Paul, yes, you are capable of acute, perceptive observations. You're *ready*. To think, analyze, burst the unreal fantasy about those girls, those poor sad girls. I feel for them. I understand so well how deeply you felt for them."

Damned if tears didn't come in the guy's eyes.

"It was their pain and your hypersensitivity which drove you to that foolish gesture, that confession."

"No. I *did* it. I'm damned. I sinned. The fact that I am able to come up with intelligent thoughts makes it all the more just, because I am *aware* of my evil."

"Don't get into *shit* like that vast abstraction, *evil.*"

"Shit? I'm disgusted to hear you say that word. It's sure as hell not *Doctor* Hillman talking . . . and it's not '*Mory,*' the 'we are poor little lambs who have lost our way baa baa baa' Mory using a word like that."

Maury aimed a sausage forefinger at him, pushed his scruffily bearded chin out and dropped his voice an octave. "Don't mock me, Borland! If I sang that Whiffenpoof Song and bleated around in a certain mood, it was half a joke because there *is* a Maury in the song. It was all to try to diminish myself, to keep rapport with you. And the *shit* is part of *your* language, so this continues the rapport. You bounced around in institutions and foster homes through your teens and were a shit-spouting bastard in many ways, although bright. I rouse contempt, evidently, because there's a touch of the bisexual in me, yes, and in you and every man, for that matter, but by God if you need an *authority* figure, I'm fully capable of turning the screws. To begin with we'll try a few Rorschachs."

"Inkblots!" Paul sneered.

"Yes, inkblots and a lot of other standardized tests, too. Session ended. Report promptly nine A.M. tomorrow."

The next day and the next and next it was inkblots and word associations and rising aggravation and frustration for Maury. Wednesday of the next week, he said tonelessly, unsmiling.

"Sit there. Address me as Dr. Hillman."

"Yes, Dr. Hillman."

"None of that condescending tone. Borland, I'm not going to be the instrument that lets you walk out of here and, for all I know, commit rape or worse."

"Now your real opinion comes out!"

"It's survival time. I've seen what happened to colleagues who put too much faith in unstructured, liberalized therapy. One of them, just last month, right out there in your own stamping grounds, let a sex degenerate go. What did the bastard do but go to the park out by Fleishhacker Zoo and put a little girl on a picnic table and rape her in broad daylight in front of her little brother. We'll work with some inkblots. You will *not* cunningly tell me that all you can see in them is the obvious symmetry. As if all you can perceive is *harmony* and *love*. I won't put up with that kind of resistance from now on."

"Resistance?"

"Resistance. It's false, totally false, that you

only see nice harmonious things. Hell, your love-and-drugs hippie cults were far from harmonious and hate-free. They were shot through with viciousness. And violence. In some cases the only thing that held them together was a hate for the whole world outside their own circle. As you damned well know."

Things had begun to deteriorate, slowly at first. Paul had still refused to see anything but harmonies and symmetries in the inkblots. And on word-association tests his responses constantly lagged and he thought over carefully every word before saying it. But the worst was how, point by point, Dr. Hillman made him concede discrepancies between his murder confession and what had actually happened.

He would have had to sound like a moron to deny that the facts made his confession read like fantasy. The doctor, and both his colleagues, had obtained official police reports of all the details of what the killer had actually done, and they had reconstructed step by step, each of the killings in sequence, with irrefutable evidence.

To a degree, the hostile atmosphere of the doctors of the larger institution had penetrated the experimental program. Loose, unstructured, undisciplined sessions were subtly tightened. Cooperation was *required*. Subtle threats were made. They kept hammering all the ugly factual details of the brutal crimes at him to show him the falseness of his confession. He'd retreated more and more, feeling these friends had become enemies. Or if they were still friends, they were more conscious of the power of *their* enemies and were beginning to conform to the older ways of therapy . . . including chemotherapy.

He was tranquilized. That didn't work because it left his mind sluggish, fuzzy. Without drugs he couldn't stand the battering, or the accusations about why he had falsified a confession that could, from a sane viewpoint, be viewed only as protecting the killer.

They ripped to pieces his quasi-religious explanations. They were merely trying to force him to understand that he had limitations, that he could not by any symbolical act wipe out evil.

"Patients used to think they were God or Napoleon. In your heart you thought you were Jesus, didn't you?"

"No. I don't know. I admit it had to be fantasy. A religious one. Leave me alone, God damn it! If you ram anything more down my throat I'm going to bust your teeth out."

That earned him a chemical straitjacket and banishment; expulsion from Eden to a back ward.

When he was allowed back, he tried to be docile and cooperative, remembering the penalties. But they started the same stuff. He became disturbed, aggressive . . . well, violent, too. More than once. Subject to rages.

The chemical straitjackets were abandoned

in favor of actual ones.

He lost ground. Months and months passed, and then over a year. The pattern of disturbance and violence and back wards then slowly starting over again threatened to go on forever. He thought he would never be free. Then he became sure, because a shattering thing happened. Maury transferred out of the program, out of Shaunautaukee, to a bigger job.

And politics among the rest of the staff won out. Paul Borland was transferred into state, not federal, jurisdiction. The old guard doctors had always considered him crazy like a fox. His disturbed states became chronic and in his growing mood of hopelessness he was more and more violent.

Threats began to be made. About a lobotomy.

The chill horror of that possibility was supposed to scare him into docility. Instead, he was outraged, and he hurled threats and got into senseless, futile fights and attacked one of the doctors.

And then, one morning, they came for him. . . .

He struggled all the way down the corridor of the Isolation Ward.

He fought against going through the doorway into the stark little operating room.

He tried to lunge out of that dreaded black chair. It was useless. The orderlies snapped steel cuffs around his ankles and tightened the leather straps around his chest and lower body.

God damn them all to *hell!* This brain-murdering operation was *illegal!* They wouldn't *dare!*

They dared.

The threat that had been hanging like doom over his head was being carried out. It was hopeless.

Suddenly there was hope. Somebody was coming along the corridor in a hurry. Word must have got to the front office and the administrator had sent someone to stop it.

It was a woman's step. Light and quick. Its rhythm affected him like an exciting pulse in his own body. The muffled sound faded to the very edge of silence as if she had taken off her shoes.

Abruptly she was there! His eyes shone with joy and filmed over.

She stood there in the doorway, a radiance. Light suffused the loose fullness of her long blond hair, forming an aura around her face. She was wearing a floor-length yellow satin robe that shone like summer morning sunlight. Her eyes, wide-set and full of childlike wonder and innocence, were the deep vivid blue of mountain wildflowers and her mouth was tender and pink, and there was a dreamlike perfection about her delicately balanced top-heavy oval face that made his chest ache.

She began to fade and disintegrate and then she vanished entirely and with her his last desperate fantasy.

He made a strangled sound in his throat, thinking no, he could not bear to lose her. He thought no no no no and then the word burst out aloud:

"*No!*"

"Shut up!" the nastier of the two orderlies snapped. "Sit still!"

He stared sickly at the nurse supervising the preparation for the grisly procedure. She stepped toward him, tested the straps binding his shoulders. She moved a lever, turned an adjustment wheel slightly, her gaze focused expressionlessly on his head.

In minutes his head was immobilized by padded steel clamps so he could not move it up or down or to the sides or forward or back. The nurse went to a sterilizer, then to a shelf inset in the wall and on to a table with stacked gowns, caps, robes, towels, sheets. She came and fitted him with a draping sheet and painted his head with antiseptic and went away without ever really looking at him.

A swing door opened. His glance slid toward the surgeon entering. The man, a broad-faced, squat figure in ducks and T-shirt came over and peered at him from several angles. Their glances met directly for one ice-cold moment.

Then the surgeon was getting into gown and gloves and the nurse tied on his mask for him.

Directly ahead of the chair were glass doors enclosing wall shelves arrayed with basins, bottles, pads, gleaming surgical instruments. He was dimly reflected in the glass. But close by was the portable sterilizer with mirror-smooth stainless-steel sides where he could see himself sharply. The left side of his shaved head was the color of diluted blood from the antiseptic. His arms were stretched out to the sides and strapped to sectional extensions of the chair in a position of crucifixion.

"Oh, my God, why hast thou forsaken me!" he said in a hoarse passionate voice.

Both the doctor and the nurse looked at him facelessly, eyes frowing above pale green masks. One of the orderlies came close, muttering, and pinched his nose shut and rammed a thick black rubber gag in his mouth.

A shroud was floating toward him. Superficially, his eyes told him that it was actually the canvas dome over the top of a tall wheeled cart being pushed slowly by the other orderly. But in its deeper meaning that canvas was a shroud. It concealed death, the murder weapon with which they were going to kill his brain.

The cart rolled past the front of the chair, turned and stopped beside it. The surgeon came over and supervised the positioning of the cart, and its suction-cup feet were lowered, securing it to the floor. The canvas was removed. He could see the drill.

A long electrical cord was unlooped and plugged into an outlet. There was a brief, rising whine of sound as the drill was tested, switched off. The nurse opened the sterilizer, brought out a tiny steel bit with tongs, placed it on a folded towel.

His gaze cornered to the left. He couldn't see what was going on out there at his side. He stared ahead at the gleaming side of the sterilizer, which mirrored everything. The drill and the bit looked like a miniature swordfish pointing at his left temple. The nurse was brushing at his temple with a gauze pad. The surgeon seemed to be marking an area of the skin there. He did not feel any of it; the local anesthetic numbed the whole left side of his head and neck.

He was not to have a general anesthetic, "for medical reasons." The real reason was punitive. They wanted him fully aware of what was happening to him. He was sure the positioning of that sterilizer had been calculated.

The drill was mounted on tracks on a carriage supported by an adjustable mechanism which moved up and down and to the sides and forward. The surgeon concentrated on lining up the target, peering and squinting and turning little wheels fractions of an inch.

The drill was switched on and moved slowly forward on the track. He could hear its high whine like a mosquito trapped on his eardrum. The point of the bit was an inch, a half inch, a quarter inch from his temple. He could not bear to look. He shut his eyes, but compulsively opened them the next instant. He felt nothing but he winced, seeing a spurt of blood when the bit punctured his skin.

He was still waiting for the horror of

knowing that the thin bone of his temple was being pierced when it was done, the mosquito whine stopped. The drill carriage backed off. The surgeon pressed a gauze pad to his head. The orderlies crouched, worked at the feet of the cart, and wheeled it away.

From the sterilizer the nurse brought a long steel straw on a towel. It was more than a simple tube; within it were tiny knives. As the surgeon prepared to insert the dreadful device through the hole in his temple he began to squirm and to strain at his bindings and to make strangled sounds in his throat, and his face became burstingly red. The nurse began dabbing some gauze below his nose and he knew he must have snorted snot onto his upper lip.

Then the surgeon was inserting the device. For a few seconds . . . or, he didn't know how long . . . he blacked out. He came back to the agony of consciousness to hear the surgeon warn him coldly to quit trying to move. The steel straw was deep into his brain. The surgeon thrust deeper and deeper. The tube was so long that he began to watch in horror for it to come out the other side of his head, afraid the surgeon might ram right on through the temple bone over there.

When the lobotomy was over and the bandage was on the wound, the gag was removed from his mouth and they began to unstrap him. He began to shout a garble of desperate words, wanting to die. For a little while the surgeon, his mask off, came and stared down at him with loathing. Finally the man said quietly, "Shut up! Just shut up and quit disgusting me. What entitles *you* to anyone's sympathies? Get him into a strait-jacket and out of my sight!"

Almost at once they were bringing the strait-jacket, a coarse, canvas affair with endless sleeves and long dirty white binding tapes attached to the closed cuffs. He stared at it, seething with rage, his eyes bulging. He was still imprisoned in the chair, legs strapped, ankles in steel cuffs, one arm bound to the arm extension. They could force his free arm into a sleeve without much trouble. Struggle would be useless; the more he fought, the worse he would get hurt. He knew that resistance under circumstances like this would be stupid. Worse, it would be the reaction of a mindless, dangerous wild animal, and would prove that he was just what they believed he was.

But the closer they came with that jacket, the more fiercely he hated them. His rage intensified and burst through his control and the world became a red smear before his eyes.

He did not know what had happened or whether it was night or day when he found himself standing alone in a silent, empty gray place tied in the straitjacket, his arms in the sleeves crossed over his chest, hands pulled back tight to his sides. He became aware of pain in his arms and jaw and skull and then he smelled something sickening and felt a cold, unpleasant sensation in the area of his groin and he knew he'd been put into short, tight rubber pants, which he'd loaded with his own filth like an infant.

Abruptly, there was a flood of light. It came with explosive speed. It rocked his senses. They settled slowly.

After a while he grasped the simple fact that a door from a lighted hallway had opened. What he could not cope with was the beautiful golden fantasy princess.

She had vanished but she was back, gazing at him, her eyes rounded. She came toward him, reaching out. He could see her forearm, bare and intimate in the shadowy sleeve, and he thought of the rest of her warm young body, naked under the yellow satin robe. His glance dropped. He glimpsed her bare foot, then her slim swinging leg flashed through the opening of the robe, showing her soft inner thigh.

He felt a twinge of sexual sensation. His eyes glittered. His face flushed. His breathing quickened. His desire for her intensified. He wanted so passionately to rip free and embrace her that the muscles of his straitjacketed arms tensed, his imprisoned fingers twitched against his ribs, and he twisted from side to side. The fever swept his whole body. he had a full, fierce, throbbing erection that was pure ecstacy and agony at the same time and then . . . then . . .

He became nauseated. The fever of his manhood chilled against the load of cold stinking

filth in his rubber pants. He felt loathesome
and wanted to back away. It was too late. She
was coming. There was no trace of revulsion on
her exquisite face. In her presence, he realized,
he was unaware of his own stink. It must be
that she purified the very atmosphere. A clean
floral scent, a fresh lily-of-the-valley fragrance
seemed to emanate from her. She came toward
him slowly, on lovely bare feet, moving with
the floating grace of pure spirit.

She paused, balancing on the balls of her
feet.

She said something in a hushed, caressing
voice.

Her beauty was a simple delusion, he knew,
and he could understand imagining the sweet
smell of her to offset his unbearable shameful
stench. Her caressing voice was more alarm-
ing, a fuller hallucination than he had ever had.
She had never before said words. In his fantasies she was music, sometimes a singer of
wordless songs, crooning softly in the night.
At other times he had sensed poetry, flowing
silently through her mind:

A loaf of bread, a jug of wine,
And thou beside me singing in the
wilderness . . .

Oh God! A minute with her was more precious than a thousand drab years of sane
reality! His throat ached to answer her.

It was insidious. He must not let himself be

trapped into speaking to her. There might be eavesdroppers outside the door, maybe even microphones in the padding on the walls of the cell. Reports would be made that he had begun talking to himself. She came another step and stopped.

Again she said something. A blurred string of indistinct words. They seemed to be making their way through heavy interference as he imagined a voice would sound over a trans-atlantic phone. He couldn't make out what she was saying. She came closer and began to hiss . . . or whisper. There was an urgency about her. He was not sure but he thought she was trying to shake him. He stood like a rock, so that she was the one who moved; she was so small against him, so insubstantial, so unreal. She stood there, very close, waiting, staring.

"*Say* something!" she said. Distinctly.

He remained silent, grimly resisting her almost irresistible force.

At last she walked away. He was relieved. Next, she had turned on an overhead light and was coming back to him. A terrible doubt assailed him. This might be a trick. They could have sent an actual temptress as a test. If he failed to perceive her, it would prove he was out of contact with reality.

She was back again and speaking in a thin, urgent voice so fast he again couldn't make out any words . . . except one.

"Joe . . ." then a blur of rushed words, then, "Joe . . ."

Or was it Joel? *Joel?* Who could she imagine he was if she was real, and she must be to be able to speak.

She gazed up at him, her lips apart, and drew a breath that lifted her chest and showed the gentle contours of her breasts under the yellow satin robe. Her vivid mountain-wildflower-blue eyes were rounded and shining and so stunningly beautiful that he felt weak. She began to blink. She licked her lips.

She started talking again, her thin, clear girlish voice high and sweet and a little desperate.

She took a deep breath and talked some more. Her voice broke. Her lips began to quiver. Her eyes brimmed. The poignant sound of her voice and the pitiful-child look on her face pierced him.

"*Joel!* You *do* know me. *Please.* I'm Pam. Pam. Speak to me, sweetheart. You're scaring me!"

She was real!

"Pam!" he cried out hoarsely.

His wife! He thought *Joel, Joel, Joel* and *Pam, Pam, Pam,* holding on to his identity and to her identity while his gaze clung desperately to her beloved face. He did not dare look away or even blink for fear of losing her. The sight of tears in Pam's beautiful eyes made him want to cry. Pam was so good. That very goodness made her innocent of evil, and she had walked into this trap. Omigod, she must get out of this terrible place before it was too late for her, too.

His alarm was acute. His glance skipped nervously past her and to the right and to the left, alert for signs of danger. He saw nobody threatening, nothing menacing. He saw little of anything. Outside Pam's immediate radiance there was a vague, murky twilight which extended much farther than the cell walls, somehow.

Alarm gave way to confusion. The room was expanding, the murkiness dissolving, his senses clearing like a lens coming into focus. He frowned down at himself. His arms crossed over his chest were in the sleeves of a patterned dark blue dressing gown with pearl gray cuffs. His feet were in black house slippers on a pale gray carpet. His pajamas were a silvery color. He shifted his stance slightly and there was no binding sensation of rubber pants around his legs or waist, and he was not carrying a filthy load. He was dry and clean.

Suddenly the lens of his senses adjusted perfectly and he saw the room in its full, true dimensions, its familiar details sharply defined by the overhead lights.

He peered around at the semicircle of four chairs with empty music racks in front of them; at the upright piano with Pam's practice violin, bow, and rosin on top; at the desk in the corner, the window drapes, the shelves of records, the record player hooked up to the stereo system through the rest of the apartment, the special tape recorder-player. And close to his elbow were the two metal cabinets which contained the special music filing system he himself had created for her.

He was here, in this converted bedroom which was Pam's studio and the heart of their world. He was not back there. It was *now*, not eight years ago. He ripped his arms free of the imaginary straitjacket and Pam came to him in a rush and he embraced her tightly and she hugged him fiercely and cried against his shoulder.

He caressed and kissed her and spoke love words and attempted to reassure her. She was loving. He suddenly remembered she was going on tour with the symphony orchestra tomorrow and anxiety swept him.

She stepped back away from him. She had to go. To the bathroom, she said.

Loss of physical contact with her chilled him slightly. He knew it was foolish. He held on to her visually. She moved slowly backward on soundless bare feet, cautiously, somehow a vague anxiety on her face. She never took her eyes off him. She seemed to be receding, like— the thought froze him—like a fantasy beginning to fade out of existence.

But no, no; that could not be. There was no doubt about Pam's reality. He must be the one slipping backward even though he seemed to be rooted to the carpet. He knew he was again in danger of losing contact with the immediate here-and-now reality. An overpowering fright gripped him when Pam reached the doorway, turned, and vanished into the hall.

The expanded room began to shrink and dim and he thought he was returning to the padded cell in Shaunautaukee. More horrible, he was suddenly positive that *he had never left the hospital.* Everything, his meeting her, courting her for three years, finally getting her to marry him and live with him, everything, all facts and details of their life together, the dream-come-true life together, had never happened at all, and he had never got out of Shaunautaukee and never would.

For God's sake, he had to get hold of himself. He couldn't be in Shaunautaukee or Pam would have called him Paul. Even if he could have fantasied the new name, R. G. Hempstead, Inc. couldn't. They made out his paychecks to Joel Danton . . . and his driver's license . . .

He alerted. She was coming back. She was wearing mules that slapped her heels. The nervous rhythm of her too-quick step told him she was still overstimulated. Scared.

She'd never seen him in such a state. How could she have? He'd never been in such a state! He didn't know how he could have got out of control like that.

He thought he had beaten those damned brain-murderers. Destroyed brain tissue was gone forever, but somehow new connections to the frontal lobe had been made and gradually the damaged areas were bypassed. New circuits had formed; complex functions were taken over by other parts of the brain. He had proved that his mind was not permanently crippled, hadn't he? Yes. He'd functioned well, very well in all areas, with growing tolerance for stress. But now. . . . ?

He mustn't panic. It would cause her more anxiety. Ironically, she had come to depend on his hard-won control, his stability, his strength. Everything was shaking now. If there was an unexciting drab plodder quality about him as against her shimmering artistic spirit, so be it. He wanted nothing better from life. To be a scary disruptive force, never! He must meet her needs, prove his worthiness to worship . . .

Worship? No, wait, no, he had to resist that dangerously unrealistic emotional state of mind. She was not his fantasy, repeat, *not* the shimmeringly beautiful golden princess who dwelt in a high tower where night shall be filled with music, but *Pam* . . .

She was here. She had freshened her face and was routinely working lotion into her hands. Across the crown of her lovely head was one of the dark blue velvet bands she wore onstage in performances to hold back her hair and show her exquisitely honed young profile. She came into the studio smiling, a picture of casual composure. A picture painted on thin glass. Darkly, behind that picture, was her knowledge that he'd been a patient in Shau nautaukee. His overcoming the ordeal of a mental illness was the only part she had wanted or needed to know about. But now? He saw the strain of her smile. He felt the vulner-ability of her exposed delicate pink ears and pale neck.

He must lie. Claim he'd been asleep, sleep-walking, which was why he'd *seemed* not to know her. He knew he could convince her, reassure her that nothing beyond fatigue and overwork was involved. Worry about him could upset her so badly she'd be unable to go on the tour.

Alarmingly, the atmosphere of Shaunautau-kee began to dominate his senses. The sinuous grace of her hands writhing together did not seem to be merely the familiar application of lotion but somehow a primitive wringing of the hands in helpless despair like silent screaming.

Something must have shown in his expression. Pam's smile flattened. Her hands became tense, motionless.

He remembered starting to say but not saying, *Don't be afraid. I love you.*

3

Joel woke to the sweetish odor of funeral flowers and wondered where he was and how long he had slept.

He sat up. He was in Pam's bed. The floral scent, he realized groggily, was from her pillow. It seemed to be night. He got out of bed and made his way cautiously through the empty apartment.

He entered the little back hall with no clear memory of anything that had happened since he had been in the studio with Pam and had intended to say but for some reason had not said, *Don't be afraid. I love you.*

He stood outside the closed studio door for the longest time, thinking nothing, absolutely nothing.

At last he opened the door. He held his breath, switched on the lights, and went in.

It was all right.

Throughout his showering, shaving, dressing, and finally leaving the unbearable emptiness of the apartment without her, Joel felt grim.

The reality was that they had come out of the studio around dawn, too late for her to get back to sleep. She had made breakfast and kept talking cheerily and not eating much and not making much fuss about his not eating much. Maybe she'd just been "handling" him so she could get away safely. She had gone on her tour, and he had gone to work. At the office they told him to go home and sleep in a bed. Which he had done.

He could account for feeling that Pam was dead on the basis of infantile fears. To a kid, absence was the same as death. But if he had not *known* after he was fully awake that he had not killed her, his mental condition was worse than last night when he hadn't recognized her.

He rode down in the elevator, went out, and got in his car. Physically, at least, he was rested. And hungry. For breakfast. Whenever a man got up was breakfast time. He disentangled himself from the maze of streets in the apartment complex and was soon on the Interstate.

He could not decide between two restaurants he had in mind. Either would do. Just so he got a hearty breakfast.

There was one place he definitely could not get breakfast at this time of evening. The

Central State University cafeteria. Without quite realizing it he found himself on University Boulevard, which curved through the wilderness of a rugged, hilly, wooded state park to the main entrance of CSU. Driving under the archway onto the campus he knew he hadn't had the slightest intention of coming here. It was a little unnerving, something outside his own will and control, in a way.

No, he thought in annoyance, this wasn't anything like that. The opposite, in fact. Because this was where he had met Pam. The loving, healing instinct in him was what had unconsciously brought him here to the beginning of all the goodness in his life. The strength of the meaning of this place, and his appreciation of it, had been greater than mere belly hunger. He should be proud of himself. And he was, he was.

The grounds of the university were almost continuous with the several square miles of the state park. It was a pretty campus, spread out comfortably over a hundred or so acres of smoothly rolling land cut through by a meandering creek and handsomely balanced with the many buildings and stands of old trees, bare at this season except for the row of evergreens flanking the central walk. He opened his window and coasted along slowly, trying to absorb the atmosphere. There was a minimum of roads and auto traffic. A network of walks connected the several colleges. The pattern of lights from old-fashioned carriage lamps along the walks and on the little footbridge over the creek showed occasional students walking or bicycling, alone, in pairs, or in small groups. Now and then voices rang out, clear, clean sounds etched on the quietness, and once, laughing shouts burst from a group throwing snowballs on the white slope behind the chapel.

He parked on the paved lot at the west end of the Commons. He gazed with an obscure, not entirely pleasant, nostalgia toward the lights inside a city bus waiting down there at the east end of the Commons. When he'd been a summer school student taking courses two nights a week in tax law and advanced accounting procedures he had come to the campus directly from work by bus, transferring downtown, to have his meal here before class. He'd get here about this time of evening. In the summer at this hour it was always daylight, and usually sunny. Walking across campus in his business suit past students playing or lounging on the fields and lawns and strolling the walks and flirting in clusters around the library and dorms, he remembered feeling unassimilated. He had thought of himself as a figure on the scene but no real living part of it, and of the girls, the girls, the innumerable girls as belonging to a remote closed world, forever inaccessible.

Cooking odors flavored the air around the solid, squarish four-story stone Administration Building as Joel moved along the central walk. Warm light from the large, steamy

ground floor windows of the basement
cafeteria spread across the snow-patched lawn
beside him. A gust of wind swayed the evergreens, and powdery snow from the branches
blew into his face and sifted, wet and chilly,
under his collar.

But soon he was inside the building and
going down the half flight of open stairs in the
cafeteria, where it was as warm as summer. It
was fairly crowded and surging with lively
voice sound. On his way to the serving line he
saw at least a dozen bright pretty faces. He
wasn't tempted to let his glance linger on any
of them. Since most of them were semishape-
less bundles of winter clothes, there was no
problem. In the summer, he remembered, their
bared bodies and tantalizing young figures had
made it harder. The pun was unintentional, but
true.

He had not allowed himself to be directly
stimulated and he never stared. But at times
he couldn't help seeing. And although he would
force his glance to scurry away immediately,
there had been one thing he couldn't shut out.
The feminine sound of their voices. He had
coped by listening as much as possible to the
sounds drifting out over the campus from the
College of Music, where students in practice
rooms and at lessons in studios struggled to
master their arts. By concentrating on the sex-
lessness of the work and study connected with
formal music, he had been able to neutralize
the exciting natural music of girls' voices and

. . . and . . .

The memory troubled him. It confused his motives. Moving along the serving line and looking vaguely at the salads, he realized there was a serious distortion to his recollection of that summer. He looked uncertainly at the soups, passed on to the entrees and studied them, thinking frowningly that it was as if he had not really listened to the sounds from the music school for their own sake, but merely as a distraction to combat lust. He moved along past cakes, pies, cobblers, puddings and realized he had nothing but napkin and silver on his tray.

"Tsk tsk!" The scrubbed-faced little cashier grinned and shook her head in teasing disapproval while she was ringing up his cherry cobbler, strawberry pie, and coffee.

He was baffled, then looked at his tray and chuckled.

"I guess it's not too scientific a balance."

She gave him change and laughed.

"That's always been my secret dream. Nothing but desserts."

Joel scanned the tables and spotted an empty space at the end of a six-seater along the wall opposite the entrance. He got settled at that table. It was not far from the exact place he'd been sitting when he'd first glimpsed Pam.

He creamed the cobbler and took a luscious bite and thought back to that summer, that special summer, and knew the *real* reason he had listened to sounds from the music school. He understood it clearly now—belatedly, yes, but truly—from this perspective four years later. It was because he had been particularly sensitive to and sympathetic with music students. Because, in a sense they, as students, were in a state of preexistence as artists, not yet arrived and touched with their art's magic. Just so he himself had been in a state of pre-existence before magic . . . Pam . . . had brought him to life, higher life. Thus, he reasoned, there had been an instinctive understanding of and identification with the music students.

Yes, Joel assured himself, that was how he had actually perceived things. There had been nothing carnal or low about his awareness. The more he thought about it, the more fully the real truth emerged. By the time he finished both desserts, his memory was as pleasant and satisfying as the sweet taste in his mouth.

He went for a coffee refill and lit a cigarette. He sat comfortably, sipping and smoking and remembering those cross-campus walks of his from the bus stop to the cafeteria here. He had felt a definite spirituality, an embracing of the whole intangible atmosphere of culture. Unless a strong wind was blowing toward the music school or its windows were closed against rain, the sounds accompanied him every step of the way. He had enjoyed them not only for their own sake but as evidence of learning and of striving toward higher goals. The different fragments had had no relationship to each other, with perhaps a vocalist singing one song while pianists, violinists, and horn players played other pieces all at the same time in a kind of shapeless pleasant cacophony. There were times when one instrument dominated, or played alone. Often it was a violin, an advanced student. On special occasions the frail and poignant sound of Pam's lone violin reached him like a distant unearthly voice singing sweetly in the wilderness.

The exquisite beauty had been so uniquely and totally and unmistakably the essence of Pam that he recognized her the first time he saw her, simply from having heard her. That seemed impossible. He hadn't known Pam existed, much less that she was a violinist. Even if he had been aware of such exquisite violin music, it was not truth to say he had recognized her physically just from having heard her play. It was better than truth. It was poetry.

He smiled. He amused himself with a better-than-truth poetic fantasy about his first glimpse of Pam: Until that special instant she had been invisible, bodiless, existing only as pure music. *Then* at the moment of magic the sound waves were converted to flesh and she materialized.

"Grow up!" he muttered half aloud.

The "moment of magic" had been nothing like that.

He remembered how she had suddenly

appeared, a petite figure within the high wide frame of the open doorway from the building corridor, and had stepped out onto the broad-railed landing at the top of the stairs.

A scowling, lumpy girl in a transparent rain hood was over there now, stomping slush off her galoshes. And crushing the whole gossamer delicacy of the mood of that magic moment, he thought exasperatedly. He should get out of here. But damned if he was going to let the force of drabness stop him from reex-periencing the joy, the *ecstasy*, of that precious first glimpse of Pam. He tried again.

She had stepped out onto that railed landing into a brightness that touched the right side of her shimmeringly beautiful golden head like firelight.

Brightness touched the right side of her head like firelight?

How could that be? Something was wrong with that image. He frowned and chain-lit a new cigarette from one not half smoked. Then he had it. What was wrong was the time of year. Of course.

It has been summer. The corridor had been dim because the solid outside doors had been closed. In here the big windows had been wide open with no blinds. There had been a sunset like a cosmic bonfire and its light had flooded this mundane basement cafeteria with a trans-forming brilliance. Coming from dimmer light into vivid brightness, Pam's beauty had hit like shock.

His left temple began to itch. He grimly prevented himself from scratching.

Abruptly he remembered Halfway House and some of Dr. Dornstadter's advice.

"Even the sweetest memories are like the smell of flowers. When they're fresh, spontaneous, fine. After a while they begin to stink like funeral flowers a week later. You in particular can't handle them."

The hell I can't!

That magic moment was a life force to him. A nourishment his ego needed. No matter how labored and even painful it was to try to break through, he was going to recreate it. True, the present conditions were wrong. It was not summer but an unpleasant schizophrenic season neither winter nor spring but both with alternating snow and rain. And the light now, artificial and imprisoned in bulbs and tubes, was not only wrong but deceptive, glossing the inner surfaces of the closed windows to conceal the reality of the darkness outside.

An unwelcome comparison came to mind. The shine on the inside of the closed windows which concealed a darkness beyond was somehow disturbingly similar to something. To Pam's vivid brightness. That blinding beauty was like a screen that concealed . . . He broke off that line of thought resolutely and put the ugly comparison out of mind. It came bursting back up into consciousness.

The itch from the lobotomy became maddening. His whole mind and will focused on resisting the temptation to begin scratching, digging it raw. He was totally absorbed with that problem so that he couldn't think of anything else or remember. . . .

In *spite* of himself he *knew* what had happened out there in the dimness of the corridor. *Before* Pam had appeared, stunningly beautiful, on the landing, rousing him to ecstasy, he had seen something that roused dread. A wispy, pale figure. It had seemed to emerge out of nothingness, materializing vaguely out there in that dark corridor. His guts had hollowed. he had thought the figure was not real, but hallucination, and that either his fantasy girl from Shaunautaukee had come back, or . . . or worse, someone else. The young, beautiful little blonde. The brutally raped and tortured dead girl from California. The one called Virgie.

A moment after Virgie appeared on the landing a second girl came and stood beside her. A girl with long straight black hair and bangs who looked exactly like another of those dead girls. The one called Cleo.

Cleo and Virgie stood there together at the railing in the light of the cosmic bonfire sunset and peered out across the cafeteria in his direction. He quickly concealed his face by lowering his head and staring blindly at the open textbook on the table beside his iced tea. Then without attracting notice by moving his head, he angled his gaze slightly upward and watched them from under his brows.

They were still there in the firelight. Their gazes focused in his direction and they did not move. It was as if they were holding their breath. Listening. He held his breath and remained silent, not moving a muscle except for the involuntary muscles of his heart. It was bang-bang-*banging*. His blood was rushing so fast he could hear it in his ears like surf or the wind through heavy foliage, and so much oxygen was being consumed that he *had* to have air. He took cautious shallow breaths silently through his open lips.

His concentration on Virgie and Cleo was total. Other people and voices slipped to the edge of his consciousness and vanished as if swallowed, and a massive narrowing circle of darkness closed in, held back only by the soft weak waves of yellowish firelight from a campfire.

Alone. The girls were alone, peering out into the impenetrable darkness. Listening. Listening for intrusive noises like brittle twigs snapping underfoot. Wanting to hear only the natural wilderness sounds, and hearing only the soothing soughing of the wind through the forest treetops. He waited, silent. He watched. Their pretty legs were bare in shorts, their breasts softly contoured in halters. Their faces were immobile. Though the waves of firelight gave the appearance of animation and shifting expressions, the only expression was fear which, like their defenselessness, gave their beauty an extra dimension of excitement.

Their lips were apart. They blinked now and then several times in succession. Mostly they stared roundly.

Finally, though, the tension seemed to ease out of them.

Cleo said, "It was just an animal or something. Don't you think?"

"Uh-huh, yes. I think. Don't you?"

"All I think is it's nerves because Judy and Marabelle haven't got back. They'll show up. They're big girls. Marabelle especially."

They suddenly broke into giggles and almost collapsed in each others' arms. Then Virgie said, "That's not nice! When she's so sweet. She can't help being so fat."

"I know, I know. I ought to be ashamed. You should be more ashamed for giving her candy the way you do."

"I ought to. But she just gets so unhappy I feel so sorry for her. I'd do anything to help her keep from getting back on those amphetamines that dirty hippie got her hooked on," Virgie said. "A little candy helps her over things temporarily. She tries so hard. Wears herself out hiking and swimming and . . . oh, gee, I'd give *anything* to see her sweet little old fat face this very *minute*. Wouldn't you?"

"Oh, *would* I. But, honeysweet, look, don't start worrying again. We both know nothing bad could happen. These state parks are carefully patrolled. You know that. Let's wait just a little while longer before—"

"Sir, the cafeteria's closing now."

The words, while enunciated clearly, made no sense in this remote setting.

The fairly loud voice was certainly a man's but there was no man in sight, and he hadn't heard anyone approach. No one could have got through the tangle of thicket and bramble and brush and vines and woods surrounding this campsite without making a noise. The voice came out of the blue, with nothing leading up to it that might account for it. The one clear path from which someone could have approached was fifty feet away, the little dock at the lake frontage was double that distance, but the voice was quite close by.

Most astonishing was the nonreaction of both girls. They were scared that someone was lurking and prowling around. Their two friends were long overdue back from a wildflower-gathering expedition in the lush meadow above the far end of the lake. They had begun to sense that they would never see them again and they were teetering at the brink of hysteria and were hyperalert to threatening sounds. They would have had to be dead not to hear the voice, but neither one of them paid the slightest attention to it.

Maybe. . . . He had the farcical idea that since the voice was addressing a "sir," it had nothing to do with them and they were politely ignoring it, keeping their distance from a matter that did not concern them. And in fact, though he didn't recall their moving, they did seem to have withdrawn to a little distance.

Quite a little distance.

He pulled them closer with the binoculars and watched them taking the sun . . . the *sun?* Had they escaped to yesterday? He held them with the binoculars for a long time, for a long, long time, all four of them in various shifting poses in different degrees of nudity, ranging from the fat girl Porky's almost complete coverage to Virgie's and Cleo's total exposure.

There came one of those innocently wanton situations when Virgie rolled onto her belly while Cleo rolled onto her back and extended one leg and drew the other knee up. Judy, the pinch-faced neuter, wearing only a crotch patch and a bra to hide the nothingness of her chest, poured suntan lotion on Virgie's round, pink, pertly upthrust bottom and then anointed Cleo's butterscotchy-tanned belly. His slow lazy lusting pleasure became rushed and as intense as rage and he was in no condition to see properly. He lowered the binoculars. And instead of delicious bodies in distant miniature there was, abruptly, inches away from him, a mustached, full-sized frowning face. Below the face was a uniform and his heart leaped in his throat and he thought *mother-fucking pig son-of-a-bitch, the goddamned fuzz, a park cop—*

The mustache-mouth was moving saying, "Sir, the cafeteria's closing now."

"M'm," Joel said.

"Are you all right, sir?"

"All right? Yes. I'm all right."

"Well, then, if you're sure you're feeling all right, it's past our closing time," another voice said.

It was, he saw a stumpy woman with a plastic nameplate:

MRS. HALFERZ
MANAGER

She was standing by the pig, whose metal badge showed the letters CSU and the words CAMPUS SECURITY PATROL.

Unmistakably he was in a big cafeteria on some campus. Workers were scraping dishes, loading carts, wiping tables, stacking trays, cleaning the steam table down at the serving line. No one was at any of the tables eating, not a soul.

The blonde was gone. Maybe he'd been spaced out on something but his head was together enough to *know* she had just been here ... dazzling ... beautiful. ... Just minutes ago she'd been right over there on that landing at the top of the stairs with another g—. But no, she'd appeared alone, like a star on a stage, alone, resplendent in the light of a cosmic-bonfire sunset. No trace of the sunset remained. He looked at his watch, frowned. Nine-nineteen. Mrs. Halferz, Manager, and CSU CAMPUS SECURITY PATROL were watching him closely.

"It *is* late, isn't it? I'm sorry to hold everybody up. I'll go as soon as—" He was going to say "as soon as I finish my iced tea." Apparently they had removed the glass. His textbook and notebook were gone too. He didn't want to carp, just get out of there. He reached down, got his hat from the shelf under his chair seat, stood up too fast, and wobbled.

"Don't feel rushed," the woman said. "Are you dizzy?"

"I'm fine."

The campus cop said, "We couldn't decide whether to call the doctor. That red place there on the side of your head. . . . You didn't slip and fall and hit your head that you remember?"

He touched his left temple briefly. *Slip?* On ice? "No. I didn't fall."

He started walking away. Steadily.

"You seem to have your balance just fine. It could've been a little concussion that caught up with you if you'd fallen . . . you sure you didn't?"

"Absolutely. Thanks anyway."

"It wouldn't take long to see the doctor in our infirmary. Be glad to go with you. Just to be on the safe side."

"What caught up with me was 'Nam. One of those Oriental fevers. I keep forgetting the name of it. It's recurrent. Never bothers me unless I drive myself too hard, get too fatigued. Fact is I'm due for a checkup at the vets' hospital tomorrow afternoon."

"Fine. You ought to. 'Night."

"'Night."

He was almost to the steps when the man

called, "Wait!"

He thought omigod, he'd given way to an impulsive ad lib. It was a matter of official record that he hadn't been in the service in Vietnam. He was unknown at any vets' hospital. If he was on the campus where he thought he was, Dr. Dornstadter from Halfway House was a regular lecturer in psychology at this university. The doctor sometimes ate in the cafeteria and would know the manager and the security patrolman and most likely had pointed him out to them. The private fuzz *knew* his Shaunautaukee background, and *knew* he was lying about the vets' hospital and 'Nam, and probably suspected he was on dope.

"Wait. You forgot your overcoat."

Overcoat? In summer? He must mean topcoat. In San Francisco he wore one in summer, when he had one. But definitely this campus cafeteria was not San Francisco State.

The campus cop brought a coat and, what's more, held it for him and helped him into it and then smiled an obscure smile.

The man did not obviously trail him into the corridor and on out the door. He had routine outside duties. Also he could seem to be watching out for him in the event he stumbled or showed any indication of needing a doctor.

At the central walk he admitted to himself that he was disoriented and must be presenting an almost classic picture of confusion. He first went a few steps to the right in the direction of the bus stop. He stopped, felt a ringload of keys in the overcoat pocket and looked blankly at the snow on the ground. He turned and walked back the opposite direction. He stopped at a lamppost, inspected the keys, saw the miniature car license tag, then resumed walking toward a parking lot. He looked behind him and the security patrolman was following. The next time he looked back, the man was gone. But soon enough the patrol car came creeping past.

Winter, somehow, it sure as hell was winter, he thought in the parking lot. He matched the numbers on the tag and the actual license plate on a white Pontiac. When he drove out of the lot, he simply followed a road, and sure enough the patrol car, which had been standing by, started up and kept on his tail.

If this wasn't summer, when and where was it? He was smooth-shaven. He had had a full beard the time he had worked at a ski lodge in the Sierras and . . . his mouth watered, remembering the joy of eating in big-appetite ski-country restaurants. Steak-eggs-potatoes-blueberry muffins. One time he ate that kind of breakfast at Lake Tahoe and walked out into the casino and beat a blackjack dealer and a roulette wheel for fifty-odd bucks and put it all on a single number that paid 35-to-1 . . . or would have, if. He got a new stake with some binoculars in a Reno hockshop, where on a whimsical impulse, he gave the right name of the owner. It hadn't been smart; impulses never were. It gave them a tiny thread to follow, because he *had* known the owner of those binoculars. A wholesome type had turned up who thought he'd seen a hippie with binoculars in the state park a day or so before bodies had been found. A vague description. Useless as testimony. Even if the fellow had gotten a close look and could have identified "the hippie," it wouldn't have linked the binocular carrier to any crime.

The campus cop's car was still hanging on. By a thread. He shouldn't get uptight, but stay loose. Threads were all anybody had had. Short, weak threads that didn't tie together or even start to prove anything beyond reasonable doubt. No one alive had seen anything. All the rest was, at best, circumstantial, mostly based on hearsay that was inadmissible in court.

True, along with thousands, he had been on the same San Francisco State campus at the same *time* as one or another of all those girls. But he'd shared no classes or cultural or social or political events. There was no evidence he had ever been in the same place at the same time with any of them. Marabelle, alias Porky, was no exception. His contacts with her had been mere transactions, but careful. No one, ever, had seen them together. She was the closest to a threat, which was ironic, because pity had led him to possible danger. She had needed help to reduce. Luckily he had been very cautious so no connection with her could be proved. She had never known his real name, nor had she moved in a crowd where anybody she might meet would be likely to know him.

As to the two beauties, sure, he knew why they were called Virgie and Cleo instead of their real names or nicknames based on their real names. Who on campus hadn't known the joke that started everybody calling them Cleo and Virgie? The joke went: Question: Who were the three sexiest women in history? Answer: Bridgitte Bardot. Cleopatra. And the Virgin Mary, who'd pulled God himself down to her bed.

Sultry, photogenic Cleo liked her nickname. She'd got it playing the Egyptian queen in a raunchy Drama Club skit, and afterward she always wore her glossy black hair Cleopatra style, straight to the shoulder with long bangs.

The unsophisticated little blonde, a child prodigy who'd entered college at 14, didn't understand her nickname at first. Her friends did, but tried to protect her. When they explained it was a compliment, a tribute to her obvious innocence and virginity, it had merely embarrassed her. But when a nonfriend had found an occasion to taunt her with the joke and the full meaning of her nickname, she had been deeply offended. He had heard about that confrontation in front of 30 or 40 students . . . as who hadn't?

Virgie went red in the face. She drew her twig figure up to its full five feet. She stood straight as a stick. She reproached the truth-bearer. She spoke well. With bone deep sincerity and intensity of feeling. But she looked like a baby and her words came out in a thin quavery voice that sounded comical. Somebody snickered. In no time there was a lot of laughter. She took flight, and whether or not she was crying, she was hurt. Some of the crowd were ashamed and tried to follow her and make up for it. Still, when the story spread about her sensitivity, the nickname was thrown at her more and more. An extra twist was added to the three-sexiest-women-in-history joke: She was not only the supervirgin Virgin Mary, but also a baby Bridgette, even though her lines were not full and sensual but delicate and exquisitely honed. Of course her three friends never called her Virgie. She was their pet and they tried to protect her from everything. And everyone.

He hadn't witnessed the spectacle of the students mocking Virgie. It haunted him, though. And somehow his imagination began to build on the details he had heard. Actually, if he had been in the crowd, he would have joined the laughter. He might even have hurled some scornful profanity at her while she was upholding her square religious principles. The hyena pack would have been with him, and in a sense they would all have stoned her for being so unhip as to get uptight and stand up and defend such nonchic beliefs. A guilty concept of frail innocence being cruelly mocked and destroyed began to torment him. He could visualize it mocking and wounding her until she broke down and wept and became even more beautiful and lovable. Gradually, she began to dominate his thoughts and plague his conscience. While he did not in any physical personal sense fall in love with her, he felt *love*. He wanted to declare that simple, unashamed truth. Every time he saw the golden light of her head on campus, he quickened and watched her from a distance with a trancelike lustless pleasure.

She was rarely alone. It seemed hopeless. He could never get near. One, or two, or all three of her friends maintained an almost constant vigil. If he approached from the flank, or straight on, whoever was with the innocent would steer her away. The best he could do was drift along in a group somewhere behind. Even then, those bitches—female watchdogs—would glance back every so often as if sensing him.

The time Cleo won the Professional Photographers Contest title of Miss Photogenic that sunny Sunday afternoon in Stern Grove, he had kept a low profile. Lounging on a grassy slope, then on a rear bench, then in stages he had improved his position till he was on the bench directly behind Judy and Marabelle and Virgie. They were engrossed with the swim-suited contestants onstage, whom he scarcely saw. He had absorbed Virgie with a slow, blurry, dreamlike sense of timelessness and bliss. At times he shut hs eyes and blindly inhaled the sweet flower scent of her, filling himself with her in a way. At the end, when all the girls in the contest but two had left the stage and Cleo was crowned, her three friends stood up and jumped and clapped and shouted and Virgie hopped-danced around in a complete circle and looked at him with those beautiful shiny eyes wide open, taking his image into herself even though she wasn't aware of it. The next minute Porky saw him and glared and Virgie was hurried out of reach to the stage to hug Cleo.

Another time, when Cleo had been a finalist in the Miss San Francisco State Contest, he had managed to get fairly close to Virgie. All in all the problem of isolating her had been too much. He had not been able to get rid of the obsession. It drove him crazy. That's what the love of goodness in an evil world was, crazy, crazy as a loon.

He got heavier into dope and lost patience with the irrelevancies and constrictions of study and drab classes and the imprisonment of his mind in mere learning which was unconnected to true wisdom, to higher, spiritual values, and dropped out of school and left the campus. . . .

The street had widened and the campus entrance was a block or so ahead. The headlights showing on his rearview mirror glided off the right edge, then recrossed to the left and vanished. The patrol car U-turned and moved away. He slowed at a SLOW sign and stopped at a STOP. He drove past the stone pillars and under the sign that arched across the street and stopped a few yards outside the campus. Cutting the ignition, he took out the keys and tried reading the state abbreviation on the tiny license tag. He got out of the car, walked back, and checked the actual license plate. Light fixtures set in the ground illuminated the arching entrance sign: CENTRAL STATE UNIVERSITY. A street sign nearby read: UNIVERSITY BLVD.

He returned to the car. He restarted the engine. He shifted to Drive. A moment later he nudged into Neutral and took the time to buckle into the safety harness. He put the car in motion and accelerated gradually along University Boulevard, which cut through and past the rough, rugged, thickly forested wilderness of the state park in easy curves and gentle rolls like the smooth floor of a roofless tunnel. His transition back to the here-and-now was gliding and frictionless, a happy waking from a dream into his dream-come-true reality. Now and then during the rest of the drive home Joel smiled at himself mockingly and indulged in a favorite poetic romanticism: Where he was going was not merely to the apartment, but to the high tower where dwelt the shimmeringly beautiful golden princess and where "the night shall be filled with music."

Be filled with music. It shall. The night.

The disjointed thought fragments amused him as he entered his apartment. To shatter an untouchable line of poetry, pick up the pieces, and reassemble them in a disorganized bassackwards out-of-sequence way amounted to sacrilege. He was not only unrepentant, but glad. It meant he was freer, less rigid, not afraid of playfulness. Which was mentally healthy. Physically, too, he felt vital. It was all because of the triumph. That's what this whole evening had been.

He hung his hat and coat in the hall closet and began to wander, loose and easy, through the apartment. Basking in the afterglow of the triumph.

He took a vaguely lord-of-the-manor stance in the middle of the front room and smiled with a faint sense of condescension, remembering the security patrolman and the cafeteria manager. To them, judging from outside, he must have seemed to be in a catatonic trance and "out." He had been "in." At the center of important meaning where he had recaptured and reexperienced that *moment of magic.* He'd brought it off against all odds. By concentrating with such an intensity of focus that he not only shut out mundane distractions of the present but squelched a clutter of unimportant shapeless memory fragments. He'd held to the magic moment, prolonged it. A simple question of values. He'd given his undivided attention to what was most precious to him and had deliberately chosen to disregard his immediate surroundings for the while only because they were of no consequence to him.

He smiled at himself, thinking he had succeeded in reliving that precious experience almost too well. He hadn't wanted to let go of it completely. He had let it linger in his senses for a time after walking out of the cafeteria and indulged himself by pretending it wasn't winter-spring but *that* summer when he'd met Pam.

Then with that patrol car following him, certain anxieties belonging to another time and place had skimmed through his mind, making so little impression he couldn't remember them at all.

He thought about art and how Pam and all the orchestra musicians practiced, practiced, reworking passages over and over till all the imperfections were gone. In rehearsals everyone labored to eliminate everything that might mar the mood or sound or tone of the perfection they strove for in performance. Composers, from what Pam had told him, almost never got the exact effects they wanted at first try. They reworked and reworked the music, eliminating everything that did not belong, polishing till it was the jewel they wanted.

He was no artist. But he'd succeeded in something like art. And if he hadn't created, he had *re*-created! That *moment of magic!* That glorious instant of his first glimpse of Pam! Her impact when she had appeared resplendent in the dazzling light on that landing, like a star on a stage, alone, all alone, had been pure joy, unmarred perfection. Like art.

Easter, he thought. That was the meaning of

that beautiful magic moment. Yes, Easter. A rising from the dead, a wiping out of all sins, a fresh beginning. Easter. That was *her* meaning. When she phoned after the concert tonight, he must tell her about his insight, his enlarged perception of her meaning . . . but no, that would be too heavy. It could alarm her. As if he'd relapsed and lost contact with her reality as a flesh-and-blood woman and was idealizing her dangerously.

He walked back to Pam's studio, stopped at the closed door. The player was loaded with records of the music she was performing in the Northern State University Auditorium. An overture. A piano concerto. And finally, a symphony, which, incidentally, was the work that had inspired her when she was 12 to become a classical musician. He frowned at his watch. He couldn't guess with any certainty just what part of the program the live orchestra was playing.

The timing was vital. There must be perfect synchronization so he would be listening to what she was playing at the exact moment she was playing it.

Of course, he conceded, that was never actually possible. But he liked to come close enough to feel he was maintaining at least a spiritual connection with her wherever she was. He had done that while she was on tours even before they were married. Then, as now when she was 250 miles away, he wanted to feel the vaguely mystical musical bond with her. There was no accurate way to do it.

He turned irritably away from the studio door. He went and stood looking at the little dining alcove. There were wall brackets with candle-shaped bulbs, and better, holders for real candles. Ah, the shimmering wispy magic of Pam in candlelight! On several occasions, one of them his birthday, they had dined here by candlelight. Sometimes there would be warm loaves of bread and cool sweet wine and a mood which evoked the lines of poetry:

A loaf of bread, a jug of wine,
And thou beside me singing in the wilderness . . .

He went back to the studio, grinning lopsidedly. Better to have her music even if it was out of synch with her than silence. He touched the knob of the shut door. He withdrew his hand. What the hell? Was he scared to go in there? Afraid of a recurrence of that out-of-control reliving of that lobotomy?

He walked away. He looked at his watch. Then at the kitchen clock.

He smoked. He began to pace and to listen. For the phone.

Late. It was time now. For it to be over. The concert.

He used the bathroom.

There was one thing to be counted on. All concerts started at the same time: late.

By now, though, by God the concert was

over, Past eleven. She *would* phone, she had *promised*. As soon as possible. From a back-stage phone. *Before* they all went to the swanky party.

Patience. Patience. He stood waiting, watching the phone, listening for the sound of his lifeline.

He switched off the lights and thought about the fact that light was the exception in the vast encompassing darkness and emptiness of universal space. He thought about time, the slow heavy time of waiting, waiting . . . the deathly cold of time stopped. . . . He felt a rush, an awesome acceleration, a compression of thousands of days and thousands of nights into a single minute and his thoughts raced with fierce intensity and meaninglessness, and everything rushed farther and farther ahead of him out of reach, out there in the void of time and abruptly everything stopped.

And it was night . . . night . . . night. . . .

Night all around except for the narrowing circle of slowly pulsing light from the fading campfire. Virgie and Cleo were mock-bravely pretending that all would be well. And then . . . then, spontaneously, they sang a brief song, a single high note in a miniduet, their throats synchronized so closely that their knifelike shriek was as one voice, one voice of terror when the *something* came sailing through the air and landed soundlessly there on the ground near their pretty bare feet.

Their wits scattered. Their attention divided

itself between the *something* on the ground
and the source of that *something*. Hopefully,
stuporously, they looked straight up in the air,
then glanced mutely at each other as if to
assure one another that the *something* had
fallen from the sky, somehow, maybe from a
plane, though there was no remotest sound of
any plane. Cleo dropped to her knees and
Virgie instantly, mindlessly, followed her lead.
Together they reached out and plucked at the
string bag half full of vivid blue mountain wildflowers which Porky and Judy had gathered
from the meadow above the far side of the lake.

Cleo yelled toward the concealing underbrush there at the edge of the woods.

"Judy! *Stop* it! Marabelle! That's not
funny!" She sounded furious. "I'm going to
slap your faces off!"

"I'm mad *too!*" Virgie yelled, that little
voice of hers high and quavering and slightly
comical. "You come right out here right now!"

They both jumped to their feet and stomped,
and pretended to think Porky or Judy had
played a game that they could cope with. But
they both *knew*. He let the paralyzing knowledge build in them another half a minute or so.
And then he came out in a violent charge and
anticipated their blind flight and outran
Virgie, grabbing her by the hair, and
commanding to Cleo, "Stop, or she's dead."

Cleo came back.

The two of them marched before him into the
little cabin with heads lowered submissively.

He told them in a quiet voice, "Strip to your panties."

He had to repeat the order. Once. *Twice!*.

They lay on their cots.

He began to speak. He had to stop three times and go back to the beginning because they listened with imperfect obedience. They interrupted him repeatedly, violating the rule of silence, however unintentionally, by muffled cries and choked sobbings. But at last he had told them all about Porky, and all about Judy, and when he was done, there was an abrupt chaos, a frenzied rush to everything, an atmosphere of utter mindless hysteria.

After a little while he was in control again.

Virgie lay bound hand and foot, but she was not gagged. In a sense she had shared Cleo's final ecstasy, their voices blending or counterpointing each other in an erratic cacophony of high-pitched screams.

Then there was only the sound of a single hoarse, raw squawking, less like Virgie's voice than an animal's.

He unbound her. He touched her hot, sweaty face. He soothed her with gentle whispers. A frosted moon through the window touched her convulsing belly and one small breast and silvered her golden hair. Gradually, gradually, her breathing steadied.

And then there was neither a rushing nor a slowness but a vast sweet timelessness.

The vastness was one with the encompassing night and he was filled with a sense of poetry and lustless love and he did not remove her panties or force her to partake of the loaf of bread and jug of wine. She could not rise, un-aided, to the intensities where pain and ecstasy fused together indistinguishably there at the heights above the world as if in a high magic tower. He transported her there, from which her spirit ascended.

In the first light of dawn she lay at peace. Her face was beautiful, but her lower body was revolting and had begun to smell. He kicked aside the broken, jagged bottle which had con-tained not wine but strawberry soda, and was now filthy with blood, gore, and traces of vis-cera, and got out of there fast, very fast.

But there was no way to outrun the dead. At times her tortured screams pursued him relent-lessly. Whenever that happened he instantly evoked an image of her face as it had been in life and at the moment of death, free of pain and transcendently beautiful. It was almost a reflex to imagine her beautifully, as if her horrible death had never happened.

He seemed to see her now, this minute, heart-breakingly exquisite. Her image must have been triggered off by the agonized raw shrill screams he was hearing again. They persisted, relentlessly.

Virgie's imagined living face became more vivid and he recognized it as the face of his fantasy girl at Shaunautaukee. Abruptly he knew he had not created that fantasy girl at all. She was simply the memory of Virgie; they were one and the same. Slowly then, almost imperceptibly, their haunting face began to combine with yet another face . . . Pam's!

"No!"

A shudder ran through his whole body.

The screams became the shrill ringing of the telephone.

He stared at it in fright. It was Pam calling him.

4

Joel had a driving sense of urgency. Next thing
he knew he was standing in the open doorway
staring out into the empty public hall. His
head was tilted at a listening angle. What was
he doing here; where had he been going? he
wondered.

His senses caught up with him. He knew
he'd been in blind flight away from that phone.
Then, while he was opening this door, the ringing quit. The pressure was off. There was no
need to run.

But she would be calling again in 15 or 20
minutes. He frowned. He shook his head.

He went down to the basement locker and
got a suitcase. In seven minutes he had it open
on the bed and began packing, determined to
be gone before the phone rang again.

He wasn't.

He braced against the sound, shut the incompletely packed suitcase. He resisted awareness of Pam's clothes and her bed and the lingering scent of her and carried the suitcase down the hall. He tried to force himself on and ignore the ringing.

His not answering *again* would upset her very badly. He seemed to feel her growing anxiety in his own breast. He smiled nervously, imagining her face. Its distress added an extra dimension to her beauty. The ringing somehow began to take on a note of desperation. It was cruel to torture her, to intensify and prolong her fright, he thought, and realized he had never loved her so much.

He went back to the phone.

"Hello . . . Pam?"

"Joel? Is that you?"

"Yes."

"You sound funny. What's wrong?"

He remained silent for several seconds.

"*Joel!*"

"I'm here. I'm all right."

"You don't sound all right."

"I'm not quite waked up. I was asleep."

"Asleep? *Asleep!* How *could* you go to sleep when you knew I'd be calling? That's terrible of you, Joel. I can't believe you'd do that to me when you knew I was already worried sick."

She talked fast. Joel listened intently and filled every pause with conciliatory words.

". . . Sorry . . . You're right . . . I don't blame you for . . . I'm ashamed of myself . . . Sorry . . .

I didn't mean . . . Please don't be mad."

She slowed down. She began, predictably, a 180-degree reversal. But while she was making the turn, she reproached him for offenses against *himself.*

"Your intentions weren't wrong; you didn't deliberately try to hurt me. But do you open your mouth and defend yourself? No, you don't."

"How can I when I deserve—?"

"I'm not always right. But do you stand up to me? No."

"I should I guess—"

"You *guess? You know* you should. But Joel, you just can't make yourself go against me, can you?"

"Well—"

"But you sure stand up *for* me. Time after time. I can always count on you. But what do I do? I go off and leave you when you need me, you poor thing. Then I got scared that something had happened to you when you didn't answer and I jumped all over you. When you were so worn out you couldn't keep your eyes open! No . . . *no* . . . you musn't say a *word* in my defense."

It was an order to be disobeyed. After he had done it, she proceeded to defend him against herself. He shut his eyes and listened to the tender beauty of her voice and there was no ugliness anywhere.

At last they said lingering good-byes and he hung up and basked in a warm afterglow.

They had reassured each other that everything was all right in both their worlds, or rather, their bubbles of fantasy. That's where everybody lived, in a bubble of fantasy, according to Maury.

He couldn't decide what to do with the half-packed suitcase in the hall. He did nothing. It would be giving way to delusions to imagine he could get in a car and be free when he got someplace else. A glorious, mindless philosophy. Paul Borland had thought, or nonthought, like that. And look where it had got him. And where it was still getting him. Because right now, right this solid minute, he, Joel Danton, was having trouble breathing. She was here, right here, Virgie. Not her image, but her essence, her suffering. It was like a dark suffocating atmosphere.

He went and opened a window. Not to jump out—it was mechanically almost impossible—but to get a faceful of cold air. This damned emotionalism! At least he had not allowed her image to plague him.

In a way he wanted to visualize her. But he was afraid if he did, Pam's face, too, would appear again and she would be inextricably connected to that California horror.

He shook his head. Why did he choose to feel it in that morbid, negative way. It could be the opposite because Pam's image had supplanted the dead girl's and she represented the triumph of the life force.

Those flowers. That broken strawberry soda bottle.

Those hard ugly details turned his guts to water and brought back the dreadful feel of that night of Cleo's and Virgie's murders. Beginning with lurking in the underbrush and causing the fear to build in them; progressing from intimidation and psychological terrorization through, calculated step by step, the physical pain, slowly and deliberately intensified in a pattern of prolonged agony that drove Virgie insane and made her beg hopelessly for the mercy of death. *Beautiful* death.

Beautiful! My God, how could anyone but a subhuman imagine any beauty in such a death. His imagination shrank from it all. He *could* not, *would* not, of his own will visualize any of it. Only the aggravation of that ringing phone had thrown him out of control, made him experience it.

The vividness, the terrible details . . . such as those flowers, that broken strawberry soda bottle, the part-loaf of bread, could not have been mere fantasy!

He would have been better off with a criminal conviction and imprisonment in California. He would be eligible for parole, or actually out, free by now. This way there never could be any real freedom.

The ghastliness of that night would always be there in him. Repressed, submerged, but never *gone*. That had been proved tonight, the way it had burst shatteringly into consciousness. Those crimes were unforgivable. He couldn't live with himself believing he was a monster.

His lustless love of Virgie, the compulsive nature of it, had become obsessive, had driven him from the campus, had driven him crazy. He had thought at the time, yes, crazy, that's what the love of goodness was in an evil world, crazy.

Mawkish, gauzy, drug-saturated nonthinking. Pure shit. Loving her symbolic goodness had been a force, a momentum that couldn't be broken by the mere act of running away from the campus. He'd sneaked and lurked and lacked the guts to approach her; or rather, he'd been blocked by her friends . . . successfully blocked. There had been no relationship, none at all, *ever!*

. . . He was back on the firm ground of fantasy. It had all been fantasy. . . .

Crumbling, crumbling, crumbling. He could feel the ground under him crumbling, the belief in his own innocence disintegrating.

He thought contemptuously about "ventilating," about "scream therapy," and remained grimly silent.

Maury, Dr. J. Maury Hillman, was to blame.

The cunning bastard had conned him into a false rapport and manipulated him. He dropped bits of counterculture jargon into his talk, affected the beard and long-hair anti-Establishment look, even getting into the jeans and sandals hippie uniform during group sessions, and posed as a kind of over-age flower child. He gave the sly impression that he was a secret soul brother, a subversive force working from within the Establishment and was not one of "them," but one of "us," a part of the beleaguered minority who shunned the world's corruption and were outcast because of superior virtues and pure ideals. He'd come to trust Maury and to think of him respectfully as "crazy, man!" Crazy like a fox!

Tricky, sneaky, sly, false, he'd had the soul of a schizophrenic pig. Most cops worked in teams . . . a threatening bastard paired with a soft-soaper who might even slip you a joint in order to soften you up and trick you. Maury had been both at once, the hard-nose lurking there all the time, waiting to pounce. Even the fairy stuff might have been calculated, a tactic to test Paul Borland.

Oh, yes, from this perspective, too late, Joel could see what Dr. J. Maurice Hillman had *really* been.

In the sessions after Maury became openly tough and authoritarian, and began to turn screws and force all the hard ugly details of those murders on him, he'd said one time, "The fantasy, Borland, was *not* the murders. The fantasy was the confession. That document was a *classic* example of the aim of fantasy—don't interrupt me!—the aim of fantasy is always, with rare exceptions, a glorifying false image, a preferred self. That's why you made that transparently false confession, to create a better image for yourself!''

''Better? I confessed to *vileness*. You're crazy.''

''Am I? Well, hear this! The unbearable part of your reality was not some grand horror, oh no, nothing to distinguish you even as a villain. The unbearable part was your nobodiness, your nothingness, your nowhereness. You were not loved and you loved nobody and you belonged nowhere and couldn't even attach yourself to groups because they were always shifting and changing and you had no identity. You didn't exist. But, by God, a grand confession like that would make you exist, and when it was proven that the confession was totally false it would be finally understood that you were some sort of martyr or saint. Because, clearly your motivation was mystical, quasi-religious, *crazy*. . . . But in the great tradition of religious fanatics through history who, like Jesus tried to take all the suffering and evil of mankind on themselves.''

''No! My confession was what it was. An admission of crime, of evil, of sin . . .''

''Don't begin *that* again. We're past that. Quit regressing! I've forced you to admit that—''

''*Forced* is the key word. A man convinced against his will is of the same opinion still. An old copybook maxim. And true!''

''*True:* Two of the girls, Marabelle Jordan and Judith Callinger, were raped and strangled to death across the lake near a field where they had been picking wildflowers.

"*Not true:* You confessed that . . . *just as in the newspaper stories* . . . you killed all four of them in or near the cabin.

"Maybe, in remembering, there was confusion—"

"*Fact:* There was a string bag containing no more than two double handfuls of wildflowers found in the clearing in front of the cabin. *Fantasy:* Paul Borland's claim that Marabelle and Judith had come back from picking wild-flowers and were carrying between them a bushelbasket full. *That's* how the newspaper stories had it. Just as in point after point, such as the colors of the panties, the truth was concealed from the general public so that loony confessors would be spotted because of the discrepancies.

"Another example. You took to heart some of the more lurid prose about the killer being 'a wild-eyed frenzied madman,' and you imagined the 'frenzy' meant 'rushing.' As if it was done in a hurry . . . you claim to have done it all within a couple of hours . . . and polygraph tests showed you *believed* it. Those deaths were *slow,* calculatedly prolonged, the work of a cold brute."

Point by point Maury had forced him to admit the confession amounted to fantasy. The harder he resisted the assault of ugly details, the more grimly Maury ground his nose in them.

The report by the pathologists who had performed the autopsies had been unendurable to have to listen to. Especially the one on Barbara Ellen McClendon. Virgie. It dealt not only with the external damage to her body from direct "insults to the tissue" . . . he would never forget that phrase, that flash of outrage within the controlled, technical, scientific document . . . but with the indirect effects. Stress and shock had thrown the kidneys, adrenals, and liver into dysfunction, engorged the spleen, and even where no external force was evident, there were intestinal ruptures and massive internal hemorrhaging from burst arteries and damaged capillaries. There was evidence of violent spasms of the heart muscles. Her system was depleted to exhaustion, and studies of nerve tissue and extensive chemical analyses of the blood and bodily fluids indicated pathological imbalances of salts, acids, endocrinal and hormonal secretions so severe that she would have died from the irreversible shock effects.

Maury pretended to read from the opinion of a "specialist" who had studied the autopsy report, to the effect that certain aspects of her condition were characteristic of advanced senility. A dubious bit of science. The "specialist" was probably the fantasy specialist, Maury himself, inventing, to make a point. Joel remembered resisting the point angrily.

"Imagine," Maury said, and looked limp. "Characteristic of advanced senility! You're

not listening!" Maury repeated his little
invention. Twice. Three times. Maybe more.
Then Maury added, "It's awesome. A healthy
16-year-old-girl. A mere child. Her whole life
used up in that seven-hour ordeal. Where the
hell do you think you're *going?* What makes
you think you can walk out of here before *I*
dismiss you?"

The next session and the next and next
Maury was more aggressive.

"Seven hours! That's the estimate of how
long she was under duress, how long it took her
to die. A guess, maybe, and questionable. But
it can't be far wrong. . . . You *will* listen and
cooperate, Borland. Stop trying to outshout
me. There, that's *better*. Face it, it *wasn't* over
so fast that it almost seemed not to happen at
all . . . or at any rate that the pain was limited.
It *did* happen, and it was *prolonged*. Absorb
the *truth*. And reflect. Reflect on the con-
sequences of your irresponsibility in creating
fantasies which serve *you*, but which protect
and shield, in effect, an actual monster! You
have sensibilities, Paul. And a good mind, at
least potentially a good mind. And you *must*
see that you violate the human best in yourself
by clinging to sickness!"

"I don't, I don't cling to it. I *accept* that it
was a fantasy. But what's the point? Bringing
her back to life and killing her over and over.
Enough! It's sadistic."

"I told you what the point is!"

"I *get* it. I *realize* the full dimensions of the

wrongness, the sickness. . . ."

"We're going to make damned sure you do."

Three blue wildflowers had been discovered on the ground where detectives had found clear evidence that the killer had been lurking in concealment. Unquestionably the flowers, which had come from the meadow across the lake, had dropped out of the string bag. Therefore the killer had been carrying the flowers. It was speculated that he had thrown the bag of flowers out into the clearing in order to increase the anxiety of the two girls who had already begun to worry about their missing friends. Such an act, seen as part of a pattern of terror, was thought to be consistent with the psychology of a torturer. The speculation had been so convincing that it was taken as fact in the total reconstruction of the case.

He had absorbed every bit and piece of the known facts. But there were gaps in the official knowledge, things only the killer could have known. Paul Borland, at Maury's urging, filled those gaps plausibly. He tried visualizing Cleo and Virgie in the firelight, and their reaction when the flowers were thrown into the clearing. He guessed at their words, their actions, and how this must have looked to the sadistic killer. Then, trying to be consistent with the psychology of a torturer, he had— with a little guidance from Maury—come to the logical conclusion that such a creature would tell them about Marabelle's and Judy's deaths. Forcing such knowledge on them inflicted devastating psychological pain, showing them their worst fears were trifling against the reality. It crushed their hopes and showed them there was no escape, that they, too, would die. Virgie, finally, had had to endure even more . . . seeing the murder of her dearest friend, her last hope.

At a certain point in time, after Maury had gone and he was in the hands of openly hostile doctors who threatened to murder his brain, Paul Borland begged to be allowed to revise his original confession. He would amend it, correct it, fill gaps, eliminate discrepancies and errors, make it perfect so the case against himself would be airtight. But asked to account for how he'd disposed of his bloodied clothes, he hadn't been able to come up with even a guess, so his plea was coldly rejected. He was accused of pure cynicism, of knowing that, because the details had been bludgeoned into him, such a confession would be legally invalid.

But it had been chiefly Maury—*friend* Maury—who had ruined him, who had implanted those killings unforgettably, indelibly, into his mind.

God damn you, Maury, he thought, but tiredly, without any real animus or feeling of any kind. Except for Maury it could all have been *really* gone forever. The positivism, the hopefulness, the future orientation of Dr. Dornstadter of Halfway House would have worked.

The mere thought of Dornstadter revived

hopes. He remembered something about that night with Virgie.

That broken strawberry soda bottle. A substitute for wine. For symbolical wine with a loaf of bread. That had been the meaning in his mind. Poetic. Connected with the beautiful lines of poetry. *A loaf of bread a jug of wine. And thou beside me singing in the wilderness.*

Imagine it, *imagine,* a torturer who enjoyed inflicting pain so inhuman it could not be borne by humans. The monstrosity of such a torturer was beyond his imagining. But it would be impossible, im*possible,* for such a creature to indulge in the mood and tenderness of *poetry* during the horror.

It was fantasy, pure fantasy to think poetry could connect with such a mind.

His imagining the alien role of murderer had been a failure. A magnificent failure. Only intellectually, from a great distance, could he experience such a thing. Emotionally he had got it all wrong. The killer's pleasure had been the sadistic infliction of pain. It was preposterously wrong to attribute to a torturer a love of poetry and a tenderness and a feeling for music.

Joel shook his head and told himself he could not, he simply could not grasp the psychology of such a subhuman creature . . . and thank God he couldn't.

He was briefly nervous, assailed by the knowledge that he was still an imposter in Pam's life. Their whole relationship was based on misrepresentation, on the deliberate concealment of vital facts she was entitled to know. She would have grounds for an annulment.

She might feel betrayed. The violation of a bond by somebody you trusted was worse than harm from an enemy. Pam loved him. She would *hate* him. . . .

He himself had been betrayed by Maury, Joel thought agitatedly.

Maury must have come to doubt his innocence. He got scared that Paul Borland would go free, thanks to him, and commit more atrocities. Real ones. What did a specialist in fantasy do if he stopped believing his patient had been fantasying? He did as everybody did, protected himself. It was professionally unthinkable for Maury to reverse himself. He had a reputation to protect. So he turned his notorious patient over to the brain-murderers. Anything Paul Borland might do afterward could be blamed on brain damage, leaving Dr. J. Maurice Hillman in the clear.

Maybe.

What did it matter if Maury had deserted him? Everybody did that to everybody.

Joel shrugged.

No more thinking. To hell with.

He needed to stay in control. He needed rest, relaxation. . . .

He couldn't sleep. He'd slept too much today. There were still hours of the night to get through. He couldn't bear to stay awake.

He had an emergency supply of barbituates taped to the back of a bureau drawer. He extricated it with a little effort.

He lay in bed waiting for the Little Blue to take hold, telling himself *I believe . . . I believe. . . .* He began to feel calm and calmer . . . and then, nothing. . . .

5

Getting up at the usual time next morning was half the battle. Then, dull routine took over and he got through the workday on pure inertia. He had no special aptitude for accounting; counselors had steered him into it because it was supposed to be emotionally undemanding. The job was no real part of him and he left the office with a sense of relief like an amputee taking off his artificial leg at bedtime.

There was a drizzle and on Tenth he started getting tire spray on the windshield. He never stopped for a drink, least of all at a sleazy dump like the Thir-Ten, but its red-neon sign had at least an illusory glow of warmth. He slowed, turned in, and came to a stop at a dirty snowbank in a space between a pickup and a jalopy with a jacked-up rear end. What the hell was he doing here? He sat staring at the rain-slicked, cement-patched grimy brick sidewall of the tavern, aggravated by the nervous rhythm of the wipers. What he was doing was stopping off for a drink. As simple as that. He cut the engine and got out.

Turning right at the public sidewalk along the front of the building, where the neon sign showed pink floaters of snow in the rain, he approached the entrance. His movement was loose and easy.

He opened the door and a bolt of lightning struck him dead in his tracks when he saw *Cleo's* face.

The shock came between two beats of his heart and was gone as he realized she couldn't be alive. The face, contrasting vividly with the murky area behind it, was only a crude mockery of Cleo's beauty. It belonged to a black-banged bitch on a barstool who was staring at him.

She was at the short leg of the L-shaped bar, a few paces directly ahead. She sat partially turned on the stool, a sluttish insolence to her pose. One bare leg extended full length in a tapering line that began at the round of her hip in a short, tight purple wool skirt, continued down the pale stretch of thigh and knee and ended at the slush-spattered toe of her shiny black boot on the floor. Her other boot heel was hooked on a rung of the stool, her inner thigh showing from the bend of her raised knee to the edge of the skirt, mere inches from her crotch. He kept his gaze up, his eyes boring into hers.

She had time to see he wasn't whoever she was expecting. But she continued to stare fixedly, without a flicker of expression, waiting for him to get out of her line of vision, refusing to see him.

He refused to be forced off course. There was an empty barstool beside her. He moved defiantly toward it. The closer he came, the grimmer he felt. He was vaguely aware of the rest of the place. Beyond her was a large dim room with booths, a few loud customers guzzling and listening to the whine-whang-jangle of juke noise. He glimpsed a quick-action-hipped waitress in a miniskirted cowgirl uniform carrying a tray. To the left a line of three or four men sat at the bar with beers watching the tube up on a shelf on the end wall. His focus centered on the frozen-faced bitch. The creature personified the whole cheap atmosphere of this joint, including the smells of beer and sweat and stale smoke and damp wool and urine.

Moving toward her, it was difficult to look amiable and loose but he managed it. There was a teasing sensation on the back of his neck as if a hair—or the edge of a razor blade—was being drawn delicately across his skin. Within an arm's reach of her, he saw her right eyelid droop. Her lips, which had been hanging open showing a gap between her front teeth, closed and rolled inward, compressing in a thin line.

Joel smiled. Before he knew it, his fist was doubled to smash that coarse, sensual face.

He caught himself just in time and made a smooth easy turn to the left. He found a seat at the bar. He stared sightlessly up at the tube, thinking nothing, absolutely nothing.

"Huh?" he said.

"I said if you wanna order?" the bartender said.

He gave his order and came back in focus and realized what a close call he had had and thought, "My God, what's wrong with me!"

That girl's staring at him had been accidental to begin with. His overreaction had been irrational to say the least. Joel was back in perspective when the bartender brought his double Scotch.

He ignored her and had a second drink. He resisted every impulse to glance around to see if she was or wasn't looking at him. A scalded-crow squawk-shriek of female laughter came from her direction. In a perverse way her laughter was a work of art, an ugliness perfected. The sound was a true expression of her essence, consistent with her whole meaning.

She ordered a beer. The bartender carried it to her. On the way back the man raised a questioning eyebrow.

Joel hesitated. In spite of himself he kept thinking about her face. That face was *not* in contrast to the murky light behind her as he had first thought, but the very essence of shadows, a gathering together of shadows. They hung in the hollows of her cheeks and beside her cheeks where her long black hair fell to her shoulders, and they formed small dark lines around her nostrils and between her lips and below the out-thrust of her underlip. Her eyes stared out coldly from under the edge of long bangs as if she herself were not there but concealed down in some cavernous dimness, watching slyly.

Joel shook his head no to the bartender, swung around, and stepped down from the stool and walked toward the door. He did not look in her direction. But he could see her. She was watching him steadily. The glow of neon beer signs back of the bar, one blue, one gold, one red, glossed her face with distorting pastel colors. The pictures from the tube flickered across her features, giving an illusion of obscure shifting expressions. But under the play of light her sensual face was as motionless as . . . as . . . His neck began to tense again.

He kept her over there at the edge of his vision. But he was increasingly aware of the insidious play of light on her face. He resisted the eerie pull of that false animation.

The distance to the door seemed endless, his pace nightmarishly slow as if he and time itself were stopping. He felt an inner urgency to get away. Finally he had the door open, one foot across the threshold. He knew in his gut that he must not look directly at her face. But he did. She was not there.

The face rushed back in time and joined a

delicate, lovely blonde. Their bodiless young faces hovered there in space, luminous against an ominous darkness. There was a void, a timeless deathly night that encompassed everything except the narrowing circle of slowly pulsing light from a fading campfire.

The waves of firelight over those phantom faces of Cleo and Virgie became again the mere flickering of jumpy light on the black-banged bar girl's face.

He was afraid he might be too shaky to drive, but he wasn't. The Thir-Ten vanished from his rearview within a half mile. Presently he was on the ramp to the freeway, heading home.

On the big road, a nowhere placelessness between places, the bar girl kept a nasty grip on his mind. But she couldn't follow him into his world. He let himself into the apartment, smiling. He put a meal from the freezer into the oven and stacked the player with enough records to last till Pam's call.

All in all his Thir-Ten experience had been positive evidence of mental health. If he were still in a straitjacket of inner guilts, he wouldn't have had the flexibility to break routine and stop for a drink. True, the girl's hair stype shocked him into imagining she was Cleo when he went in; and as he left, the flickering light on her face triggered a false memory of the horror night of those brutal murders. But he'd recovered his senses at once and recognized the morbid fantasies for what they were, and far from being shattered, he was exhilarated. Or high, as Paul Borland might have put it, Joel thought whimsically.

The Bach double violin concerto provided dinner music; afterward, stretched out on the lounger in the front room, he had some Beethoven, with Brahms coming up. He asked himself an absurd question: Could a monster guilty of unforgivable crimes enjoy the three B's? Of course the concertmaster of Pam's orchestra would answer yes . . . but then Abe was a sick man, a victim of the Nazis and he would never really get out of Treblinka, where everything but the music in him had died.

Joel shook his head gloomily. He reached for his lifeline, the phone, and set it on his lap. *The night shall be filled with music . . .* He closed his eyes and let the sound pour over and into him, luxuriating in a dreamlike bliss.

He heard the beginning of a Brahms string quartet that Pam often played with her group. The voice of the violin had a special quality of innocent voluptuousness. Joel smiled. He had had a secrety affinity with Brahms ever since he discovered that, as kids, they had each had close relationships with a certain sort of woman.

He found himself gliding pleasurably toward sleep and presently he was watching a scene of "wanton innocence" . . . *innocence?* . . . Virgie and Cleo sunning themselves naked while being oiled by Porky and Judy . . .

He woke abruptly. He looked at his watch. He'd had his eyes shut only a few minutes, but long enough to sink down into slime that sullied Virgie and violated the meaning of his lustless love for her.

He lit a cigarette and warned himself not to doze off. The danger in falling asleep was not that he would miss Pam's call. But if it yanked him awake when he was groggy, the ringing might sound like screaming.

Nonsense! How could it when he'd proved to himself he was innocent? He got up and went to the kitchen, debated with himself and rejected the idea of a drink that might loosen his control.

He returned to the front room, but stayed on his feet, pacing, alert, his attention fixed on the music. He stopped and stared out the window, trancelike, filling himself with the greatness of the music. And to think he had not known Bach from Offenbach till Pam came into his life!

The trouble was that any kind of thought, even about her, somehow threatened to . . . to . . .

He tried grimly to lose himself in the music . . . too late . . . too late . . .

He might convince Pam and himself that he was all right. But damnit, he'd been out of control last night. And the night before that. There was no guarantee that it wouldn't happen again one minute from now. He would fight, he would kill, and gladly, to protect her from everyone, anyone, including himself, he thought emotionally. But since that brain-murdering criminal surgeon had turned him into another person, he wasn't responsible for anything he might do.

He didn't know why he'd gone out of control in the first place. The night before her tour he had been very tired, of course, and strained beyond his capacity, yes, so he had slipped back emotionally into childishness. To a child, absence was the same as death, and he had *felt* Pam's imminent departure like impending death. Also, he'd been ashamed of himself for ... for ... well, *what?* His failures of manhood?

He grimaced, then shrugged jerkily. Nothing new about his being too unassertive. Pam's sex games, especially her mock protests, confused him. Sometimes when she wanted to be over-whelmed, he wouldn't know if she really did. The slightest pressure against what might be her will had the flavor of rape for him ... and it was worse when he wanted her most. In the crunch he refused to commit an unforgivable crime. Instead he idealized her like some pure bodiless fantasy and committed the unforgivable crime of failing to satisfy her. That no-win situation had been unusually bad the night before her tour.

He didn't want to think about it. He chain-lit a cigarette. He walked around in aimless agitation. The sugarcoating of sweet sound began to irritate him.

He went to the studio and stopped the music and then he was defenseless and in the silence he would feel a vague shadowy anxiety creeping over him like a shroud.

He remembered something sickening about that night before Pam's tour. Driving home past the Thir-Ten he saw dead Cleo on the walk outside. Not a ghost, but Cleo herself, coarsened and ten years older. The fleeting hallucination was so complete he'd even imagined a smell of rotting dead flesh emanating from her. . . .

Suddenly he thought about naked thighs.

"Goddamnertohell!" he whispered savagely. That bar slut he'd seen tonight was here in his world, in his senses, pulling him down.

The same girl he'd sick-fantasied seeing on the sidewalk. Or had he seen an actual girl both times?

Girls did not, repeat, not go around bare-thighed in this weather; they wore panty hose. Nonetheless, he had seen naked, unmistakably naked luscious thighs.

He shook his head exasperatedly. Face it, it didn't come off as reality. Since he'd seen her two nights ago, how could her resemblance to Cleo have come as such a shock when he saw her inside the bar tonight? He thought about that stare of hers. Hostile. Accusing. What if she was some kind of rejecting, *punishing* fantasy?

A mere resemblance to Cleo in a real girl was one thing. But if something in him had created a guilt fantasy *after* he'd proved—proved—he was innocent, what then? And what kind of proof had he given himself? Basically that anybody who loved great music couldn't even imagine the horror chamber that the mind of a torturer must be. . . . But at the time of those sadistic rape-murders he scarcely knew great music existed.

He put on his coat and hat. He had to know if that bar girl was real.

Going out the door, he seemed to pass to the other side of an invisible barrier. It was like moving through an airscreen into a doorless gambling casino. Or stepping across a floor stripe in the lobby of a hotel on the California-Nevada state line. He had the gut sense of a change—up or down—in barometric pressure. He was slightly giddy as if he were breathing thinner air, and existing in another atmosphere entirely.

Coming off the ramp and picking up speed on the freeway, Joel was nervous about the act-now-think-later way he was doing things. It was terrible to add to Pam's worries by missing her call. He should have called the bar. But how, over the phone, could he find out from a bartender he didn't know and who didn't know him whether a girl he could not name had or had not been in there when he had?

The man would remember him if he showed

up in person. Without advertising himself as a loony who didn't know if people he saw were real or not, he could ask casually . . . like a guy interested in renting her . . . about a girl with bangs.

When the Thir-Ten came into view, he was positive the bartender would confirm the fact that such a girl had been in there. But if he was so confident, why had he come down here? He remembered something. A clincher! Bartenders didn't serve drinks to people who weren't there, but he'd served her a beer.

Or had he?

Joel's beginning smile hung.

Lust was what had happened to him, he thought impatiently. There was no mystery about it. He'd lusted for that slut at first glimpse. Then, earlier tonight he'd stopped in hoping to see her again. The disloyalty to Pam shamed him, so he'd hidden it under elaborate self-deceptions. He'd torn himself apart and gone into emotional tailspins by pretending there was a serious complex fantasy problem involved. But hell, the problem was simple. Cheating when the wife was out of town was so commonplace it was normal. Instead of worrying about his mental health he should consider himself an American success story in the best upwardly mobile tradition, progressing from psychosis to neurosis. A corner of his mouth twisted in a sardonic grin.

He'd come this far, might as well check

things out with the bartender. He turned in at the Thir-Ten lot, parked, and cut the engine. He'd keep a grip on reality and think of those luscious naked thighs as the unwashed portals to a dose of clap.

The temperature was down, the wind up and pushing against the car door when he got out. He crossed to the side entrance. He stepped out of the cold into a blast of ugly juke noise, shouts, and drunken laughter. He peered through the murkiness and there she was in the flesh!

The bare-thighed, tiny-purple-skirted, booted bitch was in a booth opposite this door staring at him from under those long black bangs.

This time she wasn't alone but with a couple sitting across from her and someone he couldn't see distinctly at her side. He couldn't ask for better confirmation of her existence.

No need to go up and talk to the bartender or waste another minute breathing air unwholesome with exhaled smoke and bad smells and enduring the ugly noise. There were half a dozen couples dancing, mostly crude sweaty stompers. Two waitresses in cowgirl outfits and several customers moved along the aisles. There was a vulgar belching contest in a booth on this side. Across the way a Romeo goosed his Juliet when she came back from the john.

His gaze returned to the girl with the Cleo hair-do staring fixedly at him. She seemed somehow uninvolved with the action surrounding her. Just because she appeared to be in a booth together with three other people didn't prove anybody else saw her.

This sordid dump was so like so many he'd been in, starting with one when he was a kid and had sneaked in to spy on his big Sis, that he half doubted if it was real. Except he didn't have the imagination to invent all the details of the Thir-Ten's grubby reality. Anyway why would he go to so much trouble to flesh out a fantasy . . . especially one he basically loathed.

But after all, only last night in the campus cafeteria he had imagined himself into another time and place where, from concealment, he had watched Virgie and Cleo in the wavering light of a campfire. His belief had been so complete that when the campus cop spoke to him he had been mystified by the fact that the terrified girls paid no attention to the man's voice.

And it was a strange coincidence that both times he had come into the Thir-Ten this girl was here. Here and watching the door he came through. As if she expected him. Or else she was where she had to be to plague and confront him if she was only an unwelcome fantasy of his own unconscious creation.

Against the noisy hubbub she was a silence. And there was about her an immobility like death. Most disturbing was the quality of her stare impaling him with implacable hostility.

MANIAC

The noise of the juke and the animals faded as if silence were spreading outward from her, driving the sound into some remote wilderness. The deathlike immobility emanating from her prevented him from either turning tail and taking flight or rushing fiercely at her. He alone was paralyzed. The dancers continued to move. She had no relationship to anyone but him. He couldn't break the hypnotic power of her stare. He understood that he had not come here of his own volition but in obedience to her will. The dangerous dark power she exerted over him was . . .

"Hey, Scotty!" The thin girlish voice was very close, and so was the baby-faced blonde who went with it. She was standing spread-legged in front of him in a miniskirted cowgirl outfit, beaming a seductive smile up at him.

"Scotty?" He shook his head slowly. "You've got me mixed up with somebody else. I'm not Scotty."

"Uh huh, yes you are too. Your poison's double Scotch, so that makes you Scotty. Get it? I seen you earlier up at the bar . . . you me too, huh?" she teased.

He vaguely remembered the quick-action-hipped waitress.

"I gotcha a nice warm stall, Scotty, c'mon, I'll take real good care of you." She squirmed the hips, simpered. "C'mon."

He frowned at his watch.

"Thanks, but—"

"You don't wanna leave the barn. C'mon, I got what you want . . . what you need." She giggled, tugged, and teased. He let himself be led to a booth. She helped him out of his hat and coat, got him settled, hustled off. He avoided looking at the black-banged bitch. He'd barely got a cigarette lit when the cheery waitress was back, setting drink and chaser before him and chattering, "Back from the ranchhouse. Is that fast service, big pard, or is that fast service."

He paid, tipped generously. She gave him a history of the uniform, a brief style show featuring hip, thigh, bottom, and a spelling lesson. She advanced one shoulder, round breast, and nameplate to within biting distance of his face.

"My name is spelt D-a-r-l-e-e-n. Can you see all right?"

"Almost." He grinned, thinking the kid had delusions of irresistibility, and it was best to cater to them.

"There you go, you're cheering right on up real good. And you know what, you look lots younger when you smile. I knew I could handle you. Right off I seen you needed some fun instead of standing around looking unclaimed and frowning. Darleen'll take good care of you. Even as big a guy as you I can work you in." She backed off and giggled. "What I mean is I can work your drink orders in between other customers."

"Of course."

"You're gonna be all right now till I get back?"

"I'll try."

6

The juke was loud and fast. He could hear the ugly noise perfectly again. Thanks to Darleen's magic touch, he thought wryly. But it was no joke. He'd let himself get into such an emotional state that he'd become partially deaf, believing—or trying to believe—the black-banged bitch was a dangerous phantom force endowed with the power to impose silence and immobility. That "mysterious power" was in her panties. He downed part of his drink and without turning his head conspicuously he shifted his eyes the fraction of an inch so his line of vision connected with the third booth back on the other side of the dance floor.

Some couples clotted together at this corner of the dance floor, stomping and wagging their behinds and blocking hs view almost entirely. But there were openings, a shifting pattern of little gaps. He could see the tapping toe of her boot and her knee bobbing agitatedly to the swift beat. He glimpsed spread legs and strip of panty the shadowy color of obscurity in brief flashes that quickened him more than open staring. He pulled at his drink, momentarily losing contact. Then he was refocused and the next opening was prolonged and he could see the shimmering motion in the soft naked flesh of her inner thigh. He groped and found his cigarette, took a drag, exhaled the cloud of smoke to one side. There was something especially satisfying about this low, limited view that rendered her faceless.

The juke stopped. The floor cleared. Another record began almost at once, but in the interim he looked directly into her face. That hostile stare was fixed relentlessly on him. The thought came to him that there was nothing else for a guilt fantasy to look at and he began to frown and tense up. He finished his drink and reached for his hat.

Darleen was there in an instant.

"But you just hardly got here," she protested. "Not even one for the road?"

"No."

She gave him a solemn, wide-eyed look of injury.

"You're mad at me for slow service."

"No."

"Yes, you are, or you wouldn't go off when you just hardly got here."

The juke was wailing. Darleen's hips picked

up the rhythm, undulating almost imperceptibly while she gazed steadily at him, her underlip pouted out as if he were hurting her.

He smiled. Her mind didn't know what her body was doing.

"OK. One for the road."

"I'm glad you're over your mad, Scotty. Not that I don't like a guy with a temper."

She swished off happily and was back in a hurry, the cheery personality beaming so brightly that the shadowy promise of her one moment of depth was lost. That pouty look of suffering had been unfelt, a shallow, child-level manipulative device. Technique.

Technique. They all had all kinds of techniques. One of them, calculated to rouse and challenge the grimy fingernail lions of sewer society, was the cold stare. Like that black-banged bitch had been giving him. Maybe she still was. He quick-checked. No maybe.

He didn't let it disturb him. He was slumming and kept his intellectual distance. Fun for the crowd in this murky inferno was only a mask for something subhuman. The whining female voice from the juke was a nakedly masochistic celebration of pain, but music to the animals on the dance floor who were pasted together, writhing in slow ecstasy.

His cool analysis occupied his mind completely. He was scarcely aware that his down-slanting gaze was penetrating every opening in the moving screen of bodies. His eye, as lustless as a time-lapse camera, remained fixed on her left hand lying passively on its back on her naked thigh, the loosely curled fingers unprotesting, defenseless, motionless.

But then after a while—he didn't know how long—there was a stirring that focused his attention sharply. The hand floated upward a few inches and the forefinger began to move in languid stroking curves toward the upturned palm, beckoning imperiously, in a wordless command louder than a shout.

Goddamnertohell! She'd caught him staring. He felt paralyzed. Like in nightmares he'd used to have where he was looking down at a beautiful face in a casket and the eyes behind the closed lids saw him and he couldn't get away and . . .

But the summons was for Darleen, who went running obediently, received orders, hustled off, and was back again to serve the little Queen of the Nile and her underlings.

His nightmarish sensation vanished, leaving only a residue of sweat and a crowding in his jockey shorts. He wiped his forehead and upper lip, squirmed on the seat to ease his discomfort, and lit a cigarette. His hand was steady enought but there was still a touch of grimness on his face when Darleen got back to him.

"Oh, Scotty," she said disapprovingly, "is that any way to look, like you're not glad to see me?"

A corner of his mouth quirked in a half grin.

"Now you know good and well you can do better than that." She illustrated how wide a smile should be.

He had to laugh.

"There you go," she said.

"Satisfied? You like wrapping people around your little finger, don't you?"

"You're teasing me."

"Seriously, you know what you do? You bring out the best in people. I like that kind of a girl."

"Oh, you!" She pushed at him.

"And furthermore, you're not dumb. F'r instance, you'd never serve four beers to three people."

"Silly." She giggled. "Time for a refill, Scotty."

"Let's change to a boilermaker."

"From double Scotches?"

"I hate to lose status with you, but—"

"Oh, don't worry, that's all right. You're still OK in my book."

When she brought the order, he knew he'd made a mistake but he couldn't send it back. He gave her a twenty, guessing right that she would have to go for change. While she was gone, he poured the beer in the stein, then deftly emptied the Bourbon into the can. He timed it so that the shot glass was at his mouth when she returned.

"Might as well take out for another whiskey while you're at it."

"You don't need another beer too yet, do you?"

"Hm-mm. Still some in the can. I don't like to dilute the good booze with too much beer. . . . Tell you what. I'll chase the bourbon with a bourbon. Take out for two."

"Oh oh!" she said admiringly.

"The doubling up is really two orders at once. So I owe you three tips."

"You do not!"

"Do! Think I'd cheat my little pard?"

She argued with him like a true loser and surrendered after a remarkably brief struggle. She gave him an enticing pout as she took her defeat and his money.

What a joke to imagine he'd won. There was no way to beat 'em at their own game, or to quit playing. He knew damned well he'd had enough to drink, but he'd as soon admit it as say he was castrated.

He looked owlishly at the two shots of Bourbon. He shrugged inwardly. Once you were in the game, its momentum carried you. He scanned the crowd to make sure he wasn't observed, then dumped one shot into the beer can. He curled his fist around the glass. If—it wasn't certain—the bitch was watching . . . she saw a man down a drink neat. He barely sipped the beer.

He knew she saw his performance with the second shot a minute later. Because she had swiveled around to let somebody out of the booth and in the process of repositioning herself her stare fixed on him. He looked away, lit a smoke.

During the next he didn't know how many juke numbers—but he'd dumped two more whiskies in the beer can—he observed much about her. The out-thrust of her lower face in profile was . . . was *prognathous* the word? No . . . *primitive*. Wryly he noted that accusing fantasies did not turn their cold stares away . . . or for that matter slurp beer or accept cigarette lights or exchange words with people stopping by the booth . . . some asking her to dance and being refused.

In order to more generously share her thighs with the public, she'd chosen that outer seat. On the inner seat was a Thing which kept crawling out of the shadows to go pee and came back and disappeared. Its hand sometimes emerged holding a match flame for her cigarette, then The Thing sank back into non-existence.

The transcendental truth of the matter was exactly what he had sensed earlier. She had no authentic involvement or relationship with anyone else in this place. In that sense she was his fantasy because he alone could see her *real* reality.

Like Darleen's pout, the bitch's cold stare was technique. A challenge. Many were called by that challenge. But fewer than few were chosen. Because her special requirements could only be satisfied *once*. That knowledge was heady stuff, dangerously stimulating, a nectar of the gods to be sipped, not gulped. He must not indulge himself by too much thinking about it.

Darleen put two more shots in front of him. He wanted them for real. He was tempted. But he must not deaden his senses with mere earthly distillations.

He let the haughty queen of the Underworld see him put away a couple more drinks. In her guts she recognized the bond between them. She knew that he was chosen to accept her challenge. But consciously she did not know. It had been necessary to take himself out of the category of total stranger, give evidence that there was a rapport, that he could drink like men of her own class.

The time had come to test her. He raised his stein in her direction. He drank a toast. He smiled tightly.

For a few seconds she just watched expressionlessly. He did not know if she would deign to let him know she noticed. She'd been showing less hostility than wariness. If she felt him too strongly, she might panic. Easy does it, he thought, and waited.

Then—he wasn't sure at first because of the dim tricky light—the corners of her mouth went up. She lifted her own glass, had a good pull of beer, and set the glass down with a bang. She put a cigarette in her mouth. Presently the hand of The Thing provided a light. She blew smoke in Joel's direction and realigned her body, turning a few inches and opening her legs so that he could see directly to the crotch strip of her panties, which were the color of . . . of obscurity. . . .

She brought her knees together. She drank some beer. She dragged at her cigarette. She blew smoke toward him through a kiss-shaped opening of her lips. She held the cigarette out away from her, posing her hand in a loose-wristed imitation of elegance. She mouthed words from the juke. Her left knee began to sway outward and then inward. . . . Her thighs opened and unhurriedly closed in a lazy fanning motion, dispersing her animal heat and wafting the excess in his direction. At the same time she sang a silent song with a vague, unfocused gaze off into space as if she didn't know what was going on down below!

He was amused. She was so confident. So sure he was hooked and panting helplessly. She played the power game with the mindless pleasure of a child. It didn't seem to enter the empty space surrounded by her skull, that she was not really in command. She believed in lust—her one weapon—with a faith that was damned near pathetic.

Pathetic? Well, he thought uncomfortably, viewed in a certain light it was hard not to see that she actually was pathetic. For instance, there had been something oddly touching about the way she posed her hand with no awareness that it was not elegance, just a cheap imitation. And the stupidly sluttish way she displayed her thighs and offered glimpses of her panties like a gift. In a sense it was a gift, something nice that would be appreciated. Maybe she'd learned that sex was a power that never failed . . . or at least it disarmed people who scared her. And maybe her uninviting, unsmiling "mean" look was defensive because she was weak and unsure or sick or basically unhappy . . . this wasn't all that great a neighborhood, a decaying ramshackle dominated by poverty and ugliness. To her the Thir-Ten was no dump but a touch of brightness. A someplace where she was a somebody, where she was appreciated, even loved. She didn't know the difference between lust and love. She'd never had the chance to learn. She made the best of things as well as she could and in her *own* eyes . . . and maybe in his too . . . she was not a nothing. . . .

He had a strange dreamy memory of Sis and the loveliness of her quiet face in her casket and of Mom's bloated tear-streaked face and sad voice telling him about Sis, her baby, her precious "Valentine face" baby who had been, through her short life, pure beauty and loving sweetness and uncorrupted goodness . . . a saint no less. He felt a softness in his breast which seemed to climb and affect his eyes. In the nick of time just before the softness took over his brain, he thought, *Shit!*

The here-and-now reality was that the black-banged bitch was sending the message he'd been waiting for. She was unmistakably confirming the fact of a unique bond between them, telling him she recognized him as the one—*the* one—chosen to accept her challenge and to provide an experience of exalted pleasure beyond her wildest imaginings. She sensed that the fulfillment she craved was close at hand. Anticipating it, she was doing her seductive best to force the pace.

The pressure made him rush out of control. He let himself think about the final experience. His breath hung. He had to remind himself to breathe. His lips were dry. He could feel the beat, the quickening beat of his heart. His hand shook, fumbled as he grasped the whisky-loaded beer can. He had to take the edge off his senses, come down from the heights.

He gulped too much. He heard that ugly shrill squawking scalded shriek of her laughter. He felt cold and hot in waves. In the hot spells his whole body throbbed. His vision smeared and cleared, smeared and cleared repeatedly to the rhythm of his heartbeat. Her laugh pierced like cold steel needles in his flesh. At a certain level of intensity there was no distinction between pleasure and pain, between a female's cry under unbearable torture and an animal cry of ecstasy.

Suddenly the ice-cold needles of sensation turned into fiercely hot *zings* of sexual pleasure. He swigged from the beer can. He frowned, realized she was dancing.

She sidestepped and turned and backstepped and minced along little forward curves in what seemed to be an aimless pattern. But she kept coming closer. Soon she was right there in Joel's corner of the dance floor, her back to him. Then she simply stood in place, bending one knee and the other in a sultry rhythm that tilted and rolled her hips and swayed her tiny purple skirt, giving him a private show. He'd seen better, much better shows.

This vertical version of mattress action was crude, totally lacking in subtlety. She was deficient in grace and stupidly incapable of variation. She kept repeating the same movements compulsively and monotonously over and over and over. The steamy performance was not a solo . . . at least not technically. Dance floor rules probably required a partner so she'd brought The Thing out of the shadows as a prop. The creature with the hyperactive bladder was skimpy and barely as tall as she was even in high-heeled boots. It had stringy hair and a narrow, grinning, uncommonly silly face. The sight of it above her shoulder was disgusting . . . worse was the hand on her waist. That creep's touch degraded her.

She didn't have sense enough to know that while she was playing haughty power games and getting little kicks out of ruling inferiors she was lowering herself. *Lowering?* He'd been exalting her all along. Thinking about her in a cutesy-poo way as the little queen of the Nile and the underworld with waitress slaves and everybody beneath her. And *now,* worst of all, he was reacting *emotionally,* as if she were some kind of pure saint and The Thing's touch was a sacrilege!

What was this, *love?*

The skirt and the tilting titillating rhythmic hips and rounded bottom were swiveling around out of view. Next thing he knew it was not that narrow, grinning, uncommonly silly face he saw above her shoulder, but her face above The Thing's shoulder and her hands were on Its back. The creep was pressing Its lower body in against hers and their pelvises rolled together. Her eyes were intimately half closed, her full lower lip hanging open. Her expression made it clear she was enjoying a dry fuck.

"Enough!"

He slid to the edge of the seat and stood up with the sensible intention of getting his hat and coat.

But instead—it was absurd—he began to walk slowly toward her and she shut her loose mouth and the sleepy sluttishness vanished from her eyes and her head retreated till her chin backed in against her throat. He moved so slowly that the distance between them seemed to remain the same but for some reason she showed urgent—and comical—signs of alarm. She yak-yakked and hissed and struggled to break free of The Thing, her whole upper body tensed and leaning back. That position arched her pelvis forward. The creep imagined—a laughable mistake—that she was pushing it up harder and he held on and his skinny ass got convulsive. But not for long, because Joel was suddenly there, crowding him and saying something or other.

"*Huh?*"

Joel repeated in a quiet unemphatic voice. He forgot the exact words the moment they left his lips. Evidently they were not flattering.

"Whuh . . . whuh . . . *whud* you call me?"

"You're deaf, too?"

Joel smiled. The Thing took a clumsy half step away from him and in the process released his hold on her.

"That's better. And we'll stay friends as long as you keep your hands off of her. Shake?" It amused him to offer his hand.

"Say, if you think I'd shake hands with you—"

"The way you said *you* tells me you're a singer, right? Does she sing soprano too?"

She'd faded back out of reach and stood watching with an unreadable expression.

"None of your business what she sings, and hell no I ain't no singer and—"

"You said h-e-l-l. Tsk . . ."

The punk's eyes got jumpy and scurried over to her . . . and quickly back again. He managed a defiant scowl.

"You just lookee here, see, you can't come in here insulting me and pushing me around and . . . and. . . ."

"And?" Joel encouraged with curdling

gentleness. "Take your time. Do you mean we should go outside?"

"If you're trying to pick a fight don't think I haven't got no friends. . . ."

"Fight? I'm too civilized for that. But if you *insist* on going outside, all right. Go round up your friends. The problem is I outweigh you forty pounds and my reach is . . . well, let's check. We'll each extend one arm straight out from the shoulder. No? I was only thinking you should delegate somebody my size to fight me. Fair's fair."

She snickered. The creep's glance went to her. The look on her face stung him. He tried to eyeball Joel and make word threats at the same time. The silly narrow face became pinched; the scowl disintegrated into a puckering up before tears. Alone with Joel he'd have had sense enough to back down and cover the retreat with noisy mouthing off. But the sultry bitch was there, doing nothing to cool things. Her mere presence could goad him to hysterical false courage. If he took a swing and Joel decked him, it would be overkill. He'd look like a bully. She would appreciate him all the more for brutality, but it could trigger a brawl.

Enough! he thought again.

This was unreal. There was no emotional coherence. He was savaging The Thing but feeling no hostility toward him. It was a game. A joke. What he'd really enjoy would be a brawl. Outnumbered, he'd lose, and she respected only winners. He was doing fine with ridicule.

"Your zipper's open!"

"No it ain't neither," the creep yelped but grabbed his pants and looked down at himself. Before he could look up, Joel confused him some more.

"It *was* open. What were you trying to do, screw her on the floor and lose the Thir-Ten's license for them?"

"Hell no, by God, that's a lie."

"OK, maybe you just had it open to go pee-pee."

"I never had it o—"

"You've got a record, haven't you?"

"Whuh? No!"

"What're you dealing? Pills, acid, shit, coke, hash, what?"

"Nothing."

"That's why you keep running back to the john."

"No it ain't neither. I just go back there to use it."

"You *swear*? OK. I see you're squirmy to get back there now. Go on, then, before you have an accident. Maybe the information we've got is wrong and you're getting knifed by a jealous rival. But *somebody's* dealing."

"Not *me*. You can ask Mona."

"She'll character-witness you? And you can identify yourself, positively, and swear you've got no record, and you're not dealing anything? Man to man, I've got nothing on you, except if you perjure yourself with false information."

"You a narc or some kind of cop or something?"

"Shhh . . . not so *loud*. . . ."

The punk lowered his voice. "I never give false information . . . and I'm strictly a beer man. No dope, never!"

"He ain't no cop. Letting him bluff you, you squirt," Mona said scornfully.

"Look, miss, he and I have official confidential business. He can go back to the men's room and I'll check him out in a minute. Don't incite him to strike a federal officer."

"OK, if I see one, I won't incite him to."

"You can go on back and wait," he told The Thing. "I'll be right there."

"C'mon, Mona."

"Like where, the men's john?" she said lazily.

"Don't joke. The booth. You go on back over. I'll take you . . . c'mon." The Thing was more anxious than ever to grab the face-saver and escape. The juke had stopped; the dancers were in no hurry to clear the floor; heads poked out of booths to gawk; everybody was eavesdropping.

"Can't dance in the booth." Her low-pitched speaking voice wasn't ugly like her laugh but just as perversely exciting. It was hoarse, probably from tension, and slightly rough like fine sandpaper that teased and keened Joel's senses.

"Hell, the music stopped already anyway."

"Then start it." She took a boots-apart stance, put one fist on her hip. "Put something in the slot."

A girl somewhere giggled.

"I'll put a quarter in later, but—"

"Big deal."

"Just hold your horses, woman, and c'mon I'll take you back over to your seat. You'll have to wait for me."

The rabbit was on Its hind legs now and reached for her arm. Overreached.

"Just you kindly take your hand off of my arm."

The creep hesitated, then brayed "Haw haw!" and dropped his hand.

"Women!" The Thing shook Its head and gave Joel a man-to-man wink before turning and walking away. At a safe distance It began to swagger, heading for the john.

She watched, her lip curling.

Now, Joel thought.

"*Mona!*" The sudden rough command in his tone startled her.

"What?"

He jerked his head in the direction of her booth.

"Get your coat and things."

The smoldering eyes studied his face intently. He stared at her with unremitting harshness.

"Now?"

He nodded bleakly.

"Uh—" she began, stopped. Her mouth remained slightly open. Her tongue flicked her underlip. She started to blink nervously. She was feeling the exciting edge of fear.

Any further fright at this point would be premature and counterproductive.

She shifted her stance in a weaving, uncertain motion.

"Now! Fast." He diluted the threat in his tone, maintaining only enough firmness in his voice to break her indecision.

She hurried away. Joel put on his hat, slung his damp coat over his forearm, and watched her unhook the hip-length chubby hanging on the booth partition and drape it across her shoulders. She clamped her purse to her side with an elbow and started diagonally across the dance floor toward the door. He began to move along his aisle, adjusting his pace to her shorter step. The *thunk thunk thunk* of her boot heels sounded very fast against the dragging beat of the juke that somebody had started but nobody was dancing to.

Joel was not only sharply alert to her but tight with anticipation of what the crowd . . . or somebody in it . . . might do. The atmosphere was lighter since the "lovers' " tiff and the disappearance of The Thing. One couple began to dance; some gawking heads retracted into booths. The mood was amused curiosity, but there was still a watchfulness.

He mustn't let them sniff fear, which always encouraged bravery. He had to move with confidence, neither rushing nor hanging back. He controlled his stride to synchronize smoothly with the flashing motion of her knees, and soon she was swinging in front of him near the exit. He reached past her, opened the door, and got her out of there. It was over and done before the stumblewits knew what was happening.

Hurrying her to the car he said, "I'd call that a real *fait accompli,* wouldn't you?"

"What else?"

He got the engine, the wipers, and the defroster started. She was outside the open passenger door stamping slush off her boots. The Thing burst out of the joint in a tantrum, yelling and flailing Its arms like a demented scarecrow. Mona hopped in, slammed the door. Joel backed in a screeching arc, then gunned forward. He turned into Tenth, picking up speed, a flat smile on his face.

He didn't even know the creep slipped and took a pratfall back in the parking lot till she told him about it. Then she let go with one of those shrill, squawking, scalded shrieks of laughter that sounded like pain. The ugliness sent cold chills running over his skin, and at the same time made him throb with sexual excitement.

"Shut up!"

She stopped laughing instantly, as if he'd slapped her. She sat there sulking, staring straight ahead. She had the chubby over her like a fat bib covering her from chin to knees.

He frowned noticing an odd, agitated wavelike ruffling of the fur's surface.

"What're you doing with your hands under there?"

She gave him a petulant look, pushing out her mouth.

He reached under the coat and grabbed her wrist, clamping hard.

"You playing with yourself, goddamnit?"

"Hell, no. I got snow on my legs. I was wiping it off. I never heard such dirty talk. I oughta slap your mouth."

"Don't try it. Scoot closer," he said, keeping his hand under the coat.

"No. You're too mean. Take me back."

He glided his hand down between her legs, stroked her inner thigh, then gathered some of the soft flesh into his grip and squeezed lightly, threatening to pinch.

"OK, OK." She moved over against him.

He stroked higher between her now open thighs. He touched her panties.

"Hey!" She squirmed, giggling. She reached over and touched him. "Hey hey *hey!* What're you gonna *do* with that pants buster?"

Joel got both hands back on the wheel, began peering closely at the street signs. He slowed the car. Two blocks later he turned into what he knew was a one-block dead-end street with a storage yard on one side, a dark factory building on the other and fenced off from a railroad at the end.

He stopped the car, cut the engine and

lights. Mona turned to him, slid her arms up around his neck and hugged him, her face lifted, close to his. He avoided kissing her, extricated himself, and opened his door.

"Get in the backseat."

"I'm not gonna—" she began.

"The *hell* you're not," he exploded.

"Don't yell."

"Don't tell *me* what to do," he blasted, louder.

"I get nervous if people yell at me." She cleared her throat. "I just don't wanna—"

"God *damn* you!"

His voice rose to a bellow. She winced and pressed both hands over her ears. He leaned toward her, intimidatingly, head thrusting, eyes glittering with rage, and began to roar savagely, hurling curses, obscenities, and accusations like shit in her face. She used one hand to help herself scoot back away from him, then again covered both ears, pressing her thick, dark hair against her cheeks.

Her shadowy eyes, like an animal's lurking in a cave, peered out from under those long black bangs. He sensed her sullen resentment. He knew she was biding her time, waiting for an opening, an offguard moment. By cleverly pushing her hair so that it obscured her cheeks, changing and distorting the actual contours of her primitive, masklike face, she tried to conceal her intentions. But his senses were sharp, constantly alert. There was a hyperclarity to his vision as if he were looking through a magnifying glass. In particular he could see clearly the reality of those sensual, pushed-out lips which looked softly inviting and seemed almost to shimmer with subtle, enticing motion. That tricky little shimmer, far from erotic, was actually muscular strain from her effort to conceal venom. A tiny tic-like spasm indented the right corner of her mouth. Fleetingly. But he didn't miss it or its nasty meaning.

"Bitch. Slut. Stinking whore slime! That's the *last* vicious *grin* you'll *ever* grin. *Ever . . ."*

He began hurling filth and profanity and shocking accusations at her over and over again, his voice taking on a fervent chanting quality that lowered and rose, lowered and rose in a hypnotic rhythm, from very loud up to deafening roars and outright screams, relent-lessly, and it went on and on for how long he did not know. He became aware that he was shouting and should shut the noise inside. He pulled the car door shut. The dome light went off and her face dropped into deep shadow. With the door shut he could feel the shattering reverberation of the sound of his voice ranting like a madman and his head ached and he could half see and half feel her shrinking and scooting back farther away from him to the very corner of the front seat.

He stopped yelling. He moved at a half crawl, crouching above her, licking his chalk-dry lips, feeling a rivulet of sweat on his fore-head. He could hear her panting. As his eyes adjusted to the dimmer light from the distant street, he could see that her bangs were mussed, showing irregular triangles of the skin of her forehead. He thought he saw her chest heave and quake.

She made a queer hiccuping sound. The next thing he knew she seemed to be having convulsions, at least in her chest. Her legs and lower body were quiet except for the breathing motion through the soft flesh of her belly. He lay his hand on her skirt, then slid it up under the skirt onto her belly, bare beneath his fingers, but covered by the panty material under the heel of his hand. He stroked the naked area around and below her navel.

"You *are* nervous." He meant to speak softly. He sounded rasping. Because he'd shouted himself raw.

She didn't say anything, just lay there, her face a dim blob, looking up at him. She was panting a little, convulsing a little. He stroked her belly. He embedded his fingertips. Lightly, but beneath the softness of the flesh he felt the sudden flexing of her abdominal muscles into a defensive wall.

"It's all right. Don't be nervous. It's all right. But be reasonable, Mona. You can't do that to a man. Steaming me up the way you did back there . . . you can't deny you were deliberately steaming me up, can you?"

He waited, peering closely down at her, his hand still on her belly. When she didn't answer, he repeated, "Can you? You can't deny it, can you?"

She shook her head no. She sucked her breath in. The convulsions eased off.

"That's better. Admit it. The final worst thing was rubbing it in to me. Practically doing it with that creep on the dance floor. Right there in front of me. And looking at me that way while you enjoyed it. Spitting in my face!"

"Why I didn't either spit in your face," she cried in a thin, quavery voice. "Honest. That's dirty; I wouldn't never do that. Since I was little I never did that. Honest."

"I mean *like* spitting in my face. I know you weren't close enough to actually do it."

"I never did. Since I was little. I wouldn't do that. Oh, I just wish . . . I just wish . . . oh, it's so chilly. Can I go home?"

"Mona, don't start again! Trying to cold-cock me like a cock teaser. I don't want to get mad again."

"You get so mad. When all I did was say—"

"I know what you said. That's what did it. Set me off that way. Don't do that to me again. Don't try to pull the same stuff whimpering you *wanna go home!*"

"I'll do it with you. I didn't say I wouldn't. I didn't. I wanted to come and do it with you. Gee! You turned me on. . . . Then *now!*" She wailed and her voice broke.

She covered her face with her hands and cried.

He swore quietly. She let out a shrilling pro-test.

"Don't get mad again! Please!"

"Not at you. I didn't swear at *you*. It's just . . . oh, shit, *everything!*"

"I won't bawl. Men just hate that. I don't blame them." She burrowed in her purse, blotted and wiped her face with tissue, then said in an almost calm voice, "I'm OK now. Let's get in the backseat. Like I oughta done right off, instead of opening my big mouth. What I wanted to tell you was I didn't want to get out and get wet . . . and you thought I meant I didn't want to *do* anything."

"That's all you meant?"

"Sure, but right off you got so mad and didn't let me tell you . . . and I could still not have to get out if it's okay for me to go over the back of the seat. My boots might dirty the upholstery. I better take them off. OK?"

"Sure, of course."

"Don't get mad and think I'm stalling. I'll get them right off quick."

He backed away. She came a few inches out of the corner, faced front, and doubled forward, reaching down. He lighted a cigarette and her head swung toward him so fast that a strand of her hair sailed. The hair settled on her face and she didn't touch it. She stared in a kind of paralysis till he whipped out the match.

She brushed her hair back and started fumbling with the boots. They gave her trouble. She tugged and pulled and twisted and pushed at one and the other. He simply waited, smoking his cigarette. She was desperate to be quick and got clumsier the harder she tried. She lost her grip on a boot heel twice; both times she sneaked looks at him. Once she expelled her breath in an exasperated whoosh. He made no move and said no word to hurry her. It was not necessary. It was her problem to pressure herself—at one point she swore at herself in a hissing whisper—and to anticipate the split second just short of the dread lightning-bolt instant when his patience would be exhausted. Mindless, she couldn't figure out that her feet were probably tensed so much that they arched like the backs of Halloween cats and pushed her insteps up tightly against the vamps. He could almost feel the muscles of her arches cramping. At last the pain forced a relaxation, thus solving the dumb creature's problem.

He chuckled . . . a warm, rolling sound. She risked a tiny smile.

"I didn't think you'd want to die with your boots on," he said jocularly.

She frowned. She reached into one boot, evidently searching for a lost sock.

"Forget it. Take the other one off too."

She obeyed. She got awkwardly onto her knees on the seat, sideways at first, then turned to face the seat back. He kept the cigarette in his mouth while he reached over and skinned down her panties. She was in the process of going over the seat back, belly down when he grabbed her ankle.

"Hold still. Stay right there. Don't move." The flesh quivered at the lightest touch of his finger. "Don't even *quiver!*"

Her hand went back, fingers fanning out as she attempted to conceal herself.

"Get that hand away. Just hang there over the seat naked ass up."

He was quiet for a while. She squirmed, feeling the humiliation acutely.

"Scared?"

No answer.

"Did you know, Mona," he said conversationally, "that one time in California I confessed to torturing four girls to death?"

She whimpered.

He was half conscious of her head twisted around trying to peer at him. Her hair curtained her face so that it was all shadow, scarcely human.

"Wasn't that crazy?" he said, and ground his cigarette out in the flesh of her buttock.

Everything began rushing wildly.

She was screaming and kicking and screaming and sobbing and trying to get out of the back door.

He was opening the other back door and twisting her foot and her legs were forked around him and she was clawing at her throat and squawking and gasping and then there was silence and she was limp and she knew bliss, complete bliss, and he was in her pumping and pumping and exploding hotly.

MANIAC

He closed her eyelids and stroked her quiet head and he pressed his face down against her cold cheek and felt a sweet and loving tenderness.

7

A word he didn't know the meaning of—*necro-philia*—came to him and was gone like quicksilver down a crack.

He was disoriented in a strange shadowy nowhereness. He became frighteningly aware of but powerless to stop a senseless absurd in-decipherable swift chaotic jumble of unpleasant things happening.

He whispered and could not hear the sibilance *"Enough . . . Stop."*

He said aloud, *"Enough . . . Stop"* and could not hear his voice.

"Enough! Stop!" Even his repeated shouts remained mute in his throat.

He thought, *Nightmare, this is only a night-mare.*

And then there was a drifting and then there was a slowing and he came to the edge of a void and then there was silence, a long long silence.

A girl's face floated into his line of vision. His aimless gaze locked into a fixed stare. His detached sense of existing at some great distance vanished. He felt a painful, inescapable immediacy. The air became too thick with the smell of flowers to inhale. He stood unbreathing. Motionless.

The face, rising in gentle flare lines from a short, almost pointed chin to high, softly rounded cheeks, was capped by sleek jet hair and a widow's peak, where the dark hairline came down to a little point in the center of the forehead like an indentation at the top of a satiny white Valentine heart.

The babyishly high pink curve in the middle of her upper lip and the slight sulky out-thrust of her lower lip gave her mouth a clean innocence together with a subtle voluptuousness.

Framed within semicircles of eyebrows and lacy arcs of eyelashes were expanses of cerulean like the light of a summer sky on her closed eyelids.

The ethereal quality of her beauty was unbearably exciting.

And then the face, the Valentine face, faded. When it was gone, he knew it had been the image, the casket image, of Sis in a dress with a high ruffled collar that concealed the bruises on her throat, and he could feel the rat, the sleeping rat in his stomach waking up, maddened with fear, its needle teeth biting frenziedly, trying to escape.

One time when he was very young, 4 or 5 years old and Sis was 17 or 18, she took him to some kind of a carnival. There was a merry-go-round and hamburgers and Ferris wheel and hot dogs and cotton candy and carmel corn and shows with dancing girls and cowboys and freaks and magicians and strong men and fire-eaters and neon-tube swallowers and sword swallowers and a rat swallower. He had real good times with Sis because she was real, real pretty and loving, when she wanted to be.

A man in one of the shows had a rat, a live rat. He held it up in the air with a string tied to its tail. The man smoked a big cigar and kept blowing smoke at the rat and the rat stopped twisting and biting the air and went to sleep. Then the man opened his mouth and leaned his head back and swallowed the rat. People yelled.

Sis hated the show, which kept a lot of the men from looking at her legs and fanny in her tight red shorts.

Sis covered her eyes, then got mad at him and yanked him by the arm, and pulled him away and told him to quit looking back. He asked what was going to happen when the rat woke up in the man's stomach, would it chew its way out of the man? Sis said shut up and he had to pee and she took him back of a tent and made him do it there and said if he said another word about that rat—which he did—she would spank him bare-assed when they got home. And she did. She warned him not to get his pecker up while she was doing it. He tried not to but couldn't help it. She felt it on her leg and reached under and pinched till he yelled and Mom had to rescue him.

He squirmed, coming half awake as persistent strong light penetrated his eyelids. He tried to shield his eyes and couldn't move his arms, and his head seemed too paralyzed to turn away from the light, and scowling he opened-shut his eyes very fast and saw the raw painfully bright red-orange of relentless dawn sunlight and the comfortable numbness of his body began to give way like a drug wearing off, and he could feel pain, quick and sharp as the flick of a whip, and he half moaned and thought he must be sitting there in the car near the abandoned factory building where he had killed Mona. The terrifying thought came to him that her body was back there in the backseat and he had to get rid of it and away from here, *now*. He told himself to wake up, wake up, wake *up* and instead he sank down, down down down into oblivion, but not quite oblivion, because he hurt physically in every part of his body and he had a sore thumb as if he'd tried to drive a nail and hit his thumbnail instead. But it was strange, very strange that in spite of the physical pain he was emotionally in an easy, relaxed mood. The light on his eyelids was, he realized, a flashlight and a man, probably a ward orderly, was saying, "Wake up! Shock time!"

He was at Shaunautaukee! He'd never got out! His dream-come-true life with—what had he named her, Pam?—Pam, in the magic tower where the nights were filled with music and where dwelt the shimmeringly beautiful golden princess had never happened at all and there was no such place as the Thir-Ten. That's how Sis spelled "thirteen" and slapped his face for arguing it was *"thirte-e-n,"* and finally—he laughed, remembering—he admitted "thirten" was right so he would live to see another dawn.

Invented characters such as Mona and D-a-r-l-e-e-n would never live to see another dawn since they had never been alive in the first place.

"Shock time! Come and get 'em while they're hot! Electroshock! Insulin shock! Cold tub shock! Mom shock!"

What? *Mom* shock?

It wasn't a ward orderly but a fellow loony singsonging about shock, as if he were still running a burger stand at a carny. The bald, gray-fringed old-time carny worker always talked about onions. The smell of frying onions on the hot griddle was like a nose hook that pulled carny crowds. It was not the hamburger and not the cootch shows and not the wheels of fortune or freaks or swing rides or dodgems or the merry-go-round music that made a carny. It was the smell of frying onions. And the fryer of onions had the most important job in the carny, or in the whole world, for that matter.

What's that Mom shock stuff, he wanted to ask. But didn't let out a peep. He'd kept Maury and all the other spidery probers from sneaking in on any part of his life by lying, lying, inventing one story after another. No matter how often the cops and shrinks put him up against the polygraph it never caught him in a lie. Because he always believed what he said, completely convinced that it was Truth, capital *T*, Truth, which was superior to whatever might have been mere low-level trash scraping of facts.

Mom said one afternoon, "We're not trash like the drunken shiftless filthy trash scum around here. And don't you forget it or leave any of them ignorant roughneck bullies poke fun at you because you got your nose in a book and make good grades. There's two kinds of people that rise to the top. Scum. And cream. Cream like you and your big sister both. Things ain't easy—I ought to watch it and talk good grammar—things *aren't* easy sometimes what with money problems and what all sometimes, but cream is bound to rise above all others. You're my manly little man; you got guts like your big sister. And you're smarter and got more character strength, so the day will come you'll have to take care of her to prevent her wildness from taking her over when she ain't—hasn't—hasn't got the looks to protect her anymore. Her problem, Paul, was being so beautiful that everybody spoiled her.

She didn't have to do nothing for herself, or study or learn or hold jobs when nobody would have the heart to criticize her. Even me, now, she just winds me around her little finger so I don't make her do her share of work around the house."

"She won't even rinse out her own coffee cup."

"I know, I know, she expects to be waited on hand and foot and it's my crime against her that I wasn't strong enough to discipline her."

"No sir, Mom, you never did any kind of wrong and nobody is more strong and fair than you. And I don't know what you're always talking about, about how beautiful and all *she* is, and claiming something that is just not so, that you spoiled her because you're plain. When the real truth is you're not plain, or anything like homely, but a thousand times more beautiful than anybody I ever saw in my life!"

"Oh, well . . ." Her long, sad face got bright and she teased, "You silly child, you can't see me. It's mere blind love looking at me!"

"It's not *mere*, Mom. I see you *true.*"

She sat down and dabbed her eyes and pulled him onto her lap, and hugged him.

He was awake now. But he kept his eyes shut, to protect that memory, and isolate it, keeping it unsullied from his here-and-now reality. Such high loving hopes she'd had for him. His declaring his love that way with such depth of intensity should have embarrassed them both. But the strength of his feelings had got through, touching her heart, and that generally emotionless mask dissolved to the point she cried . . . something she very very rarely did, and those tears, joyous tears, had been precious to him and he'd grown a mile in his own estimation in knowing how happy he'd made her. He'd thought what a tiny nothing repayment to her for everything it had been. And he had marched cockily around the kitchen, showing off for her and telling her how big and rich he was going to be and how he'd buy her everything, clothes and a big house with lots of help and he would open charge accounts at bakeries and grocery stores so there'd never be any worry about mere trifles over whether they could get credit enough to eat between jobs and there'd be furs and diamond rings and going to operas and on trips to Europe and she'd have a whole library-full of great books to help complete her education. She smiled and listened and started cooking supper, enjoying with him all the great expectations and they'd had such a good time and even celebrated, playfully touching glasses and drinking to the future with not quite champagne but Kool-Aid. Lying there with his eyes shut against the hideous reality, he felt such a hollowness, such a sense of hopeless loss that he expected to feel warm tears in his eyes, but he was cold and could not cry or feel anything and simply made a wish to be dead.

He didn't want to think about Sis and couldn't stop himself, although he knew quite well that groping around through the sordid past wasn't going to change or help anything.

Sis, like D-a-r-l-e-e-n, had been a tavern waitress, now and then. Never for very long. Serving people wasn't her style. Being served was more her thing. There were always plenty of volunteers, and wherever Sis was became the center. At times she would be the special pet of tavern owners, a fixture in dumps like the Thir-Ten . . . such as Bamboo Curtain, Boom Boom Room, Fleet's Inn. . . . Where she was, was where men wanted to be to do their drinking and she'd sip whisky-colored sugar water, encouraging her companion to prove he could drink everybody under the table like a real man or prove he was a big-time sport, ordering bottles of bottled-yesterday "vintage champagne," and the cash registers rang. And maybe now and then she did a little business on the side in an upstairs room or a back room. She never admitted anything, and any extra money she came home with would be needed too much to ask questions about, and she was always "finding" money or "borrowing from a friend." Mom's jobs, in diners or unskilled work in factories, didn't pay much and weren't steady. Sis usually blew most of what she had, gambling or buying silly gee-gaws to ornament herself or getting drunk and paying for the drinks of some bum she picked up.

Unlike Mona, though, Sis soon moved up and up to the elegant hotels where the money and power were. A natural slavemaker, she could take her pick and chose to rule winners. She said she was a stakes horse, not a cheap claimer, and thought of herself as entitled to be in the winner's circle at all times.

She appealed to all men—and not a few women—whether they were weak, strong, young, old, rich, or poor, and she got what she wanted without lifting a finger. She was never known to do one lick of work around the house and she didn't walk or take a bus or streetcar; no matter how low the finances, she rode a cab to wherever she would be going . . . or had a chauffeured limousine sent for her.

She could've married a rich man or a gentleman. But money didn't impress her since she imagined there would forever be an endless supply at her disposal. She downright despised gentlemen, especially the kind who let her boss them around. A couple of rich freaks appealed to her because they begged her to beat hell out of them. They didn't have to beg very hard. Then there was a rich woman who wanted to put on a maid's uniform and pay $1,000 a week for the privilege of serving her. He'd thought at the time that it was a whopping lie. Laughable. But he hadn't known much about perversion then.

"Class ass" was what one of her lovers said about her. That slob, a merchant marine, never took her anyplace but cheap booze joints and left her with black eyes, bruises and contusions, and now and then, fractures.

Leggy, lean, and supple, she had a dancer's

body except somewhat fuller breasts than most of them. She could wear fashionable clothes and fit that class ass into the swankiest kinds of settings and she often traveled in style, on fun trips of every kind that would sometimes last a couple days or a month.

He and Mom never knew when she left when—or if—she would be back. Once in a while he and Mom would go along and get a taste of easy living. They'd sit in a box and eat in the clubhouse at Hollywood Park, with a bigshot owner of a racing stable. They lived a little while in a penthouse suite in Vegas. Once there was a fine wild weekend when they stayed in a big hotel, the U. S. Grant, in San Diego, and went across the border to the races and *jai alai* and a bullfight in Tijuana. Joel remembered picking, by dumb luck, a big winner at a race one time up north near Frisco, at Bay Meadows. He got $119.20 for $2, and Sis's rich gentleman friend had bought a bundle of tickets and gave him a $10 ticket all for himself. Sis had later, at home, punched him bloody-nosed and stole the money and took off. But for a while, for a while, there'd been high-living fun, with the Valentine face all sweetness and smiles and loving praise of him to her gentleman friend. And instead of sneering as she usually did about the 100s he'd get on tests in school and all the A's on his report cards and how he'd skipped grades, she talked him up proudly, sounding just like Mom. Sis had impulsively hugged and petted him, melting him down in two seconds flat, the way she could do any damned time she pleased, making him love the hell out of her and resent her for that power when what he wanted to keep having character enough to do was to hate her.

One thing a whore did not like to be called was a whore. How that word got out of his mouth in her presence one afternoon when he was about seven years old and alone in the house with her, he did not know. But he had been mad about some bitchy something she had done and the next thing he knew there was an explosion in his left ear and then, fast . . . she was like lightning . . . his right ear. He thought he was deaf, his eardrums busted. But he did't have time to worry about that, because she punched him one-two in the face and then, or maybe at the same time, she kicked him in the gut so hard he banged back against the wall and then doubled forward and yelled and tried to crawl away. She booted his tail, and while he was yelling for Mom, who wasn't there, Sis yanked his arms practically out of the sockets and held him hanging upright and demanded to know what the hell he had called her. With any brains at all he'd have denied calling her that, but all he did was yell the word again.

"Whore!"

She let him drop to the floor and went and sat on a chair and beckoned from him to come and promised to cripple him if he didn't obey. Then she ordered him to strip naked and lay across her naked thighs to get his spanking.

She walloped him once, very hard, enough to draw another yell, and then warned, "If I feel that pecker start to stand up I'll beat your ass bloody and you won't be able to set down for a whole week, you hear me, you filthy little bastard?"

He never wanted it to get hard there against her naked legs. He moved himself a little bit against her flesh and felt his pecker getting very warm and it felt good good good, and she kept spanking him, loud, slapping open-palmed blistering smackings over and over again until there was a rawness and fever and a terrible pain in his butt like it was being scalded with boiling water and it was such agony he couldn't stand it and all the time his pecker was getting harder and harder.

Then it was done. He was sitting on the floor whimpering. She was looking down at him, her face as red as a plush satin Valentine, her eyes glittered with excitement, and her mouth, the rouge smeared, was curved in a little smile, and he never saw anything as ugly and beautiful at the same time as that face, and she was panting and she threatened him, "You tell Mom and I'll turn you over to . . . to . . ."

Joel couldn't remember the name of the man in her life at that time. Frake? Colby? No matter. One of those rough lovers of hers that she preferred.

Ah, his overemotional-hot-stuff alternately blond and brownette and redheaded Sis.

He couldn't remember when he'd thought so much about Sis and Mom and his young childhood. Mom was long gone. Sis longer.

The "Mom shock," worse than electroshock or insulin or cold tub shock, started gently.

The night Sis died.

"I must tell you something, Paul."

"OK."

"Sit down, dear."

"You mean it's that important? They'll be here from the funeral parlor to get her any minute. You worried about what those guys down there at that place that always wanted her and couldn't have her will do to her when she can't stop 'em?"

"What did you say, Paul Borland? What was that you said?"

She stared at him wide-eyed and her thin, tall body sat rigidly taller.

"I just meant—"

"I know what you meant. It's horrible. Where do you get horrible ideas like that? A nine-year-old mere boy with sick horrible ideas like that in your head."

"I left off my ear plugs and a thought flew in before I knew it was sick. I'll go spray a germicide in my ear."

"Stop that smart-mouthing, it's not funny. Sit down."

"OK."

"She's in there dead and you can bring up a horrible thing like that. Twenty-two years old, and she's dead. What have you got to say about that, that tragic fact?"

"I don't know. It's too bad."

"*Too bad*, that's *all*, when a huge tragic thing like that happened?"

"I guess you could take comfort to know she died a natural death!"

"What are you talking about, a natural death, when that brute murderer beat her to death, a *natural death*. . . ."

"I just meant, Mom, that it was natural to her way of life, the natural way she lived was to go for mean, rough lovers, so . . . don't be upset, Mom, what'd I say wrong? I just mean it was a natural part of a life she liked that could have happened any time with some of the other monsters she lived with."

"I don't follow you. You are too smart for me. You're too smart for your own good. That poor girl lost her flower when she was twelve years old!"

"Aw, around here that's old already. The Murphy twins started in at seven. Eunice Stark said they're bragging and it wasn't till they were nine. And Eunice says she herself turned her first trick before them when she was only eight, and she is the champion."

"Trash, trash, trash." Mom covered her ears. "Don't dirty my ears. . . . I know her own drunken uncle started her."

"Sis said she could've started earlier but she was choosy, not like them. Who did Sis get to do it with her? She never would say."

"You talk like *she* raped him."

"I didn't mean he wouldn't be willing, my goodness. Everybody wishes he could get *her*."

"She was *raped* by a lunatic beast, and she had a baby."

"She did? A baby? Whew . . . she always bragged how she'd never get caught. Or anyway she'd know what doc to go to, to fix it."

"I tell you who the baby was."

"Who?"

"You!"

Mom shock! Knockout blow.

He never got over it.

Bad, the time after Sis's death was bad, very bad.

Mom's whole attitude toward him changed and instead of everything he did pleasing her, everything he did displeased her and . . . and . . .

His thought line broke off . . . as if . . . as if fatigue of the synapses had begun . . . brain fatigue . . . he didn't want to think anymore. He suddenly couldn't remember what he'd been groggily thinking one second ago. His tired nerves quit. The circuits in his mind shut down completely and he slept.

He was almost instantly yanked awake. He grimly kept his eyes shut and felt his whole face clench, trying to block out any more hateful rotten memories. The back of his neck tensed and defied his will to relax and dream.

The tension eased. Sleep came. And with it nightmare and a relentless furious rush of tiny stabbing sensations in his stomach as the needle teeth of the wakened, raging rat chewed his insides. Then somehow the rat got into an artery that led to his head and began eating his brains and the absurd joke came to him that people ate hog brains scrambled with eggs, delicious, so, tit for tat, rats ate people brains scrambled with—or without—eggs.

He woke with a shudder and lay there—just lay quivering—dry-lipped, breathing through his open mouth, which tasted vomitously foul and he thought there was no way, ever, no way he could have thought his mother was anybody but Mom. *Never never never Sis!*

No matter what any birth certificate might have said in some noplace tiny town in the middle of that state where a racetrack's name—Ak-Sar-Ben—was the state's name backward. There was an invented name for the father on the birth certificate, which some sneak thief had stolen out of the Town Records Office file drawer. A metal office file with a chip out of the olive-green paint, just above the middle of the brass handle, like a lot of finger-nails had clawed at it over the years. One summer in his early teens, he personally saw that file drawer. The day after, there'd been a robbery of stamps and petty cash and trifles.

Starting with that night when Sis died, and on and on for days and weeks that seemed like forever, Mom could not find one thing to be proud of him about. She said she couldn't make up her mind what to do with him, whether to send him to a home for retarded children or a mental hospital. Because a boy who did not mourn the loss of the most precious person in his life, his mother, but instead made ugly smart-mouth remarks, was heartless. Inhuman. An unnatural child.

One time she got so worked up she called him the bastard spawn of the unknown lunatic monster who'd raped her pure baby when she was 12.

Mom backed off a little from that, saying well, maybe it wasn't "forceful rape" but "statuary rape." Either kind it was wrong, a sin.

"It sure was, Mom. I sure feel like that. I do, honest. If you think I'm not against a terrible thing like that! I'm sure sorry, too, just like you, Mom, what with her just only a tender, sweet little child, like you say!"

"She had too much love to give. That's why she let him do it and gave him her flower. Unselfishly. Love is what she had and you have not got! It's a shame on this home to have an ungrateful unloving child in it."

When he couldn't answer some of the emotional things she said, his scared silence became evidence of some hopeless flaw, some lack in his mind and memory. For a while he had terrible dreams that he was freezing to death. Being awake during that time had been almost as bad because of Mom's coldness. She had once said that it would be better if he had the guts to run away. But he hadn't had.

He couldn't understand or cope with Mom's change. She had been the absolutely dependable bedrock, the safe certainty as against Sis's absolutely unreliable character. He'd smart-mouthed about her, making Mom laugh, while Sis was alive. Saying things like she was a woman with a thousand faces that he didn't recognize as easily as he recognized her fanny. Because he had so much experience looking at her when she was going away . . . which she was always doing, with some bastard or other. He learned early that Sis's word was no good. Her promises meant nothing. She could tell him how much she loved him one day and be gone the next. The worst part was she had the power to melt him down and make him *believe* . . . but it was never anything but a buildup to a worse letdown.

She had been at home, sleeping in her own bed for a change, when she died. He was alone with her for a few minutes while waiting for the funeral people to come for her. He was not *glad* she was dead, not exactly. But in a way it was a relief. He had stood motionless looking down at her motionlessness, at her closed eyes and silent, parted lips and he'd thought the woman with the thousand moods, the thousand faces, had just one now, and it was better than real real pretty. It was beautiful. He had walked away and that was the end of it.

Mom, though, had knelt by the bed and stroked her face and cried softly and called her

her precious "Valentine face" baby. Mom broke down at the casket in the funeral parlor and really went crazy out at the graveyard.

That very day she started changing everything about Sis's life as if she had never done a wrong to anybody. Sis was one who loved not wisely but too well. She had been, in fact, almost a saint. . . . But no, not *almost*. Mom turned against him and left him to starve and freeze to death emotionally, in a way. So he started to understand how he had been wrong and how in her heart Sis had always loved him, that she was truly all love. At times she turned it to others, but always because she was so full of that goodness. She had never never had a meanness or nastiness about her.

The unworthiness of a son who could believe anything else soon became clear, and it shamed him, and from then on, he *believed* and Mom forgave and loved him again and never, never *never* again did he let the slightest shameful ugliness creep into his thoughts about Saint Sis until . . .

Until Mom was herself gone. Then it all collapsed on him.

And now . . . everything was collapsing on him.

He couldn't count how many memory scenes kept plaguing his mind and it was like trying to draw a straight line through swirling smoke to know whether he was awake or dreaming dark dreams, except once when he was snoring and woke himself with a honk-snort but drifted off again. . . .

The pale stripe of illumination from the street light cut across one corner of the blacktop paving of the parking lot of the funeral home. There were two limousines back there when he sneaked inside. He moved blindly through narrow halls and wide spaces, first following his nose toward the strengthening smell of formaldehyde, then following his ears when he was inside the embalming room. He heard breathing. Quick, asthmatic breathing, and a muffled grunt or two from somebody on the big table, and he crouched and listened and knew that the grunting and passionate asthmatic breathing was coming from the snout of Pinky, the round pink pig of a man who was the chief embalmer and that he was violating Sis's corpse . . .

The room was suddenly overbright with glarelight that shone on the slick white tile walls and on the embalming table. Two other men, standing by, suddenly swooped down on him and he couldn't get away or fight them off and they soon pinned his shoulders down on the embalming table.

"I'm not dead," he yelled, and tried to sit up. They clamped an ether cone over his mouth and nostrils. He fought but he had to breathe and he lost strength with every breath and he heard and felt a high-whining drill boring through his temple into his brain and he lurched so violently the drill bit broke off. . . .

8

He woke with a savage headache. He knew he was straitjacketed on the floor. He realized that he had never got out of Shaunautaukee and his dream-come-true life with Pam had never happened at all and, worst, even the fantasy of loving pure goodness was lost forever, replace by another fantasy, a hateful ugliness. He strangled a cry of protest and shivered, cold with the knowledge that Mona was no goddamn fantasy.

Where he was, was at home in his own apartment, in the daylight, and he'd flung himself out of a bad dream onto the floor between beds, upsetting the nightstand. The red numerals of the digital clock glaring up into his raw eyes showed it was 2:37 in the afternoon. Pam had taken the luminous-dial clock with her. He was hung over. His memory blurred between nightmares and grim realities. He vaguely remembered getting home and muffling the phone between sofa cushions and flopping into a drunken sleep on Pam's bed without undressing.

He was still in his overcoat. His arms were crossed over his chest in that imaginary straitjacket position. Both fists were clenched like rocks. There was a wad of something in his right fist. He was too sick to move.

But finally he freed his arms and, using his left hand, managed to get himself into a wobbly sitting position. He stared at his locked right fist stuporously as if waiting for it to make the decision to open. It might as well, because he already knew what was in his fist. He shoved the pink panties into the overcoat pocket without looking.

Intensified pain bludgeoned him. For a while he could do nothing but submit to it. He lay his forehead on Pam's bed and experienced agony to the point of a masochistic revel. Abruptly he remembered his brutal sadism, especially the vicious detail of smashing the ember of his cigarette into Mona's naked buttock. He sucked air through his clenched teeth. Vomit rose in his throat and he rushed to the bathroom and puked.

He crouched, staring into the bowl, and wiped the splash of filth from his face and flushed the toilet. This time there would be no way to convince anybody that he had merely fantasied committing murder.

By a quarter past three he'd cleaned himself up and gulped seltzer and aspirins and had a stiff drink. He chain-lit a cigarette. His thoughts flea-hopped, unconnected with his actions. He decided to switch on the kitchen radio, but went at once to the front room. He got there with a sense of urgency, then stood staring blankly, baffled as to why he'd come. On the way back to the kitchen he remembered thinking he'd heard the phone. The sound of the radio surprised him. Belatedly he knew he'd turned on a newscast for some reason. His mind was mush, attention span down near zero. He tried to catch up to himself. He listened to the broadcast fitfully without much grasp. When the program ended, he was positive he would have come into sharp focus if there'd been any *bad* news.

Necrophilia!

The word that had vanished like quicksilver down a crack was back. In the dream he hadn't known its meaning. But—his scalp crawled— he remembered himself with relentless clarity in the backseat of the car.

Necrophilia! He remembered *consciously* thinking and knowing the meaning of that word while he was there with Mona's dead body.

He went over and sank down weakly on a kitchen chair. What then, what then, after that shattering moment of truth, what had he done?

Nothing, nothing at all. He had occupied himself at considerable length with worrisome

speculations about that word—like whether or
not psychiatrists in California or Shaunautaukee had mentioned necrophilia—maybe one or
two had. But only in passing. Not as a serious
possibility, he was sure. Maury never touched
it. He'd assured himself that if there had been
any evidence that Virgie . . . or Cleo . . . or
Judy . . . or Porky had been violated after
death, he'd have known. The whole world
would've known. Because the public lust for
unspeakable delights would have guaranteed
that such shock stuff would have been leaked
to some reporter somewhere, and the media
would have had a ghoulish field day.

Imagine! Joel got to his feet and paced
angrily. Imagine wasting time thinking
thoughts like that, solving an irrelevant little
problem from the dead past, just as if he
wasn't there in the grim immediate present
with a corpse on his hands. He couldn't
imagine it; it wearied the brain to try. He must
have been trying to convince himself that what
had happened hadn't really happened and he
was merely on some kind of bad trip.

And maybe he had been . . . and still was. He
stopped and stared at nothing. He lit a cigarette, noting with satisfaction the steadiness of
his hand. What if, what if . . . after not
answering that "screaming" phone call from
Pam last night he had fought off the temptation of the black-banged bitch and had got
drunk drunker drunkest right here at home?
He could have rendered himself sexually im-

potent that way, mainly as a form of loyalty to Pam. Nonetheless the lure was powerful and persistent and he'd imagined-fantasied-dreamed *everything* without stepping foot out of the apartment.

Oh, sure. That's why he'd waked up with his overcoat on and there'd been rims of mud on his shoes. To say nothing of that pair of pink panties.

He'd gone to the Thir-Ten all right. His forgettery wasn't good enough to wipe out Darleen, etc. etc. etc.

The main et cetera had been that sadomaso-chistic thinking all evening. About the pain game and how the slut would enjoy agonies to the point of an orgasm of death. Enjoy? Only sickies lost in suicidal despair could imagine they enjoyed pain. By logical extension, the line of sadistic thinking he'd indulged in would inexorably lead to actual pain, degradation, humiliation—just what he'd inflicted on Mona—if indeed that had been her name. It was suspiciously like *moan.* . . .

The philosophical anarchists spouted anarchy but when it came to action they wouldn't risk making the first bomb. So, too, with Joel Danton. When it came to acting out, he was like all neurotics. Neurotics were would-be psychotics who suffered from a failure of nerve. In the crunch, when she shook her ass that way, demanding action from him, he had thought *enough.* And what he meant was enough of the whole sordid game. He had got up and left the place and come home and taken a pair of Pam's panties to bed with him as a substitute for the real woman he couldn't satisfy anyway.

It would have been totally out of his meek character to have forced a confrontation on the dance floor! And the *idea* that he could have grabbed the prize and got her out of there so easy and so fast—with her compliant, obedient to his will, mastered—was ludicrous, a sheep-in-wolf's-clothing dream about himself. The fantasy of a little kid with big-prick ambitions . . . the way he'd sometimes imagined things when some goddamn big bully was thrilling Sis and taking her off. He grinned tightly. By God, he'd turned the tables—better late than never—by imagining he himself was the big guy, pushing the poor little son-of-a-bitch Thing around.

Beyond the point where he'd thought "enough" and got out of the Thir-Ten, the whole thing was just sick fantasy that went on and on and on step by step out of control. . . .

Next thing he'd be rushing to the cops with another crazy-as-a-loon confession.

There was a certain fact. That backseat wasn't wide enough. What had happened couldn't have happened in such cramped space. Mechanically impossible.

Since the last thing he could remember was a body in the backseat, it would have to be there now. Ridiculous. It would have been visible through the windows all day long and by now the cops would have heard about it and come up here.

He needed a drink—and had one—before going downstairs to check for any kind of evidence—boots, footlets, purse, jacket, upholstery smudges or stains—to indicate she'd ever been in his car. He would even look for her body in the trunk, if he could imagine hauling the evidence home with him.

Omigod, with both back doors open there was room enough for everything to have happened. And afterward, what he would have done was get her out of the car. Maybe by pulling her out by her upper arms. If her jaw had fallen open, it would fall shut when her head dropped back and down and there would be a loud *click* of her teeth and her wig would fall off. Wig? *Wig?*

No use to go through the motions of looking through the car. He didn't have the energy. His right thumb throbbed with pain. Was the nail turning blue? He sat down and occupied himself with detached, impersonal thoughts about little-known but fascinating facts.

An extremely interesting thing which few people realized was that there was nothing arbitrary about the circular shape of a manhole cover. Any other form—square, rectangle, triangle—could be turned in such a way that it might fall through the opening. It was impossible for a circular cover to fall through into the sewer, assuming the circular ledge onto which it fit was intact. Call it trivia. But worth knowing. It was just that kind of undeniable hard fact which a fantasist would incorporate in his fantasy in order to lend credibility to it. To convince himself that something like dumping a corpse and all her effects down a sewer and then putting the manhole cover back on—perhaps mashing his thumb in the process—and driving away *could* have happened.

To attribute such a violation of simplest decency to either himself or Paul Borland, though, would be out of character for both of them. If anything, Paul had suffered from an excess of conscience. And his own high appreciation of the aesthetic would have made such a desecration of the body—amounting to horror unnecessarily piled on ugly horror—impossible. Out of character. Totally unconvincing.

Joel touched his left temple at the site of the lobotomy. It didn't hurt. Probably the skin graft was inflamed. He must accept the agonizing truth. However much he denied that it had crippled his mind, however thoroughly he had proved to himself that new connective routes had been formed in his brain, fully compensating him so that he was as good a man as ever, the higher civilized values, the delicate sensibilities, had been weakened. To the point where strain . . . and booze . . . and dirty lust . . . could reduce him to subhuman potentials. Never again must he pretend he was whole, or push himself beyond control. Pam depended on his control, his strength. For her sake above his own he must not risk getting into a condition that would emotionally disintegrate her talent, destroy her higher world. He had had fair warning. Such horrid fantasies were warnings of a capacity for *real* evil . . . thanks to those Shaunautaukee brain butchers.

Robert Louis Stevenson was correct in his hopeful concept that if the evil within—Mr. Hyde—could be externalized, separated, and allowed to express itself, Dr. Jekyll's goodness would be thus protected.

Even if the worst had happened, if the primitive evil in his depths had broken through the weakened controls of his maimed brain and expressed itself, it amounted to a cleansing, a sort of therapy which left his far more meaningful loving self free. And he would be healthier for it, stronger. Now that the worst had been drained out, it didn't matter . . . psychologically, it didn't. Whether it had actually happened or not, there would no longer be any problem.

Actually, the deep pus that not even Maury had ever suspected was now drained. Joel recognized the full meaning of Mona as victim. He hadn't been killing *her*, except as a symbolic substitute. For Sis. No doubt of it.

That was proved by two things: First, his tenderness, his love for her *after* she was dead, when sometimes in reality he'd hated her. Second, the wig. Sis had had wigs of every kind and costumes of all sorts and every other day she changed her makeup, putting on a new face. The woman of a thousand faces.

That childhood problem he'd never let Maury or anybody guess the truth about had now, with this bizarre fantasy—or reality—had been solved. The thing to do was start fresh, like an Easter rising from the dead. The past was dead time. It could not be relived. What had been done couldn't be undone. To dwell further on it would violate the whole living spirit of Dr. Dornstadter's prescribed future orientation.

Meantime . . . well, he forgot to check on the panties to see if they'd been worn or had come from Pam's drawer.

He showered, and laundered his shorts while he was at it. Then he lounged around, resting, feeling slow and at peace.

He waited till after dark before dressing and going out. The phone had rung several times. But the painful "scream" element didn't upset him. He would have answered and relieved Pam's growing distress but he wasn't yet really in shape to talk reassuringly. A niggling question remained. Only Darleen could answer it positively. Later.

He dined expensively in a pleasant restaurant, putting it on a credit card.

He drove to a bank machine and got a hundred cash.

Then he was driving. Toward the Thir-Ten. The sign had not come into view yet. But he could see its glow, a distant pink smear in the thick wet air above it. There was an abrupt high, thin, piercing scream and a swift series of loud, fierce bellows. It took him an instant to realize the primitive jungle noises were actually the screeching tires and enraged horn-blasts from a car that had been following him, and that he was no longer on the trafficked thoroughfare but had impulsively braked and made an unsignaled turn.

He was driving over a rough surface of snow, mud, and chuckholes and crossing a rail spur into a wilderness of dumped trash, garbage, and abandoned cars. He followed unmarked trails that had once been streets, through a desolation of rubble where in another time there had been houses and small businesses. Shattered globes crowned the dark lampposts and there was no light in any of the few vacant buildings that remained standing like rotted tooth stubs in diseased gums. The whole area was a dead zone awaiting burial under the Interstate.

Near the Avenue, but isolated from it by the blocked-off direct access street, there loomed at the forward edge of the wilderness a large squarish structure within a fenced enclosure with a broken gate flanked by a scrap yard and a spur rail line. His heart quickened as his headlights brushed the grimed walls and flashed from the broken glass in the window frames.

Yes, the abandoned factory building where he had taken Mona actually existed.

He drove on past. He had not needed to prove to himself what he already knew. This whole detour was irrational, but strangely satisfying. Call it morbid compulsion or teasing himself with an exciting sense of danger; whatever, he was stimulated. He cruised the terrible streets of this dead place, this wilderness, and thought about Mona and about Darleen and about the alluring distant pink smear of the Thir-Ten sign and about pink panties. . . .

A two-story clapboard house, a big, rotted molar, with downstairs doors and windows gone, had boards on the upper windows. Behind those boards would be—yes, he saw a thread of light up there through a crack— would be a rot-toothed collection of subhuman sweepings, winos, addicts, assorted scum, holed up against the weather. The place could have been anywhere, Diego or L.A. or Frisco, and any time, because the wilderness was eternal . . . he knew, he knew, because he had been there and he still was there.

He did not slow.

Ahead, from behind a stack of something, a near-naked figure darted across his path to a tumbledown shed. He speeded up. But it was gone. It couldn't have got into the shed. His headlights would have picked her up if she were hiding outside. . . .

She?

Naked? No. Just the legs and feet. The upper body was covered by a fur jacket.

There she was again! Running like a mindless lunatic straight down the path—the
remnant of a street—her naked feet bloody.
She kept stumbling, half falling on the uneven
muddy snow. But she seemed in panic,
impervious to pain. Those vile creatures in that
house must have used her vilely. . . .

Was it? No, *she* was short-brown-haired. But
omigod it could be Mona without her wig.

Omigodomigod. He knew what had
happened. She'd regained consciousness. Her
panties had been in his pocket so he must have
removed them from her throat. When her head
had fallen back, teeth clicking shut, she'd come
to. But her oxygen supply had been cut off for
a long time. Deprived of oxygen, brain cells
were destroyed and could never be restored.
She must have—while he turned his back or
walked away—she must have slithered out of
the car and sneaked away, mindlessly running
for her life.

He increased his speed. She'd be forever at
the mercy of trash, and would be a living dead
capable of no feelings but pain and fright forever and ever. He caught up with her and
opened the window to tell her . . . to tell her . . .

The earth swallowed her up.

He shut the window and stared bleakly.
Hallucination.

He got back out of the wilderness and on the
avenue and in minutes he reached the Thir-
Ten.

Joel decided to separate facts from fantasy

by an orderly process of elimination and went first to the front entrance and looked in. He recognized the bartender who'd waited on him and served a beer to an actual girl who'd been sitting on a now unoccupied bar stool directly across from the door. Fact. He'd been in there. He backed out.

He walked back to the other entrance. From the front he'd only seen enough of the area behind the bar to know it existed. There had been a quick-action-hipped waitress in a mini-skirted cowgirl outfit, and if she was . . . no doubt she was . . . here tonight wearing a D-A-R-L-E-E-N name tag on a well-filled blouse, it would be a fact he'd been in there too.

There was no juke blast when he opened the door and no writhing animals on the dance floor and nobody in the booth where the girl had been staring at him with hostile rejection. The dim murky light seemed strangely thick, turgid. The exhaled cigarette smoke did not rise or swirl or drift but hung motionless in grayish bands. The atmosphere and tone of the place was stripped of last night's excitement and came through as simply drab. He toyed once more with the possibility that he had never actually stepped foot in here. Then Darleen was coming.

"Hi, Scotty!"

He laughed.

"Hi. Say, y'know, you'll have to show me how to spell your name again . . . and I've got another problem. You're looking too good to be real. Can I touch you to make sure?"

She giggled. "Tell you what. Things are dead and I got time. If you want to buy me a drink I'll set a spell with you."

"The inside seat?"

"O-o-h, you devil. Well, OK. We'll get your problems solved. You're real slow at spelling but you learned real good to smile it up when you see me, didn't you, huh?"

"That's my easiest lesson!"

"Don't get lonesome. Be right back."

She was. She came along the aisle dance-stepping, her lifting knees and swaying hips graceful. The knowledge of her own grace and rhythm and her pride in it and her smile at him gave her an air of a sweet-pretty child hungering for praise and confident of his approval. She wouldn't be so confident, or so warm toward him, if he'd actually rushed out of here with another girl last night. His mouth twisted in a half-regretful smile. So, he hadn't made a spectacle in a decisive manly way, only fantasied it; but the reality wasn't such a failure after all. Darleen was actually more desirable. The coarse vulgarity of her surroundings fell away from her like an alien substance, revealing a profound innocence, a purity, a virginal quality. He loved that quality above all, he thought with a sense of tenderness.

When they were settled in the booth, she raised her glass to him and they drank.

"I brought you Scotch instead of a boiler-maker. I thought you wouldn't want to get right into tough-action drinking yet.''

"Guess I'm not much of the tough-action type.''

"Ho ho ho!" she said. She took his hand and put it on her bare thigh. "Do you like that?''

"Mmm!" He stroked.

"You're not so disappointed *now*, are you, Scotty?''

"What do you say '*now*' like that for?''

"I seen you while I was getting our drinks, standing there looking around at all the booths for her.''

"I wasn't looking for anybody. Just waiting for you to come back and get in first before I sat down.''

"She's not here. I know you had it on good for her last night. I'll do, though, won't I?''

"I'm crazy about you. Why do you keep saying *her?*''

"You know good and well I mean Mona. Oh, wow, the way you toughed it out and grabbed her turned me on *good*. Like she turned you on. If she walked in I bet you'd dump me, wouldn't you?''

A strange thing happened to Darleen. She was right there talking but her face began to blur and lose shape and the next thing he knew she had disintegrated and become a ghostly gray silence.

Then he heard her disembodied voice.

"Well, do you have to think about it all night? Would you or *wouldn't* you?''

His fingers moved spasmodically. A fiery

current of joyous sensation raced into his body. He remembered Mona's touching him and asking, "What're you going to do with that pants-buster?" Darleen materialized again, the soft warm living flesh of her thigh real to his hand, her shallowly pretty pouty face coming into focus.

He touched his left temple and grimaced.

"Damn, one of those headaches hit me. That old frag wound I got in Nam acts up sometimes. I get deaf. . . . I'm OK now. But I didn't hear one word after you said 'Mona'. What'd you say?"

He realized she'd been staring intently at him. She continued to watch him while she repeated, tonelessly this time, what she'd said.

"Oh. I see. The answer is I wouldn't dump you, of course."

"For all I know it was me saying her name that spaced you out and it was thinking about *her* that turned you on and put you in *that* condition!" She looked scornfully down at his pants and pushed his hand off her leg.

His impulse was to deny, to conciliate, to reassure her. He had to be careful, and cope with the big *fact* that he *had* taken Mona out of here. People who'd known her would wonder and begin to worry about not seeing her. In a week or so Missing Persons would list her. The most casual investigation would touch the Thir-Ten . . . the last place anyone had seen her alive. None of the boozed-up animals who'd seen him distantly and briefly in dim light last night would be reliable witnesses even if they vaguely remembered him. The Thing had seen him clearly enough but he himself would be a prime suspect. Darleen alone could positively and credibly identify him.

The reality-oriented line of his thoughts chilled him. His erection slackened. But it was up again when he thought about *what* had turned Darleen on *good*. Tough action! She craved male thrust, not gentlemanly reassurances. Apology or anything with the flavor of retreat turned this class off. They liked it rough and respected power and responded only to somebody who could and would hurt them.

He looked at her grimly. He put his hand back on her leg. He seized her hand and pressed it to his pants. She doubled her fist to keep from feeling him. He said in a low, guttural, threatening voice. "Open your goddamn hand before I break your arm. And get your knees apart. Yes, she turned me on. But who the hell turned me on first? You!"

She was feeling the pressure on her hand. She pulled a long breath through open lips but kept her fist clenched. He grinned, increased the pressure till her eyes bugged with pain.

"Don't, Scottie," she said faintly. She bit her lip, blinked back tears.

"No guts!" He freed her fist, took his hand off her leg, moved to the outer edge of the seat.

"Where you going? Don't go off."

"Fuckin' tease!" he muttered.

"I'm not neither and when we close and I can

go out with you, I'll prove it!"

"I'll be back then." He suddenly laughed. "*That* made you blink. Thought I'd hang around to get hustled for tips, did you?"

"What I blinked for was because if you go off, maybe you'd see her."

"Nope."

"Promise?"

"Nope."

"Well, I do. I promise I'll go with you soon's I can, at closing."

Careful, he warned himself. This next part was tricky.

"You'd go blabbing to everybody that you're dating me just so the word would get to Mona. What turns you on isn't me, but the competition with her."

"No, that's not so."

"I hope."

At a minute or two past three o'clock he parked a block away, cut the lights, and sat watching the Thir-Ten entrance. It was possible that she'd grown suspicious about his real reason for not wanting *anyone* to know whom she was meeting. She would have to be a little leery, since she scarcely knew him, but she would come as arranged. Not in spite of but *because* of the edge of fear.

He didn't know it was Darleen when she first stepped outside in slacks and a cloth coat. He was too far away to see much of her face, with a bandanna covering her head. She turned in his direction and came along the walk, hugging a purse to her belly. Except for a low ground haze, the air was clear, and soon she was near enough to recognize. He tapped the horn a few times and she lifted her hand and fluttered her fingers in acknowledgment and lengthened her short quick step.

At the last moment, getting in the car, she seemed to hesitate. Her smile was stiff, unsure. Her face under the dome light seemed pale against the red bandanna.

"Hi! Here I am!"

"Get in."

When she shut the door, dropping the interior into darkness, and scooted close to him, he looked away and stared straight ahead, saying nothing, making no move to start the car or switch on the lights. She fidgeted around.

"Scotty, didn't I teach you your favorite lesson, how to smile when you see me?"

"I *warned* you not to tell anybody you were dating me and then goddammit if the first thing Mona said when I phoned her was that you had called her up and bragged—"

"That liar bitch! I did *not* do any such a thing. Why, of all things! That's the last thing I'd ever do, phone her up for any reason, ever. The *liar*. I done just like you told me, not to tell *anybody*. You believe me, don't you, not *her*."

"I dunno."

"Aren't you going to start the car and let's go someplace? You just hurt my feelings to believe her and not me. Whatta'd you call her up for anyway? I kept remembering ever since you left what you said to me last night. You know what you said to me, Scottie? You said I bring out the best in people. Remember? You meant it too, I know you meant it when you said it. You really *did* like me, didn't you? So how could I change in one mere day till you don't. I couldn't. I'm the same girl."

"I didn't call her up. I was just testing you." He started the engine and drove away.

"Where we're going is to a motel out by the airport. We can get steaks. And champagne. I'll give you a bath in the shower. They've got X-rated movies on the TV there. Tomorrow afternoon I'll buy you some clothes at the specialty shops out there. Including a bikini you can wear around the heated pool. They've got a sauna. . . . What're you getting so emotional and wiping your eyes for?"

"I don't know. It's just from relief. I was so scared. I thought you started hating me. But you don't want to be mean to me at all. You're being so sweet, Scottie. Now! First off, you promised me, how many times I don't know, that you'd tell me your real name. Can't you make up your mind to yet? You can trust me, I'd never cause trouble in case—prob'ly— you're married. That why you'd rather not?"

"I . . . I don't know how to explain why I've put off telling you." He peered over at her. Unexpectedly she surged up and kissed him softly on the lips and patted his cheek.

I can't, Joel thought.

"Tell me," she coaxed. "Come on, Scottie."

"OK. OK. It doesn't matter now. It's Paul Borland."

"Paul's a nice n— Hey, slow down, there's the Interstate. Ohoh, you missed the entrance. Better U-turn back. Nothing's coming."

"There's a country road to the airport that'll get us to the motel quicker."

"Quicker we get to the fun the better, huh? I can't hardly wait. Which one?"

"Motel? Skyway."

"Wonderful . . . but you have to have a reservation *there*."

"I have."

"Honest? You sure they got dirty movies?"

"Don't you *believe* me?"

"Well, sure. Only I never heard the Skyway had sexy stuff. Her and you go there last night?"

"No."

She peered at him uncertainly. He stared across his shoulder at her. After a few moments she looked away, flustered.

"Scared of me?"

"Scared? Of all things!" She laughed, opened her purse, pawed through it busily. She snapped it shut without taking anything out. Then she gave him her specialty, the pout. "I know what you need another one of!"

Before her lips could reach his, he turned his face.

"That's mean. I bet you're still mad at me for keeping my fist doubled up tight in the booth. What you wanted—" She glided her hand in under his coat onto his pants and let her fingers do the talking. Soon, he pulled her hand away. Not soon enough. She'd got the message that her touch didn't arouse him.

"Don't you *want* me?" She sneaked her hand in for another try.

"Not while I'm driving!"

He grabbed her wrist roughly, tightened, and relaxed his hold in a quick pulselike series.

"Ouch!"

"Hurt?"

"Well . . . compared to in the booth when you nearly made me yell uncle, not much."

"Sorry to let you down."

She laughed.

"It's no joke. When I wanted you to do something, you wouldn't and resisted till I hurt you. Then just now, for the very opposite reason, you defied me till you got hurt again. You don't care what the reason is, just so long as you get some pain to turn yourself on."

"Off, you mean. That's what it turns me. Off."

"We'll see."

"What's that supposed to mean? I'll tell you something. On my job I don't let myself think sexy things or feel them. Like you right now, You've got to keep your mind on driving. But mostly why I kept my fist doubled up the first time was it's not *right* to start from the wrong end and *that* kind of feeling. After I gave you a nice kiss though it was different so I could do what you wanted me to . . . or what I thought you wanted me to." She yanked free and folded her hands on her lap. "Let's make a deal; I won't touch you and don't you me."

He lit a smoke. He glanced at her.

"You're really mad."

"Yes." She sulked, looked out her window.

"Anger is the best defense against fear. You know that, instinctively. You're scared," he said flatly.

Her head swiveled quickly toward him. "Do you *want* me to be? You asked if I was scared before. When I *wasn't.*" She pulled long breath and said worriedly, "You *sure* this's the road to the airport? How far is it?"

"Not far."

He slowed to a stop at the intersection with a state road, although there was no traffic. As he started up again he glanced at the odometer. The place he'd chosen was 1.2 miles from here.

"Tell me, Darleen, wouldn't you respond very lovingly if I pulled you over and hugged and petted and sweet-talked you?"

"Well, sure, I guess . . ."

"You'd love it! And do you know why it would be *extra* pleasurable? Because of the anger, fear, and emotional pain you've been experiencing."

"You're talking over my head."

She looked out at the surrounding open countryside and hunched her shoulders.

It was hilly land, coated with a gray gloom of snow, with here and there dark splotches of bare ground and jagged upthrusts of stone. Limestone outcroppings showed more and more frequently. Then they loomed up thickly, covering fifty or sixty acres. It was as if they'd been gathered together to form an awry pattern, jutting out at irregular tilting angles like giant tombstones after an earthquake.

The entrance to the quarry was just ahead. He saw the tracks his own tires had made an hour ago, and turned in.

"What're you going in this creepy old place for? You're giving me the willies!"

The almost straight access road led between minicliffs back to the pit, which wasn't worked at this season. At one point the drop-off to the pit floor was probably a hundred feet. He'd first thought of knocking her out with a jack-handle so she wouldn't have to undergo unnecessary terror. But a bludgeoning by a narrow piece of iron would leave telltale contusions and fractures. There were plenty of chunks of flat stone around. A smashing blow from one of them would have an effect indistinguishable from the impact the stone of the pit floor would have on her skull if she landed headfirst after an accidental fall.

He stopped a dozen feet back from the edge, cut the engine. He switched the lights to high beam to shine out across the chasm, then turned them off. He flipped his cigarette outside, reclosed the window.

"It's private here. They don't work the limestone pit in this weather. But you can see the cutting machinery down there, if you'd like to get out and look over the edge."

"My God are you crazy, get out in this awful slush and look over the *edge?* No, sir. I won't. Turn back on the motor. And the lights."

"I can't wait till we get to the motel. Let's do it now."

"Do it? *Do* it? *Here?* This terrible place scares me and if you think that makes me hot, it don't *neither,* it makes me *cold.* I don't want to anymore. I just want to get out of here. *Now!*"

"You're hysterical."

"Now! Now! Now!" She beat her knees with her fists.

He reached over and gripped her arm. She bawled.

Predictable. The pattern of fright, threats, and intimidation had to break her. He thought about silencing her permanently and making love to her. He felt no slightest stimulation sexually. He thought again, *"I can't."* Because it would be meaningless. The whole planning had been mechanical, emotionally toneless. And her suffering did not rouse the loving feelings of tenderness he should have felt. Crying made her ugly, he observed.

"Dry your face. Catch your breath," he said glumly. He turned the ignition key, switched on the lights.

He thought about future orientation and Pam and her higher world. He must get out of the squalor of the environment that bred squalid motives.

He was thinking *forward* when he geared into Drive. The car rolled toward the brink and Darleen screamed and he braked and got into reverse. For a panicky instant he was more scared than she was. Then they were backing safely.

In thirty-five minutes it was over. He watched from the car as she hurried into a tacky little apartment building without a backward glance.

9

Joel knew she might be watching from inside.

No "might" about it. Darleen *would* be watching. To make sure he went away.

He had intended to leave and hadn't switched off the engine. He hesitated. He had distressed her. He should make amends. Reassure her.

There had been something particularly appealing in the way she had made the distinction about the right and the wrong way for a loving to start. It shouldn't start down there at the animal genital level, but with a sweet kiss and personal affection. He couldn't imagine Darleen letting herself do it with anybody she didn't like. She had genuinely liked him, and had been sure he truly liked and wanted *her*. It had cut her to find out he wasn't responding all the way. That had, as much as anything, hurt her.

In fact, *now,* now that he was himself again, and had proved to himself that he couldn't kill her—another "magnificent failure" in a sense—like the "magnificent failure" when it came to the fantasy about killing those poor California girls. . . . He shook his head impatiently as his lines of thought became snarled and entangled.

Joel switched off the engine and lights. It was no longer true that Darleen failed to rouse him. He was aware of a warmth down there, a mildly pleasant crowding in his shorts. Nothing intense. Just some tingling.

The feeling had filtered down from higher, concerned, tender feelings and genuine affection. And respect, too. A limited respect, yes, face it honestly, it was limited, since he considered her virtually mindless and as shallowly empty as a greeting card sentiment. Yet . . . yet . . . she had a code of decency, however false and hypocritical. And there was an instinctive goodness that he appreciated. He must repair the harm he'd done her.

The poor kid, who'd done him no harm, was in there now, watching, quaking, in the painful grip of the fear he had caused. He should be man enough to make things right. He was getting a pantsbuster. . . .

He started to open the car door. A tiny spark of static electricity jumped with a sharp *tick* of sound and stinging sensation from his finger when he touched the metal handle.

He yanked his hand back. He peered nervously at that sleazy little apartment. If he took one step toward the house, she could misunderstand. She could crack up and fly to pieces. She might kick up a fuss that would wake the whole building and cops would sure as hell be on the way soon.

He turned the ignition key. He shifted from Idle to Drive and routinely switched on the lights at the same time without thinking. He got the car rolling. After a few feet he abruptly doused the lights and drove on in the dark.

"Overreaction," he told himself edgily. She wasn't in any condition to read his license plate. Or organize herself enough to write it down even if she had pen and paper at hand.

Besides, she was practically illiterate. Maybe she *could* read and write. But he never saw her use an order pad.

Still, a lot of illiterates could read numbers. And even if she couldn't write—especially if she couldn't—she would have had to develop a fair memory to be able to get orders right for sometimes a couple table-loads of customers. That license number of his might not only be readable to her in her state. It could have seared itself into her memory like a branding iron, even if she got only a two-second glimpse.

He squinted, hunching forward, as he drove through a dark midblock with cars parked on both sides. He wet his dry lips. Sweat was popping out like busted blisters on his forehead.

It was easier to see when he got nearer the corner streetlight. He turned off that street onto another. The front right tire hit a chuckhole so deep it rocked the whole car on its springs. He turned his lights on. He opened both side windows to get a cooling draft, and wiped at his wet head and neck. His sore right thumb throbbed. He started getting dangerous throbbing sensations from the pantsbuster.

He couldn't keep driving in that condition. He found an empty residential block with some open parking spaces a few streets away. He got out and walked briskly awhile. He resorted to an old trick to cool his unwelcome lust, saying multiplication tables, not from 1 through 12, but starting with 12 through 24. He fouled up on 19 times 19, but kept going on and on senselessly through the 24s after his condition was under control.

Why he had told her *that* name—Paul Borland—he didn't know. Was he cr—?

He got back in the car and debated whether to get back to her street and find out if, hysterically, she had called the cops. He could drive over there with lights out and park a distance away and simply wait and observe if a cruiser came along.

Oh, sure, great. A big white car worth more, probably, than the whole blockful of junkers around it. Impossible to miss, it would be so out of place in that neighborhood. If a cruiser answering Darleen's call spotted it—him—and noted the license number, what then?

Maybe they already were on the lookout. The Thing had been blind with rage when Joel had taken Mona away from him, and in no condition to read the license number. *But* who knew if one of his cool-eyed buddies had clearly observed the make, model, color, and license number of his car and they had reported it to the cops and swore he had kidnapped Mona?

Bull! If a bunch of boozy belching bums tried to make a federal case out of one guy taking another guy's girl, the cops would laugh their heads off, and the Thir-Ten owner would kick them out for getting his dump infested with the law. No use for him to go hanging around Darleen's street and asking for special attention from the fuzz. Where he was going was away from here.

Now.

Within minutes he was on the curving ramp climbing up and out of this sordid world.

Coming off the curve he hit the straightaway of the well-named *free*way fast. He relished the feel of the speed pull in his gut. The surface was dry and the road was engineered for easy safe speed. The back of a big, over-the-road truck loomed ahead like a wall rimmed with Christmas tree lights. He passed it effortlessly and disposed of a couple more vehicles in the next mile or so, holding the speedometer steady at 70.

Then, as far as he could see, his side of the double-lane divided highway was unobstructed. He was enjoying the controlled power hum of the engine so much that the sign a half mile from his exit made him uncomfortable, and slightly irritable.

He couldn't bring himself to slow down and interrupt this forward flow. He must not break this momentum. Pam and her magic were not there in the apartment. If he slowed down and went into that boxed emptiness and came to a dead stop, inertia and depression could—and would—take him over.

One time at Shaunautaukee they took him out to the vegetable patch—an outbuilding closed ward—and put him in the "garden" with the human vegetables for a week. Or more. He didn't remember. Surrounded by those ex-human creatures in catatonic motionless trances, faces and eyes dead, he'd had the close-up experience of the meaning of total inertia, total living death. Those horrid masks where once there had been human faces seemed totally unresponsive to and unaware of everything. But he had been given—true or false—to understand that sophisticated tests had been made which indicated that somewhere, dimly, deeply inside, those creatures were not totally out of it but aware, helplessly aware, of what they had become, and that they *felt.* . . .

When Joel was past the exit to his apartment, he smiled. He had a sense of great expectations, of vast horizons, of limitless possibilities. Everything had the almost forgotten flavor and excitement of the unknown. Ah! the unknown, that great and inspiring realm. Its element of danger added spice. Seamlessly the freeway merged with a larger roadway, an interstate. He could imagine the splendor of the vistas in the sunlight; even now, in the night, he could see features of the gracefully hilly landscape. The road was fine, sometimes dipping and rising in graceful undulations and looping around hill bases and stretching straight and flat for miles and curving so shallowly there was no slightest sense of strain. The engineering was a marvel, the roadway subtly banked on the curves so that the car's wheels followed the turn perfectly without steering.

Literally, the finely adjusted wheels were responsive to the tilt and turn of the banked pavement, feeling their way around with no help from the steering wheel. He tested, his hands upturned on his lap at 70 mph. Actually, speedometers were always set 5 miles fast, so it amounted to only 65. He tried no hands when the speedometer showed 75. No problem. The banking was calculated to handle pretty fast driving.

How fast? He grinned.

This car, this superb power plant with God knows how much capacity, had never been driven over 80. Except once on a little down-grade he had seen the needle touch 85 and he'd quick-slowed. His right-now speed was enjoyable but carefully sensible. He was just right. In synch with the universe.

But ah, there were possibilities beyond this.

Limitless possibilities.

That's what life fully lived was all about. Scared little people settled into straitjacket routines. For the sake of security. There was no such thing, only temporary illusions of it. Fantasies. Everybody, Maury once said, including those who fantasied that there was real security, everybody lived in a private soap bubble—or was it cocoon—of fantasy.

His next future-oriented goal was 90.

He reached it fast on a straight-level stretch.

It was the fastest he'd ever pushed this car!

A tiny rise chewed his speed down a few miles. But he soon had it back up and beyond, in the midnineties!

He could see it ahead. The wall. The wall of rain. About a mile ahead.

About a half mile.

A few hundred yards later he caught the first drops and got the wipers going and sent the highbeam lights stabbing ahead. He could see the main body of the storm, thick, as distinct as a wall. A straight-down heavy downpour, a veritable cloudburst. He thought, "Slow down!" But his foot on the accelerator didn't get the message.

He got the kind of grin on his face that the morticians had stitched into Mom's cheeks and rouged mouth. After the encounter between the car she was riding in and the drunk driver who'd gone to jail a whole day and had his license suspended for six months.

Joel crashed into the rain wall without slackening speed,

The white-brightness of the powerful beams of light lost focus and instead of penetrating straight ahead mushed out, spreading to the sides and upward till they looked like a shapeless giant ghost moving constantly ahead of him. The straight-down rain was now hitting the windshield head on, and the wipers moving in a frenzy couldn't keep up with the flood. It was like shooting through a cloud as if the sky wasn't falling but had already fallen. It would soon drown the wipers and the engine and whole car along with its occupant. Which called for a new stratagem, namely more speed. Like, if possible, 100, if he could push it that high. So he could get out faster, not need to have a deep-sea diving angel come down here to this cloud at the bottom of heaven to hunt for him. Like . . . not like . . . the otherworldly helmeted salvage diver with a green oxygen tank on his back who'd gone down to the silty bottom of the river for a couple of days hunting for Mom.

Suddenly he was on the other side of that rain wall, past the storm which had left a miles-long wake of wetness on the level stretches. In the hollows were shallow pools that splashed ten feet high on both sides as he drove through.

His speed, he saw, when he had time to look, was down. He had chickened out like gutless Chicken Little running around mindlessly yelling that the sky was falling. The speedometer was way down to just over 80. In some moods, Sis used to hug and pet him and read to him from picture books and she was warm and soft-talking and sweet-smelling, and they'd have joking, laughing fun.

"Humpty Dumpty sat on a wall, Humpty Dumpty had a great fall . . . because he was a bad egg. What kind of egg are you? A good egg, are you? Want bacon with it? Yes? OK. Wolves like bacon too. What does the wolf say? No no no, no . . . *not* come right in and set a spell and give me your basket, Red Riding Hood. He says, 'I'll huff and I'll puff and I'll *blow* your house *down.*' Who lays eggs, Paul? Mom! You know what Paul says? The Easter Bunny lays eggs. That's a *good* joke. Go tell Mom your joke, and hustle back so I don't have to come twist your ear and I'll read you about that gutless Chicken Little."

He had failed in his new goal of 100 mph. The secret of positivism and hopefulness and future orientation, Dr. Dornstadter told him at Halfway House after he was free of Shaunautaukee, was to set constant new goals. Small new goals, and after reaching one, strive for another.

He reached 100. The goal was 105. Ah, he made it!

Now the orderly programmatic advance called for 110.

There had been several miles of drizzling but the air was clear now, the roadbed dry.

He had no time for thinking. He just concentrated on keeping his eyes on the road. Pink smears of taillights were constantly hurtling toward him while oncoming headlights sometimes blazed at him from across the median.

On the next downgrade he swooped past 110 clear to 120 and it took real effort to keep the accelerator on the floor.

The next climb chewed him back down to 115. But up on the level again he regained the loss. And bettered it, straining toward 125.

Excessive, this speed. Dangerous. Excesses of any kind were dangerous since those brain butchers had crippled him and made intensities impossible.

Women required intensities in a man. Even Pam.

Markings on the pavement were indistinct. Side of the road and overhead signs came at him too fast, mere blur splotches of white, green. And yellow. He had to be alert for the curves on his own.

Monkey see, monkey do. A monkey in a closet saw a naked man on Sis's naked body and then the man got off and the monkey came and mounted her and pumped away like she liked and the man howled laughing and cheering, whooping, "Ride'er cowboy!" and she got the giggles and threw him off asking what in the world did he think he was doing since he was nowhere near where he would have to be to do anything a man did. Nice try, but really a joke. A joke she shared with everybody who'd listen. All her sister whores thought it was cute, and after Sis was dead one of them gave him another try when he was eleven.

A woman's scarf had flown out of some damned car and pasted itself to the windshield!

He got the wipers going, hoping they'd brush the obstruction off without the cloth wadding and jamming under the blades. It was a sheer material. Very fine white silk, he guessed. The left wiper blade passed right over the material and it stuck to the glass. One thing he didn't need when he was driving this fast was any kind of obstacle to his view of the road.

The scarf wasn't too bad. He could see right through it. But— Then the thin material began to gather into little creases and wads that formed disconcerting lines and shadows. The position of the strange lines and dark little circles seemed to take on a definite pattern and shape . . . like . . . like . . . rounded eyes and arched brows and lower down a curve line just where the mouth of a face would be. . . . And that's what it was, a face, not a scarf but a ghost-pale face!

Then it was gone, the face, the ghost face. Virgie! *Omigod.*

He was overintense! Hallucinating.

The windshield was clear! And so was his mind. He had to watch for real, here-and-now curves. Even the shallowest ones at this speed could mean a crash.

There was a temptation, a gutless temptation to slow down. But somehow, somehow, a momentum had built up to an irreversible level and was a force in itself, as strong as his will to resist. Stronger than, he hoped. Almost hoped.

There was a momentum to situations, to relationships. A continuity, an unbreakable continuity, maybe, as if one's will had been surrendered and events themselves dictated everything. When the connection had been made, it couldn't be broken, not if there was a powerful emotional investment.

He thought about "ventilating," about "scream therapy," and wondered contemptuously if he would be able to hear himself above the high whining and roaring and screaming of the engine and the tires. He remained grimly silent.

He could feel shudders and shakes through the frame of the car. He thought with detachment that at any instant a piece of stressed metal could snap, or if he didn't let up, the overheated engine could lock and throw the whole machine out of control. He kept his foot jammed to the floor.

"Enough!" he thought, and could not ease up on the gas pedal.

If only . . . if only . . . he could just take his hands off the steering wheel. Tentatively, he relaxed his grip. There were sudden spasms in his fingers; they clutched the wheel and clung.

He thought he saw a curve, up there at the forward edge of his headlights. He switched to high beam and there it was.

It came hurtling at him. He held the accelerator to the floor. He dropped his right hand to his leg, palm up. The grip of his left hand slackened. Just before the start of the curve he took his left hand off the wheel entirely. But it hovered there, fingers semiflexed, an inch away.

There was no traffic nearby. He was in the left lane. The turn was to the left but so easy and gradual that he felt no pull.

As foolproof as these banked curves were, they would not take this speed. The forward momentum of the heavy car would continue its straight line.

There was a ten-to-fifteen-foot drop from the edge of the roadway out there beyond the guardrails to a rocky field. Once he left the curve and became airborne there was no way he could survive the smashing crashing destruction. He willed his left hand, which was hovering an inch under the steering wheel to relax on down onto his lap with his other hand.

Then he started to shut his eyes, but instead had grabbed the wheel in sudden terror and took his foot off the accelerator and fought with all the strength of his arm and upper body to swing the wheel and pull back down into the curve. But he went over the right edge of the road, and then the two right wheels were both off the pavement. He sweated and fought to stop the side skid. He gunned some power into the engine, aiming desperately at the road. At almost the last instant before he slammed into the guardrail he got power and traction and pulled onto the road. A big over-the-road monster came at him, its airhorns screaming, its lights blinking on-off in rhythm, and the crushing 100 tons traveling at 80 bore down on him and barely swerved enough to miss him. Its airhorns continued to bellow for a mile, the driver in such a rage he might be looking for a crossover so he could come back and beat him bloody.

Joel wanted to stop on the median, but he kept going—at 50 mph.

You blew it, he kept thinking. *You blew it.*

The perfect solution had been back there at that brink of eternity. He couldn't have missed. Whichever way it had come out he'd have won. Dead, he would have been home free. Alive, but crippled for life, Pam could never desert him, so he couldn't ever lose her.

He got a cigarette between his lips and fumbled for matches. He couldn't get a match lit, and with one clumsy scrape he knocked the packet out of his hand. He felt around on the floor but had to take his eyes off the road and quit trying for a smoke. The lighter didn't work. There was a kind of lookout viewing area a few miles on. Empty. He pulled off and parked and searched for his matches.

He found them there under the edge of his seat.

There was something else under there.

A brown paper sack. He let it lie and had his

smoke.

He knew what was in the sack. He'd been meaning to throw it away. When he found the right place.

The incinerator in his apartment building had seemed to be the right place. But he had had second thoughts. The chute down from his floor to the basement incinerator sometimes got clogged, for one thing.

Maybe this was just the place, a nowhere place between places, where any one of thousands of cars could have throw it out, just a few ounces of the tons of highway litter that couldn't be traced to, or be of interest to anybody. With the possible exception of far-out fetishists who bought or stole dirty panties.

He got the sack in hand. He opened the window and heard a distant engine. He listened to its sound rising and coming closer and saw the outer reaches of the headlights. Then he waited till the car sped past and its sound diminished. Nothing else was coming. Now was the time. A quick toss, a quick backup on to the road, and then away. No. He shut the window.

That truck driver could pull into the next truck stop or into a state police station somewhere in the area and report a wild lunatic passing him at over a hundred and then gunning out into the road into his path. The truck might've jackknifed and rolled over and killed the driver, so the man would have blood in his eye. And the state police could be damned interested in getting a drunk or doped-up driver into custody. If there were cruisers looking for him and they spotted his parked car here, the troopers would check him out pretty good. They wouldn't miss a paper sack out there. . . .

Joel got moving. He started worrying about possibly passing a truck stop. Or a state police barracks. He was tensely on the lookout for exit signs. He might be under electronic surveillance the whole length of this big road with a radio alert to every post and every cruiser on duty.

He saw the two-mile, then the one-mile signs indicating both an exit and truck stop together up ahead. The exit was just past the truck stop. Whether or not the big rig that almost hit him was among the parked trucks he didn't know. But it wouldn't be quick enough to get on his tail or maneuverable enough to follow and was too big for the smaller roads.

He followed a shapeless, aimless pattern over miles and miles of county and local and small state roads. He went through a handful of sleeping towns and villages and then waking towns, heading north, then west, then north, then west. Never a south turn or east turn.

Joel realized there *was* an overall pattern to his route. In general he was getting closer and closer to Keystone, where . . . he knew the itinerary of the Spring Tour by heart, as well as every work on the program of every concert . . . Pam's orchestra would be playing tonight.

He smiled.

There was a predawn glow in the eastern sky, pale, then coloring. He glimpsed the top edge of the rising sun but missed the moment when it was fully risen, when the orange-red disk would have been balanced like a giant coin on the edge of the horizon.

He considered throwing the sack in a ditch alongside one of those fenced farm fields. There was nobody anywhere to see it. He'd be long gone before anybody did. Still . . . No . . . Not here, not yet . . . He had to be sure, and avoid carelessness and . . .

Forgetting small details was bad. He was known at the office, and by Pam, too—sometimes it exasperated her—for tedious concern with small details. She hadn't been all that totally pleased by his laborious organization of all her musical scores and records, at first. She'd been habitually losing things and spent useless aggravating time and got fussy about looking for them. But she missed the disorder, the creative chaos, in a way, and complained about having her life turned into an efficiency machine. But underneath it all she was touched by what he considered a precious gift to her. He offered to dismantle the system and restore the creative chaos. He promised to quit presuming that he could understand the needs of a true artist. He would stop trying to reduce her to his drab, plodding level. Pam became agitated and very sorry and talked about being ashamed of herself.

"Ashamed?" he'd protested. "No, Pam, no, no. I can't stand it. *Ashamed?* You *couldn't* be."

How could she be ashamed? Impossible. That would mean she'd done some wrong. And by definition a goddess could do no wrong. Whatever wrong she did became right. That's what he'd felt and meant, whatever way he had said it.

But, of course, there'd been a too-muchness about that attitude, a heaviness about it that made her nervous since definitely she was an earthbound flesh-and-blood woman.

She had come to prefer his system to her creative chaos and to brag about it and about him. She considered him a strength to lean on.

Which he was and would always be.

Exactly when he'd shoved those panties into the sack without looking at them he wasn't sure, but it had been in the afternoon. At that time he had still hoped that they were Pam's, and clean.

During the evening, between the time he arranged the date with Darleen and when he picked her up after work at 3 A.M. this morning, he had gone back to the apartment. He had known by then that the panties were Mona's and must be got rid of.

Or laundered. He had no stomach for touching them in any way or looking at them for traces of semen or vaginal fluid. He'd opened the sack and sniffed, but the only odor detectable was brown paper sack.

He'd gone down to the car, carrying the sack for later disposal. He had made a thorough inspection of the car. As he had known, there was no body in the trunk. And neither in the trunk nor the passenger interior was there any evidence that Mona had been in it. No boots or footlets or chubby fur jacket, and no stains or smears of lipstick or anything else on the upholstery. Maybe he'd missed a few hairs from that coat . . . he'd have to find a car wash where he could use a vacuum cleaner before he got to Keystone. He had wiped away all smudges which could be fingerprints on glass and on the chrome and enameled surfaces.

He had jammed the paper sack under the front seat before going to pick up Darleen. It hadn't seemed smart to throw it out along a route he traveled regularly. He'd put it out of mind. His top priority had been the vital date with Darleen. Preparation for it had been far more important than the problem of the panties.

Right now the big problem had become those panties in the paper sack. Driving and frowning through a nameless two-block long town, he thought, *Oh, to hell with it!* and threw the sack out into the street.

He stopped for breakfast around eight o'clock. Ham and eggs and English muffins with strawberry jam. He had two cups of coffee and lingered over a smoke. He bought cigarettes and went outside to the filling station, feeling vital. He gassed up and had the oil checked. Two quarts low. Good lord, he'd really burned it up! The radiator was thirsty too. They had to put air in his right front tire.

He phoned the motel in the town where Pam would have stayed after last night's concert.

Everybody had checked out. The orchestra would be enroute to Keystone.

So was he, Joel thought, and got in the car smiling. It ran like new. It steered just fine. Later, with a wash and wax job, it would look as great as it was.

The feature work in tonight's concert in Keystone would be Pam's favorite symphony.

10

In private, Pam always referred to that music simply as her symphony.

It was hers more than the composer's, she'd say laughingly, because it had been only part of his musical life, but ran through all of hers. It had been there in the beginning and had, in fact, caused her birth as a musician.

She remembered the exact night she had first heard it. The second Saturday in November, when she was nine years old. It had been an occasion. A capital *O* Occasion!

Her parents had taken her to Symphony Hall for the first time. To hear a major orchestra for the first time. Not Tiny Tots or Kiddie Concert music or any kind of summer music or the Boston Pops, but the real thing, the on-tour Boston Symphony itself. Live!

Her mother had primped her, and done her

hair center-parted, with two long tight braids at the sides. There had been tiny blue bows that matched her eyes at the braid tips. She'd worn a short-sleeved, knee-length, dotted white dress and wrist-length white gloves and white ankle socks and shiny new black patent Mary Janes. She'd put on a silver locket necklace and carried a borrowed evening purse. She had felt all dressed up, and excited. Very.

She remembered her father nudging her mother and saying, "Look at Saucer Eyes."

"No I'm not, Daddy."

"Yes, you are."

"No I'm not, Daddy."

"He's just teasing, dear."

Telling Joel about it, Pam laughed.

"When my daddy would call me that, I'd do this," she said, and squinted.

"You've still got saucer eyes," Joel said.

"No, I haven't."

"Yes, you have."

"My face is so much bigger now in relation to my eyes. You couldn't call me that now."

"Yes I can, Saucer Eyes."

"You're teasing me too," she said, pleased with him. "I knew he liked my eyes. But I pretended I thought he didn't. You know. We teased. Fun. I was sure glad he did it that night. Because everything else was so . . . so . . . strange. And immense. *Beautiful!* I had never before set foot in Symphony Hall. I just couldn't get over the magnificence. Like a palace. And that was just the lobby. Thick

dark red carpets and portraits of great composers. And all the dressed-up people in
elegant dresses and jewels and furs, and everybody in a grand party mood. There were busts
of Beethoven and Bach and Brahms. I didn't
know at the time that they were known by
everybody in music as the three B's. I thought
how quick and smart Daddy was to notice all
their names started with *B* and to come up
quick like that with 'The Three B's.'

"Oh, we had records at home that I'd heard
and paid no attention to. Beethoven's name I
knew from hearing a record at an assembly in
the school auditorium. But I never had had a
music lesson. Not even piano, even though my
mother played and wanted to teach me. What I
was going to be was a nurse. Or a chef . . . for
goodness' sake . . . or a painter. I got to be the
champion water-colorist in the fourth grade.
I'd advanced from earlier crayon masterpieces.
They had a lot of busts of other famous composers there in the Symphony Hall lobby, too.
One of them was Tschaikovsky. His name was
spelled so many different ways that nobody
could misspell it, a music teacher told me. A
man on a date made a joke about the head of
the bust might fall off. They both laughed."

Pam had stopped talking. The saucer eyes
had become distant, Joel remembered. Her
silence and a trace of a frown on her face had
begun to make him nervous. Self-conscious.

"I was so dumb," she finally said, "that I
thought the bust might really be broken. But it

wasn't. I looked. I didn't see anything funny to laugh about. I was disgusted, thinking what a dumb girl to date a dumb man like that. I let it roll off my back, and walked on with my daddy to the cloak room to check his hat and overcoat. He said he usually folded the coat on his lap and put his hat in the underseat rack where it always fell out. That night he was being a big spender and anticipated buying us all orange drinks at intermission in honor of the occasion of my first concert.

"It was years later before I got the 'joke' about Tschaikovsky's head falling off. Did you know he really thought his head would fall off if he didn't hold it on?"

"No." He half frowned, then half smiled. "You wouldn't be putting me on?"

"Honest. It's so. Myrtle got the book if you want to read it. Myrtle's the cello in our string quartet. She's been here. Remember?"

"Of course. She plays in your studio with the other three of you. We never say anything to each other, but I know who she is."

"She'd be glad to lend the book to you. It's a no-holds-barred, authentic, documented biography. Whew"—Pam fanned her face—"all the loathesome psychoanalytic sexual material. Genius, yes, he's got to be forgiven for everything because of that genius. I don't hold his romantic emotional excesses against him. Nothing dry about him. His music was true beauty and the power to move. But personally the man was a horrible mental case.

Tortured. In one phase he was a conductor. A very good conductor, too, practically as great as he was a composer. But right there on the podium while he was conducting, right during the performance he was scared his head would fall off. And he held his hand on it to keep it from happening."

"Incredible," Joel said tonelessly. He had felt damned uncomfortable. He stood up and asked Pam if she could use a Choc-ola or tea or anything. He'd gone out to the kitchen.

Pam followed him. "You must be tired of listening to me ramble on. Sit down, I'll get us the drinks."

"You're more comfortable in the front room. If you'll excuse me a minute . . ." He'd gone to the bathroom, relieved his bladder, washed his hands. He never mentioned "bathroom" in relation to himself and certainly not in relation to her. Unthinkable to acknowledge in words that such biological functions existed. When he had rejoined her, neither of them mentioned the fact that her speaking of mental illness might have disturbed him.

Choc-olas had to be shaken up before opening and drinking. They both drank from the bottles. He pointed out—needlessly—that it had been the first drink they'd ever had together. And though he'd never tasted it before, he told her solemnly, it became then, and was and forevermore would be his favorite.

Too heavy. It had been too heavy a thing to say. . . .

Joel saw the Interstate in the distance angling across his road. It might be safe to get back on it. At worst, that truck driver who could have reported him to the state police would have identified his car by color, model, and make. Certainly he *couldn't* have read the license.

Even so, this earthier route was preferable. It was in touch with a lot of small towns, and provided interesting close-ups of barns and farm houses, pigs and people, to occupy his mind.

During lunch hour he stopped in a medium large town with a courthouse square and shops. He wandered, making himself a part of the slow, somehow wholesome, atmosphere.

He saw a jeweler's sign and went in the store that featured watches and watch repair. There wasn't much stock; no music-clef or musical-note brooches. Some undistinguished bracelets and pins. He'd like to get her a jeweled anklet and kneel and put it on her. There were none. He bought a necklace with a heart-shaped pendant on a thin gold chain. Down the street he saw some pretty shoes for her dainty, graceful feet, and bought her size. Carrying the shoes and the trinket he felt a sense of achievement. He was hungry. There was a restaurant at Main and First. What a hell of a good and simple thing it would be to eat in a homey, no frills, just-folks place! He went in and had a good lunch. A trifle heavy and greasy. The "coffee with" was grayish and it tasted . . .

well, earthy. No matter.

He phoned the Hospitality Inn Motel, where the orchestra would be billeted for the two nights in Keystone.

He got Pam's room number but no answer. Talking to the desk again, he found out that most of the musicians were at lunch. It didn't bother him. He was on an upswing, seeing things positively. He didn't leave a message. It was better for Pam not to know he was on his way. There was an extra kick about surprises.

When he called from the next town, the information was that they'd all gone downtown to a rehearsal in Municipal Auditorium.

He shrugged and drove on. He was only an inch away from her by the map. The upswing of his mood continued. Actually, it was higher. Almost to the point where some of the drearier sorts of psych-iatrists and psych-ologists and assorted psychos would pounce and pronounce him manic, in the manic phase of manic-depressive psychosis. God, the way they loved pasting on labels. Gave them a sense of security, no doubt. A farce. Because everybody had moods; normal minds were constantly changing, shifting like smoke. Nobody was ever the same person through even one whole day. They woke up snarling like crawling monsters in a cave but were on their hind legs and joking before noon, and by bedtime, with their cocks up, they were flying like angels.

The mental health Establishment had a vested interest in increasing its territory. It was a rare day when some spokesman didn't pontificate about how 20 million—next week 50 million—people were suffering mental disease without knowing it. "So-o-o-o, Mr. Joel Danton, you haff enurgy ven you should be tired and worried. Vot if you go through your whole life always imagining you're happy and healthy. Dot's sick."

So, all right. Dead Mona was an unpleasant reality which he did not *seem* to be facing in this vital upbeat phase which was—sorry, Doc, not manic—simply based on loving anticipation of being with Pam. Mona's death, her tragic death, was a fact. A serious problem which he should face, and which he *did* face, knowing full well that his had been the *hands* which were *physically* responsible for her death. But he had proved beyond reasonable doubt, had satisfied his own demanding standards, by logic, irrefutable step-by-step logic, that such a crime, especially the dumping of a human body into a foul sewer, would have been impossible to him, a man of sensibility, in his prelobotomized condition. The lobotomy was responsible. The guilt belonged to that sadistic surgeon and his accomplices in the murder of his brain. And tonight—or tomorrow night—with Pam and with that law professor, Dr. Webberly Treat, he would begin to establish that guilt so that when the body was discovered his defense would already be under way.

He frowned. He should not be jumping the

gun. And he must not think negatively about "when the body was discovered." He'd stay positive. *If* the body was discovered. Chances were it wouldn't be for a long time and by then the connection to him would be forgotten or unprovable, even if vaguely remembered. Darleen, for instance, would probably be in another job or married or moved out of town. So it was best in every way that he hadn't killed her. Two girls disappearing in two nights from the same place he'd been on both occasions would have started an investigation sure as hell.

He frowned. He didn't like that line of thought. It called his whole motivation into question . . . as if it might have been to his own advantage to spare Darleen. Far from it; he had felt it was in his best interests to get rid of a dangerous witness. He had not been crazy-like-a-fox, making mean cunning little calculations and deciding it might be riskier to kill her than not to. He had decently and simply chosen her life over his own.

The gold medal he was pinning on himself for not killing her was tarnished. Admitted. He'd taken her to that limestone pit with the worst of motives but he had not been able to graft those bad intentions onto his basic character to the point where he could commit cold-blooded murder. It had truly been, just as his attempts to understand imaginatively the mind of Cleo's and Virgie's torturer had been, a magnificent failure.

He checked—rechecked for the third time, in fact—to be sure Darleen hadn't dropped anything on the seat or floor. Such as a bobby pin that might not be the color Pam used . . . or a lipstick-smeared cigarette in the ashtray . . . she hadn't smoked . . . or a shoeprint . . . nonsense . . . or a raveling from coat or . . . or a strand of hair. . . . Nothing. She'd left no residue that he could see. He wiped her out of mind.

He was thinking of Pam and soaring as he approached Keystone. Maybe he was already in a swallowed-up used-to-be town with its own name, or in East Keystone for all he knew. The traffic was heavier, forcing him to reduce speed. Presently there was a shopping center, then countless blocks of grubby businesses and a plague of traffic signals, and his momentum was gone. The ground level aggravations were endless.

He kept an eye on the sunlighted snow of Keystone Heights, whose humped contour dominated the middle distance ahead. From the boulevard that circled the base he could see the streets and inaccessible mansions on the flank of Fat Hill, as it was called locally. He followed a tangent onto a wide straight avenue and soon he saw the Hospitality Inn Motel. In front a big bright fluttering banner was strung across the street, welcoming the orchestra.

He could see the leased tour buses and the orchestra members lining up to board out in back.

Joel drove on past. He could be at Municipal Auditorium in 18 minutes, he knew. He had driven from here to there often enough. He'd be there long before they began the rehearsal. Plenty of time. He slowed up, turned onto another street for a block, zigged left for a block, then zagged, left again, and was soon back to the street the buses would use. He parked to wait and be ready to turn after the buses came along and follow them downtown. The idea of tailing the orchestra and giving Pam a real surprise keened him.

In a few minutes, the buses were coming. He grinned and geared in. They passed him. He moved out and surprised himself. By making a left, not a right, turn.

What the devil had he done that for? Why was he retracing the way he'd come? He sure hadn't turned back because he didn't want to hear them rehearsing "her" symphony. It was his favorite symphony too. His reason must be that . . . well, maybe something was tugging at his memory. His mind was so full of things that he must have forgotten, some kind of something that had been registered among the must-do's but . . . but he'd carelessly let it slip away from him.

Some trifling something, undoubtedly. The way everybody had little memory lapses once in a while. There were spots of amnesia in perfectly normal, undamaged brains. It didn't indicate any big amnesia . . . or whole areas of destroyed brain cells spreading out toward . . .

toward, uh, what was the word . . . *blackout*. No, nothing dangerous, dangerous to Pam, like that . . . Just stay calm, in control. Unintense. Cool, man, that was the word. Yeah.

He'd beaten those brain butchers so far. And all he had to do was keep from getting grim and tense. The harder you chased something, the faster it would run away. Easy. Come to a mental stop. But keep driving without slowing too much.

Jesus K. Rist . . . that car behind him came up fast, inches from crumpling his back bumper. He could see in his mirror the squat glunk driving the car and loudmouthing and honking his horn. Joel boosted his too slow speed. He got off the street into a fast-food driveway. All he needed was a collision and a fight with the driver and cops coming to the accident scene, and reports to the insurance company.

Car wash! That's what he'd forgot. Easy to think of something when you weren't trying to.

There was no urgency about the car wash. There was something else. A motel he'd passed coming into town. A way-out motel on the outskirts. It had individual cabins. Where he and Pam could have privacy. Away from the orchestra. Advantages to that. And why crowd in and force Pam's probable roommate, Myrtle, to get out. No way to treat a good buddy, making her lug that cello around trying to find hole-in space with somebody else. Or get another room *if* there was a vacancy among the Hospitality Inn's wall-to-wall cells.

He brightened at the prospect of getting accommodations at that other motel. But . . .

To cut Pam off from her own world out in some dump motel would maybe be too disruptive for her and God only knew what kind of noisy drunken-partying crowds with their loud, trash music there would be out there to torture her ears and sensibilities when she was involved in creating *great* music, fit for the gods.

He headed again for Municipal Auditorium, thinking about Pam.

A goddess should have no childhood. She should spring full-formed from Jove's brow like that one in ancient mythology. As hard as he tried, Joel had not been able to visualize Pam as a nine-year-old with a mother and daddy on that "Occasion" when she'd gone to the Symphony Hall in the city where she was born.

She had tried to recreate for him the joy of it all when she'd first heard "her" symphony. The setting and the overall mood and the look and feel of everything she had responded to, including the sounds as she described them, had been easy for him to absorb. But not how she actually looked. And some of the child-level things she reported saying seemed to him to have nothing to do with her. He didn't doubt that her little girl kind of talk was the kind of things apt to be said by normal nine-year-olds. But there was no way they could be part of her specialness.

Besides, while they were drinking the Choc-olas, he'd known how unhappy she was for having brought up the subject of mental ill-ness. There had been the poisonous threaten-ing atmosphere of Shaunautaukee right there in their magic high tower.

He had become much more nervous than he dared let her know. While they'd been drinking those Choc-olas he'd had a ripping, jolting proof that Paul Borland might be buried but wasn't quite dead down there under his new Joel Danton self. Because the chocolate drinks had become—briefly, very briefly—strawberry soda. And Joel had rawly visualized that broken pop bottle with Virgie's gore on it that symbolic substitute for wine in that poetic: *a loaf of bread, a jug of wine—and thou beside me—screaming in the wilderness.*

He began to coax Pam to go on telling him about the "Occasion." But the joyous spirit of it was ruined.

There was no starting up from a dead stop.

Not that night.

Next night she was very tired. She stretched out on the sofa and wanted the room dim with no TV or music. She didn't want to read any-thing. Or talk. Or listen. Or be with anyone.

He tiptoed around, walking on eggs. He went in the bedroom and just sat. He went in the kitchen and just stood. He went in her sanctu-ary, her studio.

He fingered through a file drawer of records

and tapes. The composer of her symphony, who had one of those unspellable and unpronounceable Eastern European names, was definitely not among the greats. His one major work was the last playable music he ever wrote. Joel thought of it as *The Symphony of the Silence*. They had eleven versions of it by world-renowned orchestras with famous conductors, including a recording by Pam's own orchestra before she joined it.

Joel had a strong impulse to play it. To play it now might be the worst thing he could do.

He looked over at the record player, hooked up to stereo speakers in the rest of the apartment. She didn't want to hear anything. Maybe least of all "her" symphony. He was scared to put anything on the turntable or in the tape slot. He closed the file drawer.

He fiddled with the record player controls, setting volume, balance, bass, treble just so. The speakers out there would be just right from the first note in the first movement. If he turned the player on. He went out to ask her if, hopefully, she might feel better if she heard her favorite music . . . or anything at all.

She had told him *no music*. He chickened out at the edge of the front room. He mustn't disturb her. He had a vague, guilty sense of anxiety.

There was no direct light in the big room. Just a seep of deflected illumination from the smallest lamp in the bedroom, further muted because he'd swung the bedroom door till it was open only an inch. The big window drapes were shut. There was a hush-light atmosphere, a strange twilight atmosphere through the whole space of the room.

He gazed over at her. She was covered from chin to ankles by a glossy robe. There was a pale, ethereal glow of luminosity about her as she lay there softly surrounded by darkness, as if her supine body were afloat. Sleeping in a cloud. Maybe she *was* asleep.

He tiptoed a few steps, silent on the carpet. He paused. He peered, staying out in the middle section of the room. It wasn't certain if her eyes were fully or only partially closed. He had a sense of tingling as though there was a mild, invisible flow of electricity through the air.

Cautiously, he sidestepped closer to the sofa.

If she was awake and aware of him, he didn't want to seem to be hovering.

Her naturally golden hair was loose, luster-less in the shadows, fanning out beside her face. Her face was as still as a flower. A flower scent rose from her. Her feet were bare. He had a rushing impulse to kiss her feet and face and whole body. He was aware of the sound of his breathing. He held his breath. Listened for some faint sound of her breathing. He heard none. His heartbeat had become so strong that he could feel it pounding in his throat.

He told himself to calm down. Her eyelids were definitely closed. He mustn't wake her. He started to turn away. He wobbled, almost

losing his balance, risking a clumsy fall that
would wake her. He stayed where he was. He
started to smoke. He needed a smoke. But the
sizz-*snick* and sharp burst of light might wake
her. The perfection of her beauty at this precise
instant in time might be spoiled and lost
forever. . . .

One night she'd lain on her bed in this position. Not in this kind of strange twilight, but
lustrous in the lamplight. He'd come into the
bedroom. He had stood looking down. A sort of
panic had come over him. She'd looked so
totally motionless. He had bent to listen for
her breathing. Then he had cupped his hand a
few inches above her nose and mouth, trying to
detect whether there was warm breath. Or
none. She'd waked up! Startled. The wild-
flower blue saucer eyes stared fixedly at him.
And for an instant as fleeting as the passing
shadow of a bird's wing, fear had touched her
flower face.

No, no, he *mustn't* startle her now. He bent
down to the sofa.

"Pam . . ." he whispered.

"I'm awake! Please let me be!"

"Yes," Joel said. He started away.

"If you had something to say, say it."

He came back. "I don't want to get you any
more upset. But I think . . . well, maybe I
know . . . I hope I know what's disturbing you
so much."

"Disturbing me. Nothing's *disturbing* me.
I'm just worn out from the rehearsal."

"They don't usually wear you out."

"I don't like the new work we have to learn. That's the trouble."

"You sure? You always like learning new works. You like the challenge, and achievement, whether you personally like what you're playing or not. Professional pride. You've got that. I admire that."

"Oh, for goodness' sake!"

She flopped over on her stomach.

"Sorry. I'll let you rest."

She sat up, put on her slippers, and said petulantly, "What did *you* think was ailing me? Let's have some lights on."

He turned the lamps on.

"What I thought, Pam, was that you were worried about me. Afraid that your bringing up Tschaikowsky's mental illness last night might have . . . well . . . put the skids under me. Make me think about that period of my own mental illness in Shaunautaukee."

"All right. I don't doubt you're pretty much right."

She got up and went in the bedroom, saying her hair was a mess. He followed to the doorway and talked from there, watching her work impatiently with her hair.

"The subject of mental illness wouldn't cause me to relapse, Pam. I've read everything you've read about the composer of your favorite symphony. I know about his mental problems. It won't touch me . . . not negatively . . . to hear about the first time you heard his greatest work. Please finish telling me about that happy Occasion."

"I don't know. You *do* relieve me. You're calm about it. Mature about it. More than I was being. I'd really like to tell you all about it. Give me a minute to freshen up," she said, and went to the bathroom.

On that "Occasion" when she was nine, Pam had been in ignorant bliss about the composer of the music that had inspired her to become a musician, and specifically a violinist. She had declared after the concert that she was going to play in a symphony orchestra. She didn't say she *hoped* to realize such an ambition, but that she *would* play the violin in a symphony orchestra. Even though she'd never had a violin in her hands. She'd felt a touch of mysticism about it. It was by sheer accident that the person who'd been expected to use the ticket couldn't make the performance, and she went instead. Like people with passage on that big ship that sank who didn't catch the boat, she had the fates watching over her, and had connived to get her career as a symphonic violinist started.

When she was well launched as an advanced student several years later, it had broke her heart to read about the composer. His life had been a shuttle between madhouses and country retreats where he worked desperately at his music and "ran from the darkness."

The darkness he'd been constantly escaping caught up and swallowed him for good after he'd completed his major work. He had ended his days among the living dead in an asylum.

He had never heard his symphony performed.

But I heard it! Pam remembered saying to herself, and thinking, *I love you I love you I love you . . . you will never die in my heart . . .* and it was as if somehow his spirit would know, and her eyes flooded.

Pam came back into the room smiling. There was a little springiness to her step. She settled comfortably in her favorite chair in a buoyant mood and told him in great, enthusiastic detail about her first hearing of that symphony, a lilt in her sweet voice. . . .

Or, rather, she *started* in a buoyant mood to tell him in great, enthusiastic detail about her first hearing of that symphony and he was avidly drinking her in with his eyes and ears and his whole being. . . .

Something intruded.

He saw a big WELCOME banner strung overhead across the street ahead, in front of the Hospitality Inn Motel, where Pam's orchestra was staying.

He had an unsettling *deja vu* sense that he had driven this stretch of boulevard before. The buses carrying the orchestra were already gone, he saw, driving into the grounds and looping around the backlot. He had got here too late.

Everybody was off to rehearsal in the Keystone Municipal Auditorium. He left the motel grounds thinking he could make it down-town in 18 minutes. . . .

"So, after being the big spender and treating us to orange drinks, Daddy decided he'd made a mistake to check his overcoat and went to get it so he could fold it like a pillow for me to sit higher and see the stage better. But the buzzer sounded before he could do it. We hurried back in the auditorium but everybody else was getting back to their seats too and the aisle was clogged and I thought we'd never get there, way down the aisle to the fifth row. Such wonderful seats. The houselights had already dimmed. I'd been sitting between them. And driving my mother to distraction. He let me have the aisle seat. . . .

"Joel, you're listening so owlishly. I can't tell what you're thinking. Or how you're responding, or *if* you're receiving me at all when I'm trying to . . . to . . ." Her voice trailed off and there was a deflated, moody look on her face.

"Sorry. I *know* what you're trying to do. Give me a gift, a part of your life. If you think I don't know what a precious thing that is and am not grateful . . ."

"Please don't say *grateful*, I just wanted to share good feelings like that with you. To help keep your spirits up. Like a while ago when I was down flat on my back, emotionally worn out, you lifted me right up. You knew what ailed me, and faced it squarely, and helped me not be a scaredy-cat."

She became self-conscious. She shifted her position. She'd had her right leg folded onto the seat cushion, her slippered foot tucked under her left leg. She put both feet on the floor. She sat with composure and attempted to continue telling him about that long-ago concert.

There was a difference in her tone. Pam was Pam again.

Not that unimaginable squirmy nine-year-old who either sat swinging her feet in Mary Janes, never dreaming Mary-Jane was a hippy slang translation of Mari-Juana, or else kept twisting from one side to the other, whispering to her parents. or standing up peering over one or the other shoulder of the man in front of her or standing facing backward at the audience on main floor balcony boxes or gawking up at the domed ornamented "sky-high ceiling of the *huge* beautiful palace," and exclaiming over and over about the simply just unbelievable wonderfulness of the thrilling live music. The short, lively program opener was so fast and dancy she could barely behave and sit still and yelled *Bravo* (all alone) at the end. She clapped her hands red when the conductor bowed and went off stage, then greeting him with more clapping like a long-lost friend when he returned two minutes later for the next, longer, more substantial work.

She kept hopping around at the orange juice stand telling everybody how she had simply worn herself out and could not stand any more concert and didn't know if she could even stay awake for the main event after the intermission. All that childish silliness and uncontrolled emotionalism was inappropriate to and totally unconnected with the true Pam.

"All that childish silliness," Pam said, as if reading his mind, "must have destroyed my image."

"Destroyed your image? I don't understand how you can imagine me thinking you were anything but cute."

"Oh, *cute!*"

Wrong word.

"I meant charming. A pretty little charmer. Crackling with life. What a wonderfully appreciative audience you were."

"I wouldn't want me in *my* audience. Not at an adult concert. Well at least I wasn't noisy and never talked during the actual music. Maybe loud whispering. But I tried more or less to sit with dignity." She laughed. "Sit with dignity, that's a good one. Anyway I felt solemn, very serious when the houselights were down after the intermission. The last of the audience was getting seated. I was actually impatient with my father and wanted to shush him for making a joke."

Not "Daddy" now, Joel noticed, but "my father."

"He said nobody should clap for the conductor before he conducted the music, but wait till afterward to decide if he deserved any applause. Some conductors I could name would never get any applause at all if they didn't get it ahead of time before anybody found out how rotten they were. And when it comes to this custom of standing ovations for everything, good or bad, because it's the 'in' thing to do . . . don't get me going on that. Myrtle's the one who can really get going on *that* subject. She knows good from bad and purely hates giving inferior junk a big reward so that actually superior music isn't properly valued.

"Where was I? Yes, the famous conductor waited and waited before coming out so the itch to applaud in the audience's palms would build up. He was an old hand, a showman, but a fine musician. At last he came hurrying out from the wings and got into the spotlight. And stayed there, bowing and smiling and milking it for all it was worth. I think even the strings were tapping their bows on their music racks. Of course I and my father and mother were applauding too."

It was very clear to Joel that she was viewing the performance from a distance now. From the viewpoint of an experienced onstage performer, and no longer that of a child in the audience.

"That conductor was a legend. A magic man. When he signaled for the applause to stop, turning his back and stepping his feet apart and raising his baton, I could've swooned. It was so thrilling I couldn't breathe. And then the music began."

She stopped.

Just to pause for breath, Joel assumed, at first.

Then for the longest time Pam didn't say or do anything. He thought maybe her eyes were flooding. But she didn't blink.

She shook her head, slightly, no, and later she said it aloud: "No. I can't."

Meaning she couldn't go on. Meaning she couldn't reexperience that main part of the "Occasion." Meaning she knew too much about that tragic magician who had created her symphony.

Joel did not know what to do or say or think.

"Excuse me. Back in a minute."

He went to the bathroom, relieved himself, and washed his hands.

Without thinking, he scratched at a little itching sensation on his left temple just in front of his sideburn. The skin there was a grafted patch from his own forearm. The original skin had become permanently scarred. Because after that lobotomy, he'd kept gouging at it till it beccame raw and infected. The skin no sooner began to scab and heal than he would gouge it raw, reinfecting it over and over again. The scarred skin had been replaced with a graft over the site of the lobotomy wound. Most of the time it was inconspicuous. Unless he scratched it too much. This itching was temporary. It would pass. He lowered his head. Then he had to clench his fist against a temptation to scratch it some more. If he let himself go on, he wouldn't be able to stop. He would end up digging at it. It would become inflamed and stand out like a red flag calling attention to what it was meant to conceal.

The itching became maddening! His arm seemed to rise up of its own will. He started scratching again. It was so goddamned satisfying he couldn't quit, he thought. And then he thought how that reminder of his lobotomy and Shaunautaukee would surely affect Pam. The skin was already pink. He mustn't get that area inflamed and throw her into anxiety again.

He thought about *The Symphony of the Silence.* He hurried to her studio and got it started, putting on headphones.

It took a while, but predictably Pam came back to the studio.

"What are you doing?"

"Listening a minute to something."

"Alone?"

"You don't want any music."

"What're you playing?"

"You know."

"Which orchestra?"

"Yours."

"Oh for goodness' sake, Joel. Start it over and switch to the speakers and listen with me."

"All right."

"You poor thing. You looked so pitiful."

I know, he thought, and soon joined her in the front room.

The first movement was called "weak and wandering" by one critic. Pam loyally called it perfection . . . though not very stirring. She considered it a professional, balanced, disciplined model of compositional structure . . . not really dull and tepid. It was "healthy" music. She never quite admitted that it wasn't the composition's health but the composer's that she found rewarding. She must have had the terrible suspicion that he wrote the first movement during one of his occasional spells of sanity.

Listening to it now through the speakers, she seemed to be so pleasantly engrossed that she scarcely knew Joel was there. Yet when he began to scratch his left temple, she looked across at him and slowly shook her head no no no. He folded his hands on his lap. They smiled at each other.

Joel showed her he was sharing her pleasure. Which amounted to a declaration of loyalty. A denial of her cellist friend Myrtle's assertion that it was junk, pink confetti for a nice old-fashioned ladies and gentlemen's lawn party. A collection of pretty little tunes that didn't even include the one truly memorable, exquisite melody that formed the theme and held the whole symphony together.

"You don't understand him, Myrtle. He was running from the darkness. And searching everywhere, trying to find something he *knew* existed. He had the faith and instinct to know beauty like that existed and he found it, that pure melody."

"Good, he should've junked the first movement and started where the symphony actually
begins. With the second movement."

Pam couldn't stand up against Myrtle's
superior musical knowledge. Myrtle had
wanted to be a musicologist and took a
master's in that field but couldn't land a job. A
homely, bony neuter, she never impressed anybody favorably with her personality. She audi-
tioned while she was marking time and waiting
for a job offer in her chosen field. Convinced
she had no real talent, she imagined that she
herself was the only one who really felt that the
music she made was outstandingly good. She
was genuinely surprised—and very
happy—when she was accepted into the
orchestra several years before Pam was. It was
Myrtle who had chosen Pam to become part of
a very special string quartet when one of the
violinists in it left town for another orchestra
job.

Their chamber group now played regularly
here in Pam's studio. The music they played
there with no audience was simply for the love
of music itself. It was very important to Pam.
The threat of its breaking up had worried Joel
so much that he'd goofed. He'd stuck his nose
into something he was absolutely totally unqualified to have an opinion about.

It had been after a session in her studio and
they had been having aftersnacks in the
kitchen and talking the talk of their private

world. When he had heard Pam trying to
defend "her" symphony, Joel had walked in
and said some fatuous, amateur something or
other, like, "That first movement really is
necessary. Very pleasant listening . . . a . . .
uh . . ."

They all—Myrtle, Pam, Betty, the other
violinist, Wanda, the viola player—looked at
him as if . . . as if . . .

Well, as if he didn't really eist. The others
were polite—he was Pam's husband after all,
and their host at that, and must be toler-
ated—but . . .

With the opening of the second movement,
Joel went swiftly to the record player in the
studio and, striving for perfect fidelity, he
made precision adjustments of volume, then
treble, then added a bit more strength to the
bass. He hurried back before Pam could get
fretful about his habit of constantly tampering,
trying to improve what was fine, just fine.

She had been enjoying the first movement
comfortably, languidly. But some starch had
come into her body. As if, deep down, she
agreed with Myrtle and *now* was when the real
music was starting and it needed serious listening.

It was in a minor key, Joel knew. He'd have
had to be deaf and dumb not to absorb some of
the language of her world. It was somber in
mood. Dark, massive, heavy. At once, it stated
the melodic theme at the center of the whole.
In the very opening notes he recognized that

unforgettable, poignant, melodic line which would lead to the center of the center, to the very heart and soul of its meaning:

The Silence.

The whole movement was strong and gripping, carrying the theme in variations in one after another section of the orchestra, and then by the whole orchestra clear through toward the end of the movement.

And then . . . the massive sound of the whole orchestra began to diminish. Gradually, it became softer . . . and softer. Every audience, without fail, Pam said, held on to that fading sound, listening intently for the point where the music vanished into inaudibility.

Joel listened . . . Pam listened . . . holding on . . . holding on . . . until . . . there it was. . . .

The point of inaudibility had been reached. And they were there . . .

In The Silence.

And in the hush of The Silence, Pam had told him, and he'd experienced it himself in audiences at her concerts, there was an unbreathing, a waiting sense of anticipation through the audience and through the orchestra itself, so strong that it was an almost physical grip—like a magic fusion and bond between all. As if the whole world together held its breath, waiting, waiting in that Silence, in that void, in that state of pre-existence, waiting to emerge out of nothingness into life. . . .

And at last, at last . . . a single violin began

to play that poignant melody in a thin sweet line which became imperceptibly fuller and richer every few notes as another and another and another violin joined in in a graceful uninterrupted flow until all fourteen of the first violins were playing and then all the second violins and the violas and the cellos and bass viols came in, followed quickly by the woodwinds and flutes and piccolos and brasses, tympani and percussion, and the whole orchestral sound swelled magnificently into pure, overpowering beauty, a triumphant celebration of life. . . .

The final movement was exultant and exuberant and exalted above the world.

Insidiously the music began to build toward climax, up and up and up in a rising tempo, blaring and softening and then blaring and softening, driving forward and backing off time and time again at an ever higher and higher pitch, thrusting and pulling back, thrusting and pulling back, in an exciting, almost sexual rhythm.

The strings were rushing, the sound of the violins feverishly quick like dancing flame, and there was an urgency to the heavier tones of the cellos and bass viols blending in with rich woodwinds, shrill flutes, and piccolos and the loud, raw, passionate bellowing of the massed brasses. Through it all came the hard, fast-driving beat of the drums, bang and bang and bang bang *bang,* and all at once the whole orchestra at full throat swept into a frenzy of deafening sound.

Then *chop!*

Right in the middle of an uncompleted phrase, everything stopped at once and it was all over.

The sudden total silence was stunning!

Nobody knew for sure if that ending was deliberate.

Or if the darkness had caught up with the composer right there at his worktable.

Either way, his celebration of the triumph over The Silence there in the middle of his greatest work had been premature.

11

Joel reached Keystone Municipal Auditorium. It was a tall, squarish, handsome building with a solid look of strength. It seemed profoundly significant to him that this edifice, this symbol of exalted human striving toward beauty, this monument to culture, was built of limestone.

He parked alongside the tour buses near the stage entrance and got out and drew his lungs full of cold clean air. He approached the door, and put out of mind the memory of approaching the Thir-Ten side door. He was himself, now, and in full control.

That episode, when the creation of those Shaunautaukee brain murderers had taken him over, was past, that whole sordid world safely behind him.

Just ahead was the shimmeringly beautiful golden princess in her higher world. He paused outside the door, needing another long breath. Then he went in.

The immediate problem was to get out of sight before anybody backstage challenged his right to be there. He moved as inconspicuously as possible along the side wall toward the double doors to the auditorium about twenty yards ahead at the foot of a shallow flight of steps. The orchestra, visible through the wings off to his left, was on stage in a lull, the conductor saying something barely audible at this distance, the musicians turning pages of the scores on their racks.

He searched for Pam, his repeated glances increasingly jumpy, but failed to catch even a glimpse of the back of her golden head.

He frowned. He stretched his stride, grasped the iron stair rail, and hurried down the half-dozen concrete steps, thinking she might have bent down out of view. He pushed the crossbar of one door. Locked. The other door opened. He stepped into a wide, carpeted passageway, then zigzagged toward and entrance to an inner aisle from which he could see the stage. He heard a battery of muffled drums, a blare of horns, and a soft undertone of strings. What if—his gut hollowed—Pam's violin was not among them?

Omigod, what if she wasn't there? She'd put up with extraordinary stress this whole past season with a different conductor to adjust to almost every week while candidates to replace the retiring maestro were trying out for the job. Then he'd got into that state, worrying her sick, the night before she left on tour. The tour itself was full of big and small dislocations and problems that made working conditions more tiring. Worst, his son-of-a-bitchery in not answering her phone calls had added pain beyond her endurance. If those final blows of his had silenced her music, it was *true* that each man killed the thing he loved.

Then he was in the hush-lighed auditorium. He turned his face toward the bright stage but shut his eyes. If she was not in the place she had earned in the first violins, Fifth Chair, outside row, and he did not see her exquisite right profile, he would . . . he would . . .

In the dead gap between two beats of his heart he opened his eyes and made visual contact with his lifeline and the world went on.

He made his way unobtrusively to a seat well back in the shadows and sank down to worship from afar with a pure and lustless love. If a man killed the thing he loved, he was killing his own reason for living, so it would not be murder but essentially a bungled suicide.

The conductor rapped his baton on the stand. *Tick tick tick.* The music chopped off. Started again. Repeated.

Pam's golden head leaned to the left, elongating the delicately vulnerable line of her neck and tilting her right profile up into the full flood of overhead lights, and the subtle sway of her body and the grace of her hand on the bow and the suppleness of her wrist and her arm floating in space had a dreamlike quality and he reflected that she knew this passage so well she could play it in her sleep, and perhaps, with her cheek pillowed on her instrument and shoulder, she was sleeping, sleeping and dreaming. . . .

The maestro's stick went *tick tick tick*.

Pam's glance angled up and to the right toward the conductor then slid to the score on the rack she shared with the Sixth Chair. The lineaments of her body from her faintly bulged loose blue sweater and gray slacks to her brown loafers and white-socked ankles crossed under her chair came into clear focus. She unhooked her ankles, leaned forward, feet firmly on the floor, watched the score, and played something in quick tempo, nodding her head briskly.

Intermittently, the orchestra sounded very loud. High decibel bursts, then silences. A soft pretty passage featuring woodwinds and strings began to flow in a sweet melodic line. Abrupt stop. The last few bars were repeated two times, both exactly the same. Senseless. The rehearsal was all fragments without continuity. Incoherent. Parts taken from finales and openings and middles of three different works with no sequence at all and there were disconnected mood jumps from somber to lively to passionate.

There were spasms of starting and seeming to go somewhere, then stopping and going back over the same ground again. Nothing ever completed. Nothing ever exactly right. Frustrating. Gruelling. Rehearsals wore her down, used up more nervous energy than a performance. Three or four times she reached behind, her tugging her sweater up, trying to cover the back of her neck. It was a fact of life that, just as all conductors were bastards, all stages were drafty.

Pam must be nervous to notice a draft; nothing bothered her when she was absorbed and really "in" her music. He couldn't make out her features. In fact, from this distance she was not recognizable individually, seeming rather to be the impersonal embodiment of the beauty of music itself. Irresistible. During the next orchestral passage he moved under cover of the sound to a seat many rows forward. During the lull he fixed his gaze on her and remained motionless, edgily aware that he must not call attention to himself.

He had an eerie sense of the emptiness of the auditorium. Nobody else was there. It meant the rehearsal was closed to outsiders. If he was caught and the maestro ordered him out and Pam agreed with the bastard that he did not belong in her world . . . The thought was unbearable. He blanked his mind.

The orchestra was playing again. He had a teasing, keen, visceral sense of danger and advanced as quietly as shadow through shadow. He settled down very close to her in a third-row seat. Dimness concealed him. He watched her.

She looked very pale, somehow depleted of energy. He detected signs of stress such as the strain line at the edge of her mouth, the faint frown around her eye, the slackness of her cheek. The anxiety he'd caused gave her a depth, a look of suffering that added another dimension to her beauty, made her all the more lovable. Of course, more realistically, her lovable look of suffering might simply be due to concentration on difficult work. Her bow was moving very fast, her left hand slid up and down the neck of the violin, her fingers moving frenziedly on the strings.

The advantage of watching from concealment was that the person observed was not self-conscious and one could glimpse true spontaneity. His thoughts drifted into a kind of bright timelessness through space. He was in open sunlit air in a row directly behind Virgie. Cleo had just won the Photographer's Day contest. Her friend's victory made Virgie clap and jump in childish joy and she turned around full circle. She was unaware of him but her wide-open eyes absorbed him, his image imprinting on her senses so that he became a part of her goodness and . . .

What was happening? Something was happening. The whole orchestra seemed to be playing but the sound was fading out more and more toward the very edge of silence. And then there was silence. An end to the passage. But the musicians did not relax completely. Pam rested her hand and bow on one knee but kept her violin on her shoulder and watched the podium. The whole orchestra's attention focused on the maestro. That whatsisname up there on the podium just stood holding everybody in a kind of paralysis. Months ago, early in the season, he'd conducted one of the regular subscription series concerts. Forgettably. All he'd inspired in the musicians was suspicion that his tedious perfectionism and polishing of small parts concealed failure to understand the whole of a work. He'd been considered weak, unqualified to command, and had got only minimal professional cooperation. But now he was apparently holding everything together tightly to the point where they didn't even dare relax until his official *tick tick tick* stick permitted.

Joel frowned. He heard a thin faint sound. A violin. Abe's. Abe Hambul, the concertmaster there in the first chair, was playing an unaccompanied solo, vaguely familiar and vaguely unpleasant. Pam's bow rested on a string. After a while the music from the violin beside Abe flowed in with his and then another pair playing together joined in, a little louder, followed closely by the two in Chairs Five and Six . . .

Tick tick tick.

"What are you using, cotton strings? I can't hear you."

Pam. The conductor was talking to Pam. He said something more that Joel didn't catch. There were titters of laughter from the orchestra.

"Quiet, please. Let's take it over. There *may* be concertgoers who come to listen as well as look and would like to hear the violins. All of them . . . if you don't *mind*, Chair Five."

Pam stared at him. Her neck and cheek became pink. Abruptly she jumped to her feet. She weaved her way back through the first violins then bolted out of sight into the wings.

Joel was indifferently aware of somebody saying to somebody *How did you get in here?* and *You, there, I'm talking to you, whoever you are.* He was on the move and, in passing, caught snatches of irrelevant words but had no curiosity about their meaning or desire to eavesdrop. *Where do you think you're going?*

Joel climbed a short stairway, stepped onto the stage. He stopped and turned his head to the right.

"Are you speaking to me?" he asked on the off-chance that the silly question had been directed at him.

It had.

"I'm going to my wife, you son of a bitch," he said.

But only in his mind.

Because.

Because suddenly he was unsure. That answer, while true, was perhaps not the whole truth. There was the possibility that something else had priority, and that, before going to his beloved to heal the injuries to her pride, her dignity, her sensitivity, he had meant, as the first step in the sequence, to avenge with the swift justice of death the unpardonable shame and humiliation that had been visited upon her.

Joel looked at the man thoughtfully and then he was backstage, gazing softly into Pam's overbright gorgeous mountain-wildflower blue eyes listening to the music of her hushed, rushing voice. He touched her shoulder and stroked her golden silk hair and wanted to kiss the tender round of her cheek but instead caught one of her gesturing hands and kissed it and then chafed her cold fingers and when she paused for breath he said quietly, "It wasn't all that bad."

"You just kept standing there like that."

"Maybe I did stare a little too long. Wondering . . . uh . . . what to do. Whether I should bull into things and maybe make things *worse* for you or—"

"I spoke to you three times. You didn't hear me. I had to finally nearly drag you off that stage," she whispered. Her eyes kept cornering to be sure nobody in the area was close enough to hear.

"Ah-h-h, you're oversensitive. After all, I didn't say one threatening word or take the first step toward him. So, actually, *you're* the one who created a commotion." He chuckled.

"Please, Joel, don't be cute."

"Sorry." He frowned and looked away. "You never walk out on a rehearsal. You consider it unprofessional. Weak. He forced you to walk out. *You,* a *real* musician! The outrageous injustice of it! For a minute I couldn't take it. On principle. Not just because I love you."

It moved her. She rubbed her throat, then caught his hand and gripped it. "I understand; I understand how *much* you care . . . but . . ."

"But? No but. I was angry, yes. With good reason. I was in control of myself. I *heard* you all right, don't think I didn't. I simply was not ready to let that bully off the hook."

"You really heard me?" She wet her lips. "And knew me?" she said, barely aloud.

He nodded decisively.

She flicked a glance at and away from his left temple.

He touched the skin graft over the lobotomy. "Is it red?"

She shook her head no.

"Pam, you think I was in the same state you thought I was in in your studio when you caught me *sleepwalking* the night before this tour started. I wasn't. Don't worry."

"Joel, I kept phoning every place till I was frantic. You weren't anyplace, the office, home, anyplace. Where *were* you, what *was wrong?*"

"Later, I'll explain it all, later. But definitely I'm all right now. God, I hate the stress I've put you through. And it must've been an added shock to suddenly see me, Pam. But I had to come, I couldn't wait to be with you." He paused, then went on bitterly, "I'm *sorry* I came. Because right away I bulled in and made things worse for you."

"You didn't *mean* to."

"The road to hell is paved with good intentions. I don't deserve you. I don't belong in your world."

"I wouldn't even *be* in my world as you put it, except for *you*. If you think I could ever forget *that*, you poor thing, my goodness, no."

First, he thought in a rush, there was the buildup of his ego, then the indescribable sympathetic sweetness of her voice saying "you poor thing," while the irresistible face dissolved him with a somehow forlorn expression and the stunning eyes aimed a pleading look at him. The incredibly swift timing and force of her blows staggered him and he had no will to counterpunch. Negative feelings could not exist in the mood she created; it was even hard to remember what he'd been angry about. Sis used to turn him to mush that way whenever she took a notion and he never could stay mad at her. But he always had to try. There was no parallel, of course, since he never got mad *at* Pam, and he wasn't a kid.

He must stand his ground, show her some maturity by saying an unsayable truth out loud.

"I'm only *one percent* responsible for your being in the orchestra. As you very well know," he told her, and instantly regretted it. A low blow. She looked at him indignantly, reproachfully. He had violated a certain tacit agreement. It was suicidal to violate it. The whole basis of their relationship—what else was there, really?—rested firmly on a fact that was 99 percent fiction.

"As I very well do *not* know. You were ninety percent responsible."

"One percent."

"Really, Joel, it's childish to keep repeating the same silliness. Ninety-nine percent!" she said firmly.

"I suppose pretending your own talent didn't count for more than one percent isn't childish. I repeat, ninety-nine percent."

He was attacking something precious—what Maury would have labeled their "shared fantasy"—and Pam made it clear she was there to defend it.

"If I wanted to point out your error, I could. But surely, Joel, I don't have to explain the obvious. You prevented the misdirection of whatever talents I may have. Now, I don't think we need to waste any more time or energy on the subject."

She had the last word. She waited, watching him with at least the *look* of total composure. He opened his mouth. He sighed. He shut his mouth.

She rewarded him with a warm but brief kiss on the lips. Then, knowing he was no longer dangerous, she walked away, explaining that she must finish the rehearsal but would be back soon.

He watched her cute bottom going away from him, rounding and tilting rhythmically from side to side and thought for a moment about Sis, his mouth twisting in wry amusement.

Pam's parents had stinted to provide an education which would give her security in the world she loved, as a teacher. She'd had her recital and earned her master's and had already got a couple of job offers, when the orchestra had scheduled auditions to fill openings including two in the second violins. At the time his relationship to her had been semi-existent at best; he hung around somewhere near the edges of her awareness. Dr. Kronstadter had introduced them in a casual way and had evidently told her a little of his history. His past "emotional problems" had evidently roused her interest . . . after all her favorite composer had been insane.

Now and then she'd notice him and speak or smile or let him share a table in the cafeteria. Once—gold star day—she hadn't had change for the soft drink dispenser and he'd been allowed to buy her a Choc-ola, which instantly became his favorite drink. A few other times they'd been at the same events, mostly recitals, and she'd let herself see him. Then an arty movie together, where she misunderstood most of the symbolism, enjoyed the free coffee, but remarked wistfully about the absence of popcorn. He'd not dared touch her hand in the taxi.

Then! astonishingly! she'd appointed him to walk her across campus to her dorm one evening. On the way she confided her secret childhood dream of one day becoming a part of the "greatest musical instrument of all," a symphony orchestra.

Next evening, she told him she would soon be accepting a teaching job in another state and how happy it made her . . . although she was sad to be leaving everybody here. Her happy feeling was because she loved her parents so much and would never repay their sacrifices by worrying them about her future. She'd looked so forlorn about all that happiness that he couldn't stand it. He'd dared to blurt out, "But, Miss Ellender, how about your dream? I mean . . . what do I know about music, but you said a symphony orchestra is the greatest musical instrument in the world. That has to be true. Didn't you tell me they were having tryouts? Auditions?"

She said, and he dared deny, that she did not have enough talent to ever try against professionals. Then she said she was so scared of auditions she shook. She showed him her hand trembling. She slipped her foot out of her moc and wriggled her toes and said she actually had cold feet just from thinking about it. He did not drop down and kiss her sock. Because she did not at the moment require him to be at her feet or at her knees but to rise up and give her strength to lean on. And he'd done it. He'd argued, lectured, pleaded. Finally, he even *ordered* her, at the last minute, when they were outside the stage door, to go in there . . . because he'd known absolutely that she could not fail.

She got the job, of course, next to last chair in the second violins. This season she was up there in the Fifth Chair of the Firsts, as good as Abe Hambul. Abe himself said so.

She kept improving. In Joel's eyes it was a natural ascendance toward stardom. But Pam could not see herself as a concert soloist. It wasn't that she put a ceiling on her potential but she loved the feeling that the growth of her talents contributed to the whole orchestra. This was not selfless at all, she argued with sweet solemnity and ridiculous logic, but the very opposite because to leave the greatest musical instrument of all would be a step down. And petty personal ambition would tend to separate her from and encourage her to imagine that she was somehow above music itself.

She worked hard and disciplined herself (because she didn't want to lose her job . . . the grubby thought intruded and was banished) because she was a dedicated idealist, and, he reflected proudly, she could endure anything. Including conductors.

Among conductors there were big talents, no-tal stick wavers, temperamental show-offs, oily politicans, Mr. Nice Guys, outright Prussians. They only seemed different. All had giant egos; all were bullies. They loved imposing their own warped meanings onto the music and crushing the wills of musicians who were superior to them. Each came in like an assault, one after another, all season, attacking the headless orchestra, destroying the harmony that had been built through twenty years with the real maestro. They caused clashes and conflicts within the orchestra, lowered morale, turned some of the rehearsals into hell for almost everybody. Pam felt deeply that the weakened orchestra needed her and she stuck through everything, refusing to give the bastards the satisfaction of breaking her down publicly. But she'd come home and pour it all out. Twice, she'd cried in angry frustration. Once she had been so torn up and hurt that she'd sobbed. Afterward, always, she'd tell him she couldn't have stood it, except for him.

This time though, after that no-tal with the little *tick tick* stick had abused her, Pam not only hadn't wanted to be comforted, but had been practically horrified by his coming to her rescue. No—he tried to check his rising irritation—that's not how it had been; he was distorting the whole situation. He fished a cigarette out of his pocket, got it between his lips, saw the NO SMOKING sign.

12

Joel's attention focused abruptly on a thread
of sound from the stage. He frowned. Wasn't
that Abe's violin beginning the passage that
followed that strange prolonged silence and
which had led to trouble for Pam? He stood,
head tilted, listening intently, abdominal
muscles tightening. Soon, very soon, any
minute now, the thin line of sound would
thicken with additional violins. And if, when
Pam's music flowed in, it was interrupted
again by that *tick tick tick!* . . .

He waited.

He waited.

He stopped waiting.

He went outside and lit a cigarette. He was a
little lightheaded. Tension. He started to walk
it off. He stopped beside his car. He just stood
jingling the keys in his pocket, thinking

nothing, absolutely nothing. He sneezed. He got moving briskly. He fired his cigarette into a snowbank at the end of the parking lot. He wheeled and marched back toward the stage door. He veered away. No, he wasn't going back in there till that rehearsal was over. Masochism was not his thing, he thought grimly. Not that it was her thing either, of course. Anyway, he detested that particular music, whatever it was.

He kept walking around the edges of the parking lot and crisscrossing it from the corners in *X* patterns. He couldn't keep from imagining the worst about what might be going on. He'd shared the pains of rehearsals after they were over; he was a shoulder to cry on. But the pleasures? No, they could not be shared, or even understood. They were beyond his comprehension. Special relationships existed in that closed-off world. He shot a furious glance at that stage door, like . . . like . . . a kid outside a bedroom door behind which *something* went on.

Enough! He lit a cigarette shakily.

He found a cleared walk along one side of the building and hiked up to the front. He stopped at the corner of the building. He felt dizzy. He should and *did* understand: When everybody had worked hard and the result was a splendid performance, there was a certain mood of joy in the moment, an earned *high*, and everybody shared in the triumph. They all existed on a higher artistic level that transformed everything at such a time. Pam would feel that she and the conductor had gone through hells and climbed together to the mountaintops of pure ecstasy where he became a god, the *maestro,* who had given her a special experience and fulfillment that no other man could provide. Least of all a nonmusician. Not that she ever said anything like that in so many words. But underneath it all it was how she felt, whether or not her nice-girl mind permitted her to know it. Also, the *more* she was made to suffer—by, for instance, the one who'd made her *sob* on Joel's shoulder—and the greater the triumph and joy of the climax at a performance, the higher her respect—if not downright worship—of the bastard *maestro.* The kind of pleasure she got from the roughest of the bullies was worse than outright sexual thrills. He was clenching his teeth and sucking in cold air. It made his teeth ache. Good! He had pain coming to him for vicious sexual fantasies like that about Pam.

He went over to the outer lobby doors and entered, feeling ashamed. There were posters, displays, pictures. There was one of Pam onstage, in performance, looking as earnest as an infant. He gazed fixedly and lengthily at her image, filling himself with its magic, and was cleansed and restored. He even became capable of whimsy, observing that her photo was actually a trifle small. And it was somewhat cluttered by all the other members of the orchestra. But it was a work of art nonetheless.

He went outside smiling and hiked some more, feeling healthy and genuinely future-oriented. He congratulated himself for having avoided avoidable trouble by getting away from that rehearsal. It was just breaking up when he went back inside. Perfect timing. Somebody up there must like him. Or anyway somebody up there liked *her,* and her happiness was contingent on *him.*

Fifteen minutes later he was alone with Pam, deferentially helping her into the car. He gazed at her lingeringly and marveled over the fact that the aura of goodness surrounding her was actually manifest in the scent, delicately laced with lily-of-the-valley cologne, emanating warmly from her sweet flesh. He was breathing her in while his eyes were absorbing the nourishment of her into his depths, he thought poetically. He toyed with the shapely idea that to possess an angel was to experience timeless bliss. His head was in the clouds, but it was also just under the car's roof, and the earth-bound fact was that time passed and while he was enjoying her she might be getting chilly. He backed off, shut the door, went around, and got in the driver's seat.

"Oh-oh." He snapped his fingers. "I forgot. Maybe *you'd* rather drive. Hm?"

"Uh-uh. You know what a good driver I think you are compared to me."

"Usually. Except, maybe now, you might be worried about my control."

"No.

She scooted closer to him. He started the engine, got them rolling.

"I won't try one-armed driving, but I will get a little fresh." He patted her knee, fondled her lower thigh, and said, "I brought you a little gold-chain necklace with a heart. And wait'll you see your pretty little new shoes."

"You silly," she said, sounding pleased, "you know you can't buy shoes for a woman without her trying them on."

"If I showed poor judgment, I'm sorry."

"Don't be; I'm sure not," she said tartly.

He drove to an exit and displayed reassuring caution before swinging into traffic. Safely enroute to the motel he said, "I'm sorry if you kept worrying during the rest of the rehearsal that I might make another spectacle. I wasn't there. I went outside and didn't hear anything more that went on. I hope he didn't give you any more trouble."

"No, it was all right." She patted his hand on the steering wheel and smiled at him. "It was sensible of you to leave and not have to be disturbed on my account. Anyway, Abe spoke to him and maybe defended me or gave him a better grasp of that passage."

"That's like Abe! I'm really relieved that he came to your rescue. I'm sorry as hell letting myself get out of control and—"

She cut in. "Don't keep saying *sorry,* Joel, when what your intentions were is so clear to me. And don't you think for a minute that I meant to give all the credit to Abe. You're the one who let that conductor know I've got a protector! And believe me I worked better and felt more confident afterward, thanks to you! Sure, yes, at first I was scared you were in a bad mental condition and didn't even know I was there. But you sure did! And the more I think about it the prouder I am and the more I love you. If you think I could be mad at you for showing the whole world how much you love me, no sir!''

Those eyes sparkled and shone on him and he basked. He was incapable of anything beyond a fatuous smile.

She gave him a teasing smile and said very softly, "Do you plan to *show* me how much you love me when we get to the motel?"

"I'll try."

He chuckled. He gazed at her.

"Could you also try to watch the road now and then?"

"Mm-hm. Know what I did when I left the rehearsal? Had a religious experience. There's a picture of you up in the lobby . . . the one with the orchestra. I communed with it, like an old-time Tschaikovsky peasant with his icon."

She snuggled closer.

Another half hour passed before Myrtle, the cellist she'd been rooming with, cleared out. Pam chainlocked the door, grinned, and kicked off her shoes in his direction.

It was literally a kickoff. Play had begun. It was his move. However the games started, there were rules. Unstructured spontaneity was dangerous. He squelched an impulse to showboat and surprise her with an immediate direct run for the goal: ripping her clothes off, hurling her down, ramming inside her naked body, and exploding in a sweeping rush so fast and irresistible that before she knew what was happening she would be in the convulsions of a powerful orgasm and crying out in wild, mindless joy. His pleasure was building to an almost painful intensity when she excited him more by stripping off her socks. He looked away from her bare feet, grimly determined to contain his heat.

He moved toward her slowly. He must proceed with great care and exalt the mere mundane act of undressing her to the level of a ritual unveiling of beauty. The process would be lingering, his hands caressing, his lips savoring each part of her nakedness as it was revealed to his adoring eyes. If he was worthy of his privilege and indulged in his own joy with sufficient artistry, it would serve as the foreplay necessary to arouse her to the point where she would bestow her favors upon him and accept his animal passions. This would be the first time he had ever made love to her. The wedding night. Although that was not the literal fact, it was the higher truth. Always, whenever he made love to her, it was the first time, because there was about Pam an essence of eternal virginity.

And at *this* time, in *this* state of preexistence awaiting rebirth, the cleansed, future-oriented new beginning, there must be no trace of low brute violence or even the slightest abruptness which might startle her.

It was in intention to achieve perfection. That was his intention, but . . .

He was crouched over her, panting. Her frenzied writhing slowed and her naked sweaty body became slack, inert. Her glazed eyes stared, sightless, at him. Her mouth was partly open. His senses focused. He started to back away, a dull witless expression of horror on his face. Abruptly her knees locked around him. Her eyes flashed and crinkled as her cheeks squeezed upward in a smile. Her mouth opened wide and she laughed and laughed and laughed.

It was such a delicious sound he began to chuckle. She grabbed and twisted his ears and pulled his face down and gave him a hot wet kiss, then broke for air and laughed some more. Gleefully.

He got the idea, finally, that *they*—and not just *he*—had had a damned good time.

He rolled over onto his back beside her.

And thou beside me singing in the wilderness. The wispy lines of poetry hovered in his senses, then vanished when her laughter subsided. The strange cold thought came to him that pleasure had lost its voice while her body was losing heat.

He drew the sheet up over them. She turned and fitted her body against his side, sliding her leg onto his stomach and draping an arm across his chest. Her cheek rested on his shoulder.

Her eyes angled toward his face for a moment, which was suddenly poignant as he realized her glance was a mute, frightened plea. His hand answered with loving tenderness, a gliding gently over her gold silk hair. Soon she was reassured. Her lids closed. He thought, *Do not be afraid, my darling*. The brave and trusting mask of contentment she wore was sadly beautiful. Undoubtedly she was in shock. And soon the effect of the natural opiates in her system would wear off, and the aftershock would be terrible.

He understood that her laughter, while not entirely out of character, had been excessive. She had had the instinctive knowledge that the sound of pain signaled distress and invited attack. So a defense mechanism operating like reflex produced an imitation of laughter, which was really hysteria.

There was a humming, mewling little sound in her throat. Then he felt a sighing exhalation of her warm—fevered?—breath tickling the hairs on his chest. She stirred restlessly. She opened her eyes and her glance darted about nervously.

"I guess I better quit enjoying being lazy and get up."

"Rest, sweetheart," he soothed. "You're not up to it."

She propped herself on one elbow, tilted her top-heavy dream-sweet, wide-eyed face above him and giggled softly.

"I'm up to being down."

Her words made no sense. It was painful to see that the connection between her good mind and those beautiful but overbright eyes had broken. He looked away and murmured in a kindly voice, "I appreciate the way you are trying to bounce back."

"Bounce *back?* Oh, boy, we're witty today, aren't we? If you don't quit being so cute, *I'll* get carried away and you'll be pregnant because you'll be underneath . . . *Joel!* There's a rule. If I make a joke, you go ha ha ha."

"Ha ha ha," he said indulgently. "Seriously, Pam. You would be entitled to get carried away. I confess that *I* got carried away. I am sorry."

"Listen to him. Completely deadpan!" She got a mock solemn expression on her face. "After due deliberation I tend to disagree that you are sorry you got carried away."

"I swear I am! I know I hurt you. . . ."

"It's a shame I didn't notice. Here I was imagining I had a great time!"

She laughed. She was not *refusing* to accept the gravity of the situation; she was emotionally shattered and incapable of accepting it.

"I swear, Pam. I *meant* to prepare you. Not to neglect the foreplay."

She grinned widely, but began to sober and stare at him uneasily when he continued to frown. She hunched her shoulders. "I can't keep up with the deadpan style. I guess I belong in simple-minded audiences where they hold up a laugh sign so you'll know when to."

"Seriously. The neglect of foreplay. . . ."

Her attention span ended. She couldn't hold to a mature line of discussion and began a childish scatterbrained babble about trifles.

"I've got to get cleaned up. You too. Boy, do you need a shave. While I'm showering you better go out and get your suitcase . . . after first putting on some clothes, I'd advise . . . I'll play just this one last round of the game, then I'm done. I'm getting hungry for one of those steak sandwiches I've been hearing about and dying to have an appetite for. Tell me, lover. When a man tells a girl she's his icon and gets her flying a thousand miles an hour, how much more foreplay do you think she can take? I'll be ready for an illustrated lecture on the subject when we have lots of time after tonight's performance. Meantime . . ."

"The performance will have you flying a thousand miles an hour. Like the rehearsal did after the emotional welts the maestro inflicted on you."

"What? Emotional welts? On, I see, I see, yes. *After that trouble happened, you were there and got me flying a thousand miles an hour and making me feel I really am* your icon . . ."

"There's a profound question psychologically about whether the pleasure of being soothed is not intensified by the degree of pain previously inflicted, and . . ."

"I don't follow you. I don't want to. To me it's Chinese, like my granddaddy used to say. Inscrutable. Right now, I'll leave you to your postcoital philosophizing, while I rise and shine."

She didn't sound sick or look crippled as she uncovered herself, rolled-turned into a sitting position, bounced to her feet, and scampered naked around the foot of the bed into the bathroom.

He detected no sign of injuries or bruises, although he looked at her so steadily and concentratedly that just before shutting the door, she said gleefully, "Voyeur!"

"*Voyeur?*" he began, and shut his mouth. No use trying to explain to a door that a man whose thinking was "postcoital," as she'd so airily put it, wasn't in a lecherous mood.

He sat up, frowning. The room, with their clothes flung all over, had a postdisaster look about it, which was entirely deceptive because no brutal rape had actually occurred. But he'd insisted on believing that she was suffering grievously. Her attempts to convince him otherwise had seemed to him to prove she was shocked out of her mind . . . by his savagery.

He remembered thinking of her as not just his icon but as some impossible figment of perpetually restored virginity. At worst it had been a gentle, romantic fantasy. He didn't know when it had degenerated into the ugliness of a rape fantasy. . . .

But yes he did know! It was after she'd

bared her feet . . . not *when,* but *after.* Then instead of letting him enjoy undressing her, she began to fairly rip off her own clothes in a frenzied rush. She didn't quite order him not to waste time but get out of his own clothes hurry-up-quick, but that was her meaning. Then in a flash, she was on the bed, in position, hot and waiting impatiently, craving *action,* a ravaging man's *thrust.* It amounted to total rejection of his slow, unaggressive style. It asserted contemptuously that he had always been an unsatisfactory lover and that she was fed up with being dominant and that she required mastery.

His own inadequacy had enraged him and he'd known she demanded rape and respected nothing less. That's when he'd got carried away and came on strong. No use to keep grimly refusing to acknowledge the happiness his gentle Pam got out of him as a rough lover.

He went glumly over and snapped on the TV, thinking about Mona. He stood there wearing nothing but socks and switched irritably through all the commercials on all the channels two or three times. At last he found out there was no newscast on yet.

Meantime he had immediate worries. Pam would soon be in her own postcoital phase. She'd remember the two days and nights of scary hell he'd put her through. She'd expect a full explanation. The hardest part would be to make her believe he couldn't somehow have phoned from somewhere or had somebody else get word to her.

He couldn't think naked. He found shorts, shirt, pants, put them on. He couldn't think dressed either. He located one shoe, stepped into it, fished around, and found cigarettes in a jacket pocket. He lit one, spotted the other shoe, and put it on.

Nobody ever wanted unpleasant truth; to hit her suddenly with this one would be crude sadism, an overkill that might make her panic and want to escape from him.

To tighten her bond to him he must tell her nice things, not necessarily happy things, but at least hopeful. It was no joke that a man who really cared, cared enough to lie his best. Her will to believe would be working for him. Catching him in a lie wouldn't make her mad but sad. And the unwritten law with her type was that if the intent of the lie as a whole was loving, trifling inconsistencies would be accepted in the same spirit.

He tried the TV again and got a weather report. He listened distractedly to temperature readings from here and there, and a news wrap-up of no interest. His mind was on Webberly Treat, a partner in one of the state's biggest law firms and a professor at the university here in Keystone. He was an old friend of Pam's family and had a special avuncular, somewhat innocent, feeling for Pam, and he was an officer of the local Symphony Society. Joel was sure he could count on Treat being at the annual party in the art museum honoring the orchestra after tonight's concert.

Pam had always been indignant about what had been done to him at Shaunautaukee and wanted Joel to fight back, take legal recourse. Joel shrank back from a trial where his past would have to come out. She understood the decision to change his name legally and remove the stigma attached to a record of mental illness. She hadn't wanted to pick at old scabs and had not pressed to know his dead name. So of course she had no idea that Paul Borland had been sordidly connected to a rape-torture-murder case in California . . . or even that he'd ever lived there. She had assumed that—like her favorite composer—the emotional stresses that had landed him in a mental institution were due somehow to higher sensibilities which made it difficult to cope with gritty realities. She was proud of the dependable emotional balance he'd achieved. She didn't try too hard to deny her own importance as his main incentive.

He'd known that if she discovered how much he had concealed and how many of her wrong assumptions about his past he'd let her believe, she'd feel deceived, to put it mildly. Her image of him would change. Instead of a reassuring figure he would become a stranger. Untrustworthy. Maybe dangerous. As hard as she might try to absorb it all, the marriage would collapse.

Last spring when she went on tour, Pam had been in some kind of mood and was determined to tell Webb Treat all about what those savages at Shaunautaukee had done—or *tried* to do—do his brain. The fact that he personally had overcome the damage made no difference. A principle was involved; villainy must be exposed to protect possible future victims who might not have the good luck to save themselves. He had calmed her down, pointed out that to be publicly labeled as lobotomized would convince people he was a mental cripple. And the newspapers and TV might blow up the trial, especially one involving a photogenic wife. They'd jump on the fact she was a violinist with the symphony. It could smudge her with notoriety by association that would invade and ruin her music.

She'd waved away that possibility, but understood that he would be embarrassed and might be handicapped in *his* work.

Pam had promised not to start anything "real," but wanted to discuss it with Webb Treat. She'd laid the whole situation out as a hypothetical case, though she suspected that he suspected she was talking about her husband. As a lawyer he assured her that, definitely yes, lobotomies were against the law. And absolutely, if he were retained he would, with relish and full confidence, sue everybody involved including Shaunautaukee and the State itself on behalf of the victim of such a criminal procedure. For millions. The probable damages awarded would depend on many factors, including degree of incapacitation, lifetime earnings potential, whether the case went before judge and jury or judge alone, and the impression made by the victim himself.

The money part of it would be irrelevant. What was vital now—before Mona's body was discovered and possibly linked to him, if it ever was—was to have it established, officially and legally, that while physically it was his body that had committed murder, the mind capable of such monstrousness was the creation of those criminal Shaunautaukee surgeons. That was true! They had weakened the civilized element of his brain irreparably.

He must release Pam from her promise. And tonight, hopefully, Treat would meet Pam's husband, the real, not hypothetical, victim. It would be best, Joel decided, to give the lawyer an impression of himself as pleasant, not too bright, a little bit out of it. A sort of amiable grunt.

He nodded yes, feeling organized, and set about straightening up the room. He was picking up her clothes when she came out of the bathroom.

"I'll do that," she said. "Didn't you bring your suitcase in yet?"

"No."

"You'd better. It's getting a little late. We've got lots of talking to do." She didn't look at him but stood in a towel and scuffs getting panties, slip, bra out of a drawer. "I'll get these on in a jiffy and let you have the bathroom. I'll finish dressing out here."

"I don't know how to tell you, Pam, but . . . uh. . ."

She gave him her full attention. Her expression was as earnest as a baby's. Expectant. When he didn't go on, she said, "Well?"

13

"The fact is I forgot to bring a suitcase."

"Forgot?" Her eyes widened. They narrowed. "Forgot to bring a suitcase? Joel Danton, you don't mean to tell me you came on this long trip without a change of clothes or . . . or . . . even a *razor?*"

"It was spur-of-the-moment. Unplanned. I just didn't think. But," he finished weakly, "I could use your razor."

"I'd slide my eyes away too, if I were you." She mimicked him lightly. " 'I didn't think . . . I could use your razor!' That's really funny. Still, we'll just have to make do. The motel guarantees valet service for the orchestra. Probably I can get that suit cleaned. You launder your shorts in the shower. I'll borrow a hair blower to dry them. That shirt . . . mm . . . it wouldn't hurt you to loosen up and buy a new one."

"There's a big shopping center near here. I'll buy a suit, or anyway pants and a jacket that would look all right at the concert and party afterward."

"Big talk, but wait'll you face those price tags. No, if it's too late for the valet service I've got a can of spot remover if we need it. I'll check . . . and if I have to, I know where I can borrow an iron."

"I'm not going to reduce you to grubby little chores like that. Forget it, Pam. What's money for if not to provide freedom from worry about necessities like new clothing?"

"Oh, boy! Suddenly he's Mr. Easy-Come-Easy-Go!"

"I do have a sense of occasion. Civilized amenities can't be observed in shabby clothes."

She gave him an oblique glance. She said in a calm, very calm voice, "I'm going to dress. And then you are going to tell me what's been going on that kept you from observing *civilized amenities* . . . or having even the simple courtesy to let me know *anything* about what was happening to you or what you were up to."

She walked away into the bathroom, leaving the door open. He followed to the doorway and stood looking in at her.

"Up to? That accusing tone isn't like you at all. Your starting out with a presumption-of-guilt attitude disturbs me."

Her answer was a naked view of her backside as she hung her towel. He lit a cigarette.

He watched her step her feet daintily into her panties.

"The key point, Pam, the operative factor at this crucial stage is that everything is all right *now*. The brighter future begins at this moment. Unless it's approached in a negative, punitive way."

Silent, Pam tugged upward on the pink panties, bending her supple body from side to side. She tilted her hips provocatively and wagged her bottom with a certain insolence. She peered at him in the steamy mirror, frowning.

"Joel, I can't help thinking that you are being evasive *deliberately*." She wiped at the mirror, switched on the humming ventilator fan, then slipped her arms in the bra straps.

"Why are you pretending nothing you've done—or *not* done—calls for an explanation? What I really do not *like* is for you to shift the blame to me. You turn everything around and accuse *me* of being *punitive*."

She turned herself around and was punitive with a vengeance, haughtily thrusting those soft, pale-skinned, pink-nippled perfect conical breasts at him, offering their succulence, then swiftly making them inaccessible in their satin cups. She hooked her arms behind her, squirming her shoulders, and angled her face up at him in the attitude of a scornful temptress.

"Well?" She frowned at him. She pulled a half-slip down over her head to her waist, hiding her slim pretty thighs from him. She frowned more insistently and compressed her lips into a thin line. She sidestepped past him into the room, flicking a glance at his left temple.

"Is it red?" He scratched it.

"No, it's not and don't scratch it raw, if you please."

She took up the phone. He waited and wandered while she spoke to somebody. She hung up.

"The cleaner's truck is here. I'll have to take that suit to the lobby."

She sped into skirt, blouse, shortie coat, emptied his jacket pockets, goaded him constantly till he surrendered his pants. She instructed him to shower and was gone, carrying the room key.

In the shower he reflected moodily on the symbolism of being stripped of his pants and confined. There was something remarkable about the conversion of dreamy floating artistic princess into a pragmatist who relished functioning in a no-nonsense down-to-earth, take-charge role.

Could her enjoyment of such a role indicate an underlying lust for power? Unlikely. But if so, her eventual aim would be to nail his balls to the wall . . . unless he retrieved them. He shrugged. The good sensual feel of lathering

and scrubbing himself in the warm flowing
water made it difficult to concentrate on anything. It was harder yet to face unpleasant con-
trasts between his fantasy-girl image of her
and the real Pam. He used shampoo, got soap
in his eyes and stopped—or tried to stop—the
lazy drift of his thoughts. A mental game.
Childish. Pointless. Unamusing. He resisted,
grimly at first. But bits and pieces of evidence
from their whole relationship accumulated,
and a case built itself in spite of him, step by
irrefutably logical step, which forced a startling
reevaluation of her character and motivations.
From the first she had exercised absolute
power over him and could have destroyed him
anytime she chose. But she had known he
could not get away, and like cat with helpless
mouse, she had prolonged the joys of power
and indulged in a kind of morbid foreplay to
heighten the final perverted ecstasy of the kill.
He was frowning, his mouth set in a straight
lipless line. A sensation kept tickling a corner
of his mouth.

No! he told himself. There was nothing to
grin about. The idea of Pam as some kind of
dangerous closet sadist waiting to pounce
fiercely was, admittedly, so shocking as to
seem funny. One *preferred*, of course, always to
accept beauty, to believe that the surface
sweetnesses was consistent with the whole.
But beneath that gentle mask there might
be—there *was*—a sinister leering malevolence.

He clapped a hand over his mouth to muffle a howl of uncontainable laughter.

He laughed himself weak and thought about a true loony at Shaunautaukee who imagined all the cakes and pastries his wife brought him were loaded with mysterious undetectable poisons. He'd run out of the communal room when his not-quite-so-loony fellows gorged themselves on the delicious poison. Time after time nobody dropped dead. The fellow had real problems trying to hold on to his belief. Whenever sanity threatened to take over and he was on the point of taking back his treats, his buddies would encourage him to hold on characterfully to his belief in his own truth, assuring him the poisons acted only on *his* special body chemistry.

Joel remembered Maury's smart-ass congratulation: "Paul, I admire men of conviction like yourself. True believers. It is very very difficult to achieve a state of lunacy, and harder yet to sustain it for very long. The way sanity keeps poking its nose in where it's not wanted!"

Once upon a time, Joel thought, half wistfully, he'd had the power of absolute belief. It was harder and harder to get into loony states. Like this last one. You had to totally misinterpret every goddamn thing Pam did to bring it off. Even then it didn't work. It was like putting horns on a baby and pretending she was the Devil.

Pam came back to report his suit would be done in an hour, then she was off again to get the hair blower and bring them steak sandwiches. He shaved, used her deodorant and mouthwash, and eyed her toothbrush guiltily. He used it and threw it away. He pondered: Could a mere fantasy girl hurry-up-quick get his suit cleaned and lovingly help get him straightened out in all ways? No, by God, and she couldn't play the violin either. He smirked.

Twenty minutes later he was ready with his alibi. He sat propped up in bed, covered by the spread, aiming the hair drier at his shorts on a chair back while he waited for Pam. She was unwrapping sandwiches and uncapping drinks over at the counter.

"I can't eat now, not till I've squared myself with you. How to start? Well, to begin. The reason I missed your phone call two nights ago—"

"Wait. Let me get set where I can hear."

He switched off the blower. "There, that's better."

She nodded and swigged from her bottle of orange. She took his shorts over and spread them on the room's heating unit. She started to sit on the adjoining bed, then shook her head.

"No, I'll just kind of walk and listen and not stare and make you self-conscious. And," she added with a nervous laugh, "I'll eat. With my mouth full I can't interrupt."

She took a bite and chewed solemnly and walked back and forth past the foot of the beds as he began to talk.

"I worked late two nights ago. Because I was slow and kept making mistakes. There was still a correction or two to make before I even started out to the airport. To get signatures. From both the president and treasurer of a company whose returns we file for them. Tergel Corporation. A very big account; I didn't dare mess up and lose it for Hempstead. You know. The signatures were necessary then. Both men were headed for a conference in Europe and wouldn't be back before deadline. One man was there . . . the other found out the flight was delayed an hour . . . turned out to be two hours. He didn't show up till very late."

He paused, noted her zero reaction. She didn't glance at him directly or in the mirror. She walked and fed herself and heard him out. Not unreceptive. Not impartial. She was rooting for him, of course. Just waiting for him to make a convincing case.

He threw in lots of tensions and uncertainties he'd had to undergo. And how shaky he'd been after locating the man and finally getting the signature in a bad-tempered rush. He'd rushed to get back home, even though he knew it was too late. He'd driven too fast, skidded, nearly crashed. Shaken, he'd stopped for a drink. Didn't get home till past two in the morning. He was afraid to yank her out of sleep alarmingly with a call. And afraid not to. Afraid she wouldn't understand why he'd missed being there. He'd felt hopelessly incompetent. Next morning he'd been too sick to go to work. Not physically. Mentally. He'd been positive he couldn't handle the strain, doubted he was up to the accuracy demanded. He was afraid he couldn't even grasp what it was he was supposed to do. He'd dreaded letting it be discovered on the job that he was in a bad condition, incompetent.

He tried a long silence that she could not ignore.

"Were you afraid that that condition you were in in my studio the night before I left was coming back?"

"But I wasn't in any condition except sleep-walking."

"If you can't feel free to be totally honest with me, Joel! Please. Don't feel you have to look away, ashamed of something not your fault!" She came and took one hand between both of hers and gazed intently at him. "Look at me. Look at me," she urged softly. "You can admit it to me. You didn't really know me. Not at first. Did you, you poor thing?"

"I didn't want you to ever have to know what insanity is *really* like. I thought I was slipping back into that."

"That's too big a word, *insanity,* as you know good and well. Dr. Dornstadter doesn't believe in even thinking of problems in hopeless terms like that. Like it's some incurable forever thing. You *did* think I wasn't me. Was it that fantasy girl you used to imagine back in that awful place? Is that who you thought I was?"

"No."

"Joel."

"Yes. But only briefly. Pam, I swear to God. Listen, what happened that I didn't make phone connections with you was because I went to pieces because of the lobotomy. Beyond a certain stress point I knew I couldn't go. But I thought I'd gone over the line and the damage to my brain *hadn't* really been permanently bypassed at all, and my mind would be worse . . . I couldn't think with any grasp. I was scared I'd be inarticulate like a bumbling half-wit and sound crazy on the phone. I called the motels in the last town and in Keystone here. But I didn't leave a message, because I had to be sure of myself. I started to drive to you early last night. Then I stopped and holed up in a motel. I got drunk. I fell asleep. All I needed, I guess, was a full night's sleep. I woke up early today, rested. In perspective and control. Needing only one thing . . . you!"

"Your hair's still wet. Keep the bathtowel on it." She went to get her sandwich. She picked it up, frowned at it, put it down. "If you phoned Keystone, that was today after you were all right."

"Yesterday." He corrected the slip. "I was

mixed up on your itinerary and thought you were here already. Today I didn't leave a message when I called because I was so close I knew I'd be here soon. I guess I should have got word to you here that I was OK and on the way."

"Yes."

"Sorry."

"The big thing, I suppose, is you're all right now." She frowned, hunched her shoulders. "Where'd you nearly crash?"

He ad-libbed a location and gave some details, throwing in a full 180-degree turnaround and broadside sideslip toward an oncoming farm truck.

"Oh my goodness! What you've been *through!* You poor thing. Look, you've talked all you have to, Joel. Here, I'll get your sandwich and Coke."

"Well, if I can manage it . . ."

He managed. He wolfed his own and the uneaten two-thirds of her sandwich. She watched with melted eyes. Finishing, he said:

"There's only one nagging little residue. A *possibility* that that lobotomy could really be trouble sometime. The weakened areas could—who knows?—rupture, cause a stroke. Or turn me into a vegetable. *Then* . . . no, no, it won't happen, but just what *if* . . . where would *you* be? Pam, I've changed my mind about bringing legal action. Suing. You can tell your law professor friend, Webberly Treat, if you see him."

"There's no *if*. He's planning to drop by the motel to see me before the concert. But I don't know. Are you really sure you want me to bring it up? You were so dead set against it."

He hadn't expected her to balk. He said offhandedly, "Oh, well, if you don't want to do it."

"It's not that. But if I brought up a big professional problem that took up all our time when we haven't seen each other for so long . . . you understand . . . this wouldn't be the best time."

"I see."

"The way you say it, you don't."

"Sure I do. Why spoil a reunion with your *doting* uncle?"

"You make it sound nasty! You don't like him just because I do. You're jealous."

"So what else is new. So *don't* use your influence with him. I'd rather have a *good* lawyer, anyway."

"Talk about childish! All I asked you was were you sure you wanted to change your mind. You made such a good case *against* legal action and a public spectacle that'd hurt us both. Now, suddenly, you start to worry that *maybe*, someday, there'd be trouble with the lobotomy and you'd be a vegetable and all. After telling me how all right you really are now! There's no hurry. You can think it over some more. But . . . well, meantime . . . well . . .

if you're sure you won't be embarrassed and you want me to, I'll mention it, say you're the 'hypothetical' case."

"No. It *seemed* important. You're right, it's not important. Sorry to bring it up."

"Joel, the way you back down and won't stand up for your side against me exasperates me out of my mind sometimes."

"All right. I'm disgusting. Not a man. But like a kid against you. Scared to cross you and lose *everything*. You want my side? You want to know why I suddenly wanted to sue and strike back at everybody at Shaunautaukee and the whole damned world? All right. All right. I'll tell you. Tell you what happened right *before* I thought you were that dead fantasy girl in your studio. I had just gone through that lobotomy! I was dragged, yelling and fighting, into that little back ward surgery. Tied down. Gagged. Helpless. I saw them doing it to me in the mirror surfaces of some damn stainless steel instrument sterilizer or something. All they did was deaden the surface pain and kept me conscious throughout, so I could *see* my blood spurting as the hole was drilled in my skin and temple bone. Then when it was over and they'd crippled me I was so violent, so enraged, that they put me in a straitjacket and rubber pants to go to the toilet in in a locked little punishment cell. And *she* was there, the fantasy girl, at one stage and another, through it all, wanting to save me somehow. And then when it was over she was there, the only consolation, the only loving hope. And no, I didn't merely *remember* it. I *relived* it. The whole horror. It was so much realer than anything else that I couldn't dare believe you were you and I was safe. . . . Don't *do* that! God damn *everything* to *hell,* I can't *stand* you crying."

She wiped her face. But more tears streamed down her cheeks. She tried to talk. She couldn't. She walked away, came back. She stood by him, wrapped her arms around him. She hugged him fiercely. He could feel the quaking of her stomach muscles against his arm. She managed to speak, but just repeated, "It's all right. It's all right . . ." over and over and over mindlessly.

By God he had clobbered her into mush. He hadn't been entirely sure he still had it in him, but it was all there: his full power.

She withdrew a few inches and gazed at him with grieving wounded eyes, silently participating in his suffering, and absorbing it into herself. The bond of pain gave them a special new awareness of each other.

Without yet fully understanding and appreciating the immensity of meaning involved, she sensed that there was another, exalted, expanded dimension to their relationship.

Her lips touched his forehead, then the wound site of the lobotomy in an instinctive honoring of pain. Then, in tribute to his mastery, she sat down humbly so that her head was on a level below his. She lowered her eyes and for a moment her lids closed and her dream sweet face had never, never been so beautiful. She looked up and mirrored his smile. She petted his cheek. He turned his face and kissed her palm. Then he nipped it lightly with his teeth, giving her the merest suggestion of real pain and her eyes sparkled joyously.

14

Pam was in an upswing, waiting for Webberly
Treat's call. She changed into her formal
concert gown in the expectation that he would
invite her to dinner. When Joel's suit got back
from the cleaners, he put it on in the bathroom
while she waited near the phone, watched a TV
newscast, and told him her plan.

"While you're buying the new shirt I'll have
time, before you join us, to tell him you're
actually the 'hypothetical case' and that we
want him to represent you and bring suit. That
way, he'll know before you meet each other,
and nothing more will have to be discussed in
detail till you would see him professionally in
his office. OK?"

"Fine."

"Things will be started and relieve your
mind."

"Yes."

"Then we can be relaxed and friendly. You'll like him and he will you, don't worry. Offer to pay the check, but let him, he really wants to give us a treat. Don't mind if he says nice things to me."

"I won't, don't worry. I shouldn't have made that nasty *doting* uncle crack. What's happening on the news?"

"I guess it was summer at home today."

"I heard earlier the temperature got up to seventy-two degrees."

"Looks like lots of melting. Did you hear the announcer say the street's like a river? Gosh, you ought to see the bunch of cars flooded out at the curbs and traffic crawling bumper to bumper in the middle of the street."

"What street?"

"I don't know. Oh, yes; he said Tenth Avenue. Why, that's the one you go to work on."

He came out to look. The scene had shifted.

"I can't understand why it would flood."

"I think he said it was partly because of a big backup from a sewer."

Sewer? Sewer *backup?*

"Impossible! Storm sewers are enormous!" The protest strangled in his throat.

The phone screamed. He immobilized himself. The floor would collapse under his next step and drop him into a bottomless pit. There was a hollow fast-falling sensation in the pit of his stomach. Suddenly he saw a stranger,

a man with dead-white skin and shadowy eyes
glittering beneath a jutting browridge staring
at him hostilely. The enemy stranger's bony
face asserted a formidable will and implacable
strength so far beyond his own that—

Enough of that scary kid fantasy! He
warned himself to quit playing mirror games.
This was survival time. The melodrama left his
mind; the color returned to his face.

Yes, he thought coldly, it was impossible for
a 120-pound body to clog an enormous storm
sewer. But a secondary line carrying overflow
from smaller outlets toward the main might be
no more than three feet in diameter. Mona's
body, dropped into it from above, might have
wedged and blocked most of the passage. All
sorts of debris could have accumulated around
her and formed an impenetrable mass, a
dam, closing the conduit, and the flow from
God knew how many feeder sewers could have
backed up, turning a stretch of Tenth Avenue
into a river. If the dam didn't break by itself,
the source of the trouble would be located and
Mona's corpse would be discovered too soon!

He watched Pam, his lifeline, while she
spliced a strong extension of that lifeline,
roping Uncle Webb in carefully with the girlish
music of her voice.

She nodded and smiled and hung up.

"It's all right," she said brightly. "He's
taking us to dinner here. I'll meet him in the
restaurant in a half hour."

The moment Joel reached their restaurant

table an hour later, Pam smiled and nodded imperceptibly, letting him know she'd done her part and everything was all right.

Webberly Treat had a firm handshake and his broad, intelligent face looked amiable. In his fifties and gray at the temples, the lawyer had a trustworty air of substance about him, an appearance of respectability and authority sure to inspire confidence in a jury. There was no mention of legal matters during the meal.

Pam and "Uncle Webb" had memories to share dating back to the years when the families had lived in the same city. Her musical progress was the center of their bond and they talked of her early recitals and the current season's problems, and touched on the fact that tonight's concert featured "her" symphony by her favorite composer. They made conscientious efforts not to exclude Joel but to weave him into their pleasant mood. Joel was responsive, nodding or smiling or saying a few appropriate words when they drew him in but he tried to stay out at the edges, not intruding. Most of the diners in the restaurant were orchestra musicians, and there were several friendly interchanges with people passing their table or sitting nearby. The atmosphere of her world was nourishment, and the happiness she exuded touched it all with a magic beyond his best fantasies.

There was only one discordant note, as if a cold sliver of the night had penetrated the radiant warmth. It lasted less than a minute, while Abe Hambul, the concertmaster, stopped and spoke to her in his corpselike dry-husk voice about a technical matter. His and Joel's glances met. There was no glimmer of recognition or acknowledgment in those eyes of the existence of Pam's husband. It was Abe who had once said—after Pam had spoken of Joel's love of great music—that the commandant of Treblinka, the Nazi death camp, had formed symphony orchestras of the condemned because he genuinely loved great music.

When Abe left, Pam touched her breast with one fist, her eyes briefly anguished, and shook her head.

"I love Abe so much!"

Webberly Treat nodded gravely. He was well aware of Abe's concentration camp experience.

"His suffering is what you love," Joel said.

They both looked at him. He knew he should not have said the unsayable.

Treat changed the subject smoothly. The remark was forgotten. Maybe. Callous? Had he sounded callous to the lawyer? That might be bad. Or maybe good. Evidence that a lobotomy could destroy higher sensibilities. Joel had discarded the plan to present himself as an "amiable grunt." If he seemed too far out of it, too stupid, he couldn't have held a job. Opposition lawyers would point that out. His own lawyer might judge he was faking the brain damage and was less interested in justice than a big money settlement.

Pam slid a small envelope across the table to

Joel.

"That's your ticket for tonight. I'll see you after."

"You're not leaving?"

"Uncle Webb wants to discuss things. Legal details. You know. So I'll give you time alone together for some man-to-man talk. You needn't hurry to get me to the auditorium. I'll go on the bus with the others."

"But—"

"It's all right. I don't mind. Uncle Webb and I already decided we'd do it this way."

She got through the thank-you's, hugs, and good-byes. For several seconds he and Treat watched her go before they looked at one another. Joel smiled. Treat did not.

Instead, he gut-punched him.

"I'm not going to handle your case."

"*What?*"

"I'm not—"

"I heard you," Joel cut in. "But I don't get it. You were going to take my case; you told Pam you were. What made you change your mind? Was it that crude remark about her feeling for Abe Hambul?"

"Certainly not; it was perceptive and close to the truth. I *didn't* change my mind; Pam misunderstood. I let her misinterpret my telling her she had nothing to worry about and that I would be giving you good news. The good news is that you do not have to suffer constant anxiety because of the mistaken belief your brain is damaged. There was no lobotomy . . . so there's no case."

"You say there was no lobotomy."

"Exactly."

Joel managed a stiff-cheeked smile.

"That's really good news! The bad news is that Pam's Uncle Webb that she thinks the world of, is not a friend. And not a fool. Only fools go with the losers. They'll never call Professor Treat Judge Treat if he antagonizes the whole damned state, will they? So they've told you I fantasied it all!" He laughed sourly.

Treat poured the dregs from the coffee pot into his cup with a shaky hand.

"I'm very angry," he said quietly, frowning. "I assumed you trusted me and knew that I'm incapable of selling out to the opposition. You insult me. I will expect an apology when I've explained fully. If you don't want to wait and listen and take my word, I advise you to go directly to the local hospital and arrange for X-rays. The odds are thousands to one that there's no hole in your head. At least," he added nastily, "in the technical sense."

"You don't mean—" Joel began, and started over. "You don't mean . . ." He took a long breath.

"I do mean. You were tricked into believing the temple bone had been penetrated. A show was put on for you. The skin was penetrated, there was bleeding, there were bandages. Basically it was a form of shock therapy. As I understand it, the surgeon at Shaunautaukee allowed you to see in some sort of mirror, that a long tube was being inserted into your skull. At a certain point, he blocked your view with his body and substituted a very short tube which looked to *you* like the end of a long tube inside your skull."

Joel sat dumfounded, staring sightlessly, his inner eye seeing that operation. He realized that that's what could have happened. His lips were dry, open. He shut his mouth.

"I'm going to do just that! Right now. Get an X-ray. I'll *prove* they're all liars."

"By all means convince yourself. However, that surgeon would have been a fool to perform an illegal operation which would leave X-ray evidence against him. Irrefutable evidence." Treat paused, and after a moment spoke in a warmer voice. "You can't absorb it, I see. You don't yet grasp the fact that it *is* good news. When the long-range meaning to your future becomes clear, Joel, you'll be—as will Pam—very happy to know you're not maimed."

"But, goddamnit to *hell*, it's all the *same*, the shock, the belief they implanted in me that I was . . . was . . . was maimed . . . is as bad as . . . as the real thing. I . . . I . . . ."

"That's an excellent point. I've considered the possibility that we could make a case on that basis, that the shock of it was equally damaging and may have held you back in your career. However . . ."

"Yes?" Joel urged him on.

"We'd be on flimsy ground. You've done well in adjusting to a demanding job and to your marriage. They have neurological tests on record to prove your nerve functioning was unimpaired after the 'operation' and before your release. And we're up against medical expertise in the question of whether the so-called ghost operation was or was not justifiable. They have discretionary power when it comes to any form of shock therapy. A majority of staff at Shaunautaukee concurred that it was called for."

"Sure . . . sure . . . they hated me. I just don't understand why Dr. Dornstadter never leveled with me, though. I don't know how you found out, or when or why, . . ." He broke off, fumbled, and found and lit a cigarette. His hands were steady, he noted grimly.

Treat explained.

Joel listened with an air of attentiveness but he had a feeling of resignation. It didn't matter *when* or *how* the lawyer had found out if *what* he'd found out was true.

But it wasn't true and he had proof that it wasn't. He resisted an impulse to touch the lobotomy site because it might give Treat the impression that he had doubts and was re-checking the evidence of his own senses.

Treat began to run out of words. He kept leaving openings for Joel to apologize. Joel kept missing them.

The final minutes were heavy, barely civil,

and their parting was a sort of mutual escape.

He knew the orchestra buses had long since left, carrying Pam away. His rushing back to the motel room to see her after she was gone was absurd. He went in and for a little while or maybe a long while he simply existed blankly. Then the emptiness of the room began to feel like a trap.

He hurried out to the car and got away, driving in the direction of the auditorium, toward Pam. After a few blocks he imagined he smelled beer, or beery breath . . . Mona's.

He could not trust himself to drive, so he cut into a side street and parked. He tried to fend off thoughts of her and calm himself with a cigarette. The minute he lit it he reheard that raw scream when he'd mashed his cigarette ember into her naked buttock.

He touched his left temple. His hand was shaking badly. He waited. Steadied. He began to explore the lobotomy carefully.

He located the exact spot immediately and pressed the pad of his forefinger against the skin till he could feel the circular hole in the temple bone distinctly. A protective sheath had grown over the opening; some kind of membrane that was tough but resilient. As usual he felt a slight give when he pressed harder. At one point, at the edge of the slightly sunken area, there was a tiny, hard protruberance where the bone had reknitted imperfectly, leaving one rough spot on the rim of the circle. That little bulge of bone was a telling detail that confirmed the reality of the lobotomy. Unmistakably.

He didn't know why he needed to prove to himself what he already knew. Unless . . . well, face it. Treat had shaken his confidence.

Why would a surgeon risk performing an illegal operation which left irrefutable hole-in-the-bone evidence detectable by X-ray? He'd have to be crazy. Maybe he really was . . . at least sometimes. That wasn't so farfetched. He could have spells of actual insanity, and the other doctors would gather round to protect their outlaw colleague.

Could that tiny lump be a fiber mass or a grainy bit of cartilage or a blood clot or a scar or injured muscle fiber, or a calcium deposit or some other something besides bone? Sometimes it seemed to move when he rolled his finger a bit from side to side. But that could be the mere sliding sensation of tissue and fluid moving over the motionless bone.

He rolled his finger, testing. Yes, that's what it was. There was only a deceptive illusion that the bone lump itself moved.

That rough spot on the rim was as real in his mind as the hole itself, which he had *known* was there from the day of the lobotomy. He had reinforced his unshakable belief in that hole with a mental image of it, which he repeatedly verified by touch. But what if the whole construct, so unshakable in his senses, was based not on what he really knew but on what he thought he knew? There were muscles under the skin and networks of blood and lymph vessels and nerves and tissues, including gelatinous squashy fats. Pressing into shifting substances like that could give the impression that he was probing down into a slightly sunken area. Besides, under pressure there was some give to the padding of his forefinger, which he could misinterpret as the give in a resilient membrane across a hole. In this mood of doubt he was thick-fingered clumsy and his touch was off and he could not be sure he was in contact with that membrane.

It was as if . . . no, he wasn't going to believe a thing like that . . . as if . . . the temple bone was intact.

No.

He refused to believe such a thing. It would prove that he himself, not some stranger rendered subhuman by a lobotomy, had abused, raped, and murdered Mona and vilely desecrated her corpse. No. No. That would link Mona to him and to Virgie and Cleo and Marabelle and Judy. Their spirits and the agonizing memory of their screams seemed to invade the car suffocatingly, crowding out his breathing space. He felt himself sinking into oblivion and thinking it no longer mattered whether he had been crazy as a loon to confess those torture murders or crazy like a fox.

He shook his head violently, thinking *no,* no, it was suicidal to believe there'd been no lobotomy.

In time, in due time, no hurry, under the

supervision of his own trusted doctor, he would have his own X-rays made.

Meantime, he switched on the lights and got going. He gradually rose out of his scary, demoralized state. There was a physical remnant of distress, a slight chilliness through his body. Even that was gone when he reached Pam . . . or at least reached where she was, Municipal Auditorium.

It was still early. He had nowhere else to go, nothing better to do. Scores of even emptier people had arrived earlier yet. They had formed lines at either end of the outer lobby, thereby organizing and structuring their dead time to give it and themselves an illusion of meaning while they waited, passive, for the doors to open. He chose to become the tail of the longer line, and soon enough he had become the middle without moving one step forward. He felt philosophical. He perceived himself objectively as in, but no real part of, this scene.

In due time he was wandering over the rich carpeting of the inner lobby, observing the crowd impassively. Some showed animation verging at times into excitement at a low level of intensity. Most were on the move toward aisle entrances and he caught only transient flashes of glossy hair and sparkling eyes and jewelry and colorful dresses and there were sweet scents and flower faces, he noted with detachment, as if from a great distance.

The flower face was seated onstage tuning up with the orchestra. The moment he made the visual contact that reestablished his life-line, the "great distance" began to close rapidly. It vanished when he reached his sixth row aisle seat and Pam flashed him an enchanting on-off smile.

She resumed practicing something he couldn't quite hear since dozens of musicians were doing muted run-throughs of different passages simultaneously, canceling each other out. The pleasant cacophony was not unlike those summer evening sounds from the practice studios in the College of Music on the CSU campus, where he had felt himself to be no real part of the scene. Just as he had felt here until a few minutes ago. But now he was definitely a part of this scene where the night was literally filled with music. There was no better place to be than in the here and now, his mind clear and in contact with the higher reality.

At the mundane level, he repeatedly had to swivel to one side or half stand to let people pass in to their seats. When his row was filled, he sank bonelessly into the cushion and remained inert, rallying only when Pam gave him a glance. She was, of course, occupied and preoccupied and a little nervous in anticipation of the performance. It was not good for her to let herself be too aware of the audience or think of personal problems. She could spare him very little attention.

In the empty spaces between her brief glances, his thoughts tended to drift darkly and sink into ugliness. Once he let his lids close tiredly and had a split-second nightmare: Mona's face with her eyes bulging, her jaw dropped, her mouth wide open in a silenced scream.

He stared at his shimmeringly beautiful golden princess, telling himself that where she was, no evil could exist, and imagining that her cleansing goodness was filling him. Like magic he was free of that horror image of Mona and was drifting back in memory to summer evenings on campus near the music school.

In that time, that long-ago time, in his state of preexistence before Pam, he had sometimes heard a lone violin as sweet as the dream of perfection. And lo! the dream became manifest and the truth, the poetic truth, was that he recognized her as the embodiment of beautiful music the moment he first set eyes on her. But now the sound of her violin was indistinct. It became silent as she finished practice. He was having trouble maintaining steady visual contact with her. She seemed to recede into the distance, then come in close in a strange rhythm as if he were alternately looking at her through the right and the wrong ends of a pair of binoculars. *Binoculars?*

He frowned. He was letting himself drift dangerously. He snapped out of it. He looked at his watch.

It was way past eight-thirty. The minutes crawled. Pam waited, the orchestra waited, the audience waited while nothing happened.

Finally, the lights sank and a wave of applause rose and *Tick Tick* hustled out to the podium, took a bow before anybody heard him conduct, then turned his back and raised his little stick and the music began.

Joel heard it all right. It reached his ears. It didn't get through.

At least not during the two works in the first half of the program. Mere preliminaries.

His left temple itched. He didn't scratch. His scrotum itched. He couldn't scratch at his crotch here in public.

Pam was playing animatedly, bowing arm pure pale poetry in motion, left hand fingers dancing on the strings, her body unconsciously swaying forward and back in short arcs, her golden head glossy. She sent out sparks of light. Glints from the little heart-shaped pendant on the thin chain necklace he'd brought her, along with the pretty shoes, which, of course, were unsuitable for wearing on this occasion.

Itch, itch, itch, he couldn't stand it. He had to stand it . . . or sit it . . . sit it out. . . . His squirmy tension was beginning to annoy the woman in the seat beside him.

His program booklet fell, *splat*, to the floor. There was a bar in the lobby. He groped down for the program. Found it. He squinted at the page listing individual musicians. First Violins, fifth name Pamela Ellender Danton. They'd finally got around this season to stop listing her as Pamela Ellender. Third in the

Violoncello listing was Myrtle's name. He looked at Myrtle, loverless Myrtle, with her instrument clamped between her legs, enjoying ... poor gal, lucky gal ... a purer finer love.

Just one drink ... double shot ... and he'd be OK.

He could get up and move unobtrusively up the aisle and get into the lobby without bothering the audience. Then ... his foot itched ... after having one for the road he'd head out. For somewhere. He should. Anywhere. She had grounds for annulment. Misrepresentation of his whole pre-Shaunautaukee life. Withholding of some—all—the facts she would have been entitled to know, which, if she had known ... There would never have been a marriage. A fraud, betrayal. She'd married him only because—not in spite of—his mental problems ... like her idealized composer's mental problems.

He half turned on his seat, preparing a swift rise and turn and then he'd be on the move out before anybody onstage, fully occupied, would notice. The first violins were resting for a few bars. The stage lighting spilled over the first few rows. Any movement would attract and distract her attention. Whether she saw him go or not, she'd soon know that his seat was empty.

But by then he would be gone ... gone into nowhere. But where ... ?

He stayed. He added to the thunder of applause. When *Tick Tick* motioned for the orchestra to stand and get their applause—especially since there was no special soloist, the orchestra being *the* performer—Joel himself yelled *Bravo* and started it. The standing ovation. The crowd was primed and ready to show they were no hick yokels but *in*. And up they came . . . *whee* . . . Pam couldn't resist, even Myrtle couldn't resist, smiling . . . beaming. Everyone in the whole orchestra, however they scoffed about it, liked it and was secretly flattered. Pam simply glowed on him. Maybe the rest of the orchestra knew it was he who had started it. That's one good thing I did for you if you can remember me. The standing ovation for *this* work was *nothing* compared to what it would be after *her* symphony. . . .

But he wouldn't be there.

Pam wiggled two fingers, a little good-bye wave as she went offstage for intermission. Joel hurried to get away with no good-bye feeling at all, just a sense of . . . of . . . something . . . nothing. He banged his sore right thumb on the lobby exit door, and swore.

He headed for the outer lobby door. But he veered off. He had a drink. An orange drink. Maybe he'd turn it into a screwdriver. No. He needed no stimulants, no mere alcoholic stimulants.

Pam would worry if he wasn't there for *her* symphony.

Afterward would be time enough to . . . to . . .

At the open doorway at the head of the aisle he had a morbid hallucination of a beautiful

Valentine face above a stand-up collar and caught a scent of funeral flowers. He collided with the "hallucination" . . . a glancing blow, almost knocking the woman—a perfumed beauty—down. He apologized. Profusely. She laughed that it was nothing, nothing. He gestured for her to go ahead. She did. She smiled at him from her row as he went down to his seat.

He sat listening to "her" symphony. He became increasingly aware that something was happening to his feel for music, some sort of disconnection. . . .

What was happening to that orchestra anyway, he wondered in annoyance. Were they running out of steam? He could hardly hear them playing at all.

Then . . . what the hell! Had they forgotten the music, or what? they were just sitting there. Doing nothing. Not playing at all. What was it, a strike or something? It would be months before the new contracts were negotiated. Was the union giving a warning, showing its muscle, reminding management who it was that made the music?

Hell of a time, right in the middle of something to pull a dead silence bit like that . . .

A violin started to play.

Not Pam's. She was sitting there, motionless, her bow at the ready. A couple more violinists started up. Then Pam and the punk beside her both began to play at the same time. Then all back through her section more violins got into action.

Finally the whole damned gang, every place, tubas, trombones, trumpets, drums, bass fiddles, got going. Everybody was earning their keep. But oh, man, overdoing it and getting loud and wild and playing too fast . . . the raw naked brass, unmuted trumpets and trombones, and the piccolos and flutes shrill and shrieking to make themselves heard, screaming.

Pam had told him what it was like in the line of the battering percussion sound and with the horns aimed full blast at her section.

She couldn't hear most of the other violins; she could barely hear her own. All she could do was saw away, playing notes like disconnected fragments, cut off from her sense of the music as a whole. Cut off from her meaning. The idea of her, lost and in distress that way, affected him profoundly and his chest melted with tenderness, his throat choked up, the corners of his eyes burned with tears.

He felt her slipping away from him.

Joel was quivering. His left temple began to itch. For a minute there was a rage in him. He was getting a pantsbuster. He kept thinking of those feminine violins being overwhelmed— raped, goddamnit—and enjoying it. He clenched his teeth, bulging his jaw muscles.

He tried grimly to hold on to his sense of her.

Instead, he kept hearing those violins, those frenzied, feverish, feminine violins, quicker and hotter than dancing flames. He thought about them being overwhelmed by the harsh aggressive brass noise and assertive drums.

And in that passionate irresistible sweep toward climax, the violinist with the shimmeringly beautiful blond hair who yak-yakked about music abandoned all pretense of a sense of music and meaning.

True to form, to bitch form, she surrendered her will to the bullying overpowering "maestro." She even slipped up sometimes and called him that; Maestro. *Master.* She gloried in mindless submission to his strength, to his brutishness, and reached an exalted state of joy, of *ecstasy!*

Joel had a torturing image of her luscious naked body writhing in heat. . . .

The fuckin' imposter! All those cultural pretentions and spouting about high, selfless ideals of subordinating herself to the beauty of music, when, of course, it was nothing but phony rationalization of her love of groveling in the slime of masochistic perversion!

Orgies! That's what she actually indulged in in that orchestra. Lots of disguised foreplay. Rushing with twitching pussy to rehearsals where whip-cracking maestros raised emotional welts, forcing her to endure humiliation and pain that made her cry but gave her secret orgasm after orgasm! Then, right out in public, she was *shameless.* During finales of symphonies when she was deafened, her own pretended identity so completely abandoned that she could exist only to do the bidding of the bully *maestro,* she joyously degraded herself and obeyed his will and was blind to everything except his commanding *stick!*

She fairly convulsed in uncontrollable orgasms in the grand climactic finale. *That* was her highest thrill, that perverted sexual ecstasy brought to unendurable pitch by all the pain she'd enjoyed.

Oh, yes! That was her ugly *inner* essence. . . .

In the finale the whole orchestra swept into an insane, chaotic, deafening frenzy so shattering that the sudden silence at the end came as a *shock.* . . .

He refused to be any part of the ovation. He kept his hands on his lap and his butt on the seat.

He sure as shit wasn't going to be any part of a standing ovation for *her* symphony!

He hated it!

15

He endured the standing ovation.

He went backstage. He moved through the noisy shifting crowd slowly but directly toward Pam.

She was surrounded by her world. She was unaware of him, advancing closer and closer, until he was right there. She was on one of her postperformance "highs."

She got one look at his bleak expression and her spirits plunged, the excited, laughing animation going out of her.

"What's *wrong?*"

"It's private."

He looked coldly at the girls around her, violinists mostly, and very soon they had other things to do, other places to be.

Pam looked at him, astonished, and said indignantly, "What did you make them feel unwelcome like that for and hurt their feelings? That was plain mean and—"

He stopped her curtly: "They never cared about my feelings. To your gang I'm nobody. Just Pam's clone, with no ideas of my own, or—"

"No *musical* ideas is all they mean, for goodness' sake. Why, they think it's cute the way you always loyally feel the same way I do about any piece of music."

"Cute!"

"You know good and well they don't mean cute that way, putting you down. They think it's nice and warm and romantic and shows how much you *love* me. You're not acting like you do *now*."

She studied him intently, waiting for a declaration of love. And waiting and waiting.

"Are you ready to go or not?" he said.

She blinked. She gestured oddly. She looked away from him and back at him, uneasily.

"I'll get my coat. And put my violin in the case." She managed a strained smile. She patted his hand. "Don't be tense. Be right back."

Hurrying off, she almost bumped into someone, veered away, and wobbled off-balance. When she peered anxiously across her shoulder at him before turning out of view toward the lockers, he remained expressionless.

She reappeared. Evidently she had got her composure back.

"You can carry it for me," she said girlishly,

handing him her violin case.

He took it, unsmiling, and said dryly, "What a privilege."

She pretended to be amused. She tucked her arm in his while going out to the car. He started to put the case on the backseat.

"I'll take it, I'll take it," she said, and laughed nervously. "You know me. I always worry it could fall off if we had to stop suddenly."

"Don't I know! Here it is. Take it. Hold your precious baby on your lap."

"Not on my lap, silly, just close at hand where—"

He slammed the door before she finished. When he got settled at the wheel and started the engine, she scooted over. She sat so close that he could feel her upper arm and hip and thigh pressing against him through their clothes. He got the car moving.

"We're not going to that fancy society party."

"Of course not when you're so unhappy, Joel." She slipped her glove off and lay her warm palm on his hand on the wheel, her soft fingers stroking. His fist clenched against the sensation.

"You're sure you can bear it?" he said harshly. "Not being in the sacred presence of your little god, the *maestro?*"

He heard her sharp intake of breath. He turned his face to see her looking at him in utter consternation, the stunning mountain-wildflower blue eyes widely rounded.

He stared ahead and laughed humorlessly. "I suppose you've had all the orgasms you want in one night?"

"I didn't say anything about anything like that, if you think I won't want you or would reject you. I don't know what in the world you're talking about."

"What I'm talking about," he said deliberately, and braked, carefully approaching a yellow-turning-red traffic signal, "is the fulfillment you were getting onstage tonight . . . as usual . . . during that *orgy* of a climax to '*your*' symphony. Sharing the experience, the exalted level of masochistic ecstasy you were experiencing under the command of the *maestro's* stick."

"My *God*, Joel, what horrible kind of thing are you thinking?"

"The meaner they are in whipping you into line, the more you worship them after you come through a great performance with them. The hell you have to go through up there with those horns aimed right at your section till you're deaf. All that percussion battering at you! You admit you can't hear the other violins; you can barely hear your own during all that noisy frenzy. You lose your own sense of the music. . . ." The light changed; he gunned away from the stop. "All you can do is saw away. You lose your own mind and will. You're reduced to watching the maestro's stick, obeying his will, mindlessly enjoying the pain, the humiliation. Oh, how great it is, your idealism. Your faceless submission of self to music. What does it amount to but a glorying in helplessness and pain? The experience is greater than any mere physical animal ecstasy. But is it *high?* Or is it lowness, underneath the rationalization, mere naked, shameless, wallowing in masochistic perversion?"

"Slow down. Stop the car!"

"Face it. You crave degradation. You enjoy brutes. The worse bully a maestro is, the more you respect him. *Sit still.* . . . Get your hand off that door latch."

"Stop yelling. Let me out!"

"I'm not yelling." Maybe he had been. He modulated his voice. "I'm only pointing out that you've had nothing but *contempt* for me because I was on my knees to you, a *worshiper* when what you *respect—*"

"You're getting loud again. I won't listen till you're calm. You don't know what you're saying. Stop it, right *now,* Joel! Stop hurting me with all that *ugly* talk. I can't *take* it. At a time like this. After a performance, when you *know* I'm very sensitive anyway. And *then,* you come and look at me the way you did, that *mean* way, upsetting me, when I *know* you don't want to and you don't know what you're saying. You don't mean it, I know you don't, because you *love* me, Joel, I *know* you do. I—I" She started to cry.

He remained grimly silent. He couldn't shut out the muffled sound of her crying and buried it under a blast of radio music.

"*Oh!*" she said furiously, and shut it off.

He turned it on. She turned it off. It went like that, on-off, on-off, for a couple of blocks.

Darleen, too, had instinctively resorted to anger to combat her fear. No doubt about it, he'd scared Pam. He smiled faintly. He decided to let her win this one and left the radio off. It instilled false confidence and did wonders for her sense of security.

"That's better . . . that's better. I know one thing, Joel. You turned it on because of one thing. You love me so much you couldn't stand hearing me cry."

Yeah! The sound was starting to give me a real pantsbuster, he thought. He had to control himself to keep from saying it out loud. To clobber her with crudity when she was still shaky would be poor timing and might take the fight out of her prematurely.

"Wel-l-l . . ." he said.

"I know you're sorry for hurting me with all those terrible accusations. Even if you're not ready to admit it yet, you couldn't look me in the eye and *deny* it . . . could you?"

The forward edge of the headlight beam picked up the Welcome-to-the-Orchestra banner above the street in front of the motel. He pointed toward it.

"Look, we're nearly there," he said, giving her the comfortable impression that he was avoiding looking at her and was trying to distract her. A clear pattern of retreat.

"Fine," she said. "I don't know what happened after I left you with Uncle Webb that upset you, but we'll get it straightened out." She patted his sleeve.

By the time they entered the motel room, their proper relationship was restored. She had the upper hand. A gentle hand. But firm, she let it be known by withdrawing the privilege of carrying her violin case in, and helping her out of her coat.

She crossed the room, carrying herself with a haughty air. She paused before going into the bathroom and told him, "We'll talk when I come out."

Her voice was not warm. But there was an implicit promise to understand all and forgive all, Pam being Pam.

His backing off about the radio music and his shamefaced manner as if he couldn't look at her had definitely reassured her. She believed she was back in command. She believed she was still his shimmeringly beautiful golden princess. She refused to believe her world could be shattered.

He closed the drapes and switched off the lights and shut his eyes. The darkness obliterated all sense of place and space and freed him of the confinement of this minute in time. He let himself drift, unanchored. Soon the unrelieved blackness dissolved into thick swirling fog smeared with faint ectoplasmic light and obscure constantly changing shapes. An exciting scene came into vivid focus. In a blissful state of dreamless sleep he watched Virgie and Cleo in the narrowing circle of fading firelight, surrounded by the encompassing night but pretending the scary things that were happening weren't happening. . . .

He alerted abruptly . . . an odd metallic sound . . . a door unlocking. He saw a door opening. He stared at Pam in the entrance backlighted from the bahroom. He had not realized she'd locked the door on going in. He'd thought she was over her fright because of that haughty air as she walked across the room. Not haughty, but brittle. A fragile pretense.

She peered warily out into the darkened room.

"Joel?"

He switched on the light. He looked at her without speaking.

"Were you standing in the dark?"

He didn't respond. She answered herself.

"Silly question. Obviously you were. What I meant was, were you brooding and gloomy?"

He merely smiled cryptically. She began to feel the weight of his silence. She tried to reduce it to a trifle.

"Needless to say, you're not *cheery.*"

She went over to the dressing table counter. She peered at herself in the wall mirror as if her appearance were the first order of importance. She fingered a lipstick without uncapping it. She smoothed an eyebrow. She shifted her weight from one leg to the other. She stalled, frowned, decided to remove her blue velvet headband. She fussed needlessly with her hair. She reached both hands behind her neck and began fumbling with the clasp of the threadlike gold chain necklace with the glass heart pendant he'd given her. Her upraised arm blocked off her side view. But at the first step he took she quickly twisted her upper body around to face him. He continued toward her.

"So you were keeping an indirect watch on me in the mirror, alert for any sudden moves." He stopped close behind her.

"What are you *doing?* You keep acting like . . . like . . ."

"A dangerous lunatic?"

"Not *that.* Like a stranger!"

She quick-stepped to one side. He'd anticipated. At once he moved forward, pressing just enough with his lower body to pinion her against the edge of the counter.

"Stop it! I don't like this at all!"

"Hold still. Can't you trust you back to me long enough for me to undo that clasp for you?"

She was holding her shoulders high, rigid. Her arms were at her sides but unrelaxed. After a while, reluctantly, she tilted her head partially forward. In the mirror he saw that as her face lowered, her eyes climbed, continuing to peer up at him under the lids.

He gazed at the exposed back of her lovely neck, smiling. His hands were steady. He opened the tiny clasp deftly. He pulled the chain tight around her throat and loosened it several times in a teasing rhythm. The pressure was so light she scarcely noticed it while he breathed warmly on the tender skin and then kissed it repeatedly with growing fervor.

She sucked her breath in sharply.

He whispered, "Am I giving you goose-bumps all over?"

"Oh-h-h, *are* you!"

"Thrills or chills?"

"Thrills *and* chills!"

She laughed. He laughed. He handed her the necklace.

"The two opposite sensations are indistinguishable, you know, sexy thrills and scary chills." He paused, changed tone abruptly. "Incidentally, you're right. I *am* a stranger! Somebody you don't know. And never did. My name is Paul Borland."

"Will you quit crowding me? It's making me uncomfortable." She turned, bumped her hip against him, and moved away as if escaping a trap. She stood near the door and wiped the back of her neck, looking at him sullenly.

"You ignored what I said."

"I don't like the ominous way you said it, or the nasty little smile on your face right now. It makes you feel fine, just fine, doesn't it, to see how I'm taking it . . . not so good. *Imagine,* telling *me,* that I don't know you. And hurling a strange name in my face. I suppose Paul whatever was the name you had before. Legally, you're Joel Danton, that's who I married, so what you're saying is you don't honor the marriage because you're somebody else. Well, good. Get out. Here's the door! My God, in my wildest dreams I couldn't imagine the way you've been hating my music that I thought you loved just like I did. And all the time you've been festering with resentments and hiding your hostility when I thought you were on my side, always, and . . . oh . . . oh . . . that's what *really* hurts. How could you be so false, so, so . . . You *never* loved me, did you?''

"You've got it all wrong. I've always loved you. Seeing you in distress this way makes me love you more than ever. I *want* you this *minute*, Pam—"

"Don't *touch* me, don't come *near* me. When I'm hurt, by *you*, you get turned on, you admit a terrible sadistic thing like that?''

"Call it sadistic. Actually it's the opposite. Sympathetic sharing of your pain. Isn't that the highest form of love? Isn't a concern for suffering at the very heart of the healing professions . . . and all religions?''

"I can't *believe* this. This mockery, this cynicism.''

"But it's not cynical mockery. I'm serious.''

"Sadism's an ugly perversion and you're practically calling it a beautiful virtue.''

"I must really be crazy.'' He looked at her with sardonic amusement. "But so was your favorite composer. The thing you played tonight . . . 'your symphony' was the last thing he wrote before the darkness swallowed him for good. He finished in an asylum. The living death. You *know* that. You're as pale as death."

"I'm leaving."

"No. No you're not. I'd run you down."

He moved intimidatingly close.

"And don't scream."

He lit a cigarette.

"Your knees are going to collapse under you . . . better sit down."

He indicated the armchair, took her elbow, helping her.

She sat. She hugged her arms around herself, chilled. He went and got her coat, put it around her shoulders. She stared ahead stuporously.

"Truth is beauty, the poet says. You must know the truth about Paul Borland. . . . Are you listening?"

She nodded.

"Do you want aspirins?"

She shook her head "no." She looked forlorn and it touched him.

"Don't be afraid. As far as your music is concerned, I didn't ever resent or hate it. I *was* with you in all ways and loved your music. It was only tonight I didn't. Before that, the magic was there, solid, and your beauty and goodness and love sustained me. You were my lifeline, my icon, goddess, the perfect fantasy. You made it possible for me to believe in my innocence."

Tears began to glide down her cheeks.

"I don't understand." Her voice choked. "I

don't understand, Joel."

"Paul. Paul Borland. Years ago, in California, I confessed to—"

"I don't want to hear any—"

"—the brutal murders of—"

"I won't *lis*ten to—"

"—four San Francisco State College coeds. You *will* listen! Their bodies were found in a state park. They'd been raped—"

"*Stop*—" She wiped her eyes with the backs of her hands.

"—and strangled with their panties . . . and tortured—"

"That's what this is, all this ugliness you're forcing on me, torture—"

"One of them, a delicate beautiful blonde, was subjected to prolonged torture. There were mistakes in the confession. Deliberate mistakes, some people thought, and called me crazy like a fox. Others decided I was crazy as a loon. My doctor at Shaunautaukee was sure I'd fantasied it all because I'm nobody and wanted to be big and Jesusy and take the punishment for somebody else's crime. He convinced me, but—"

"Did they catch him?"

"No. The surgeons decided I was a fox and killed my brain." He laughed harshly. "Your Uncle Webb found out they didn't actually do it. Just convinced me they did."

"What? What? How could he find out any such thing?"

She had innumerable pointless questions,

which he answered with growing impatience.

"Enough! I'm tired explaining. I accept it. Forget it, it's true. There was no lobotomy. I believed there was, and that was the whole point of it, to shock me and scare me into virtue. It worked, by God; I thought only good thoughts and I believed I didn't dare risk any kind of violent intensity. Or I might end up totally out of control, really crazy as a loon."

She watched him unblinkingly. He paused, chain-lit a cigarette.

"You shouldn't have come on this trip and left me. Everything started to unravel. I had flashback memories of killing those girls. I buried the truth again under a lot of plausible explanations, rationalized it, and felt innocent again. As long as I kept a good hold on you and fantasied that I was part of you and your world and that where you were no evil could exist, I could believe it had all been fantasy. I *had* to think that way . . . but then, two nights ago I went out and murdered a bar girl."

She sat erect, shook her head, stood up. "No, no. Don't say that. The terrible state you're in is really dangerous. Making you have dreadful, morbid fantasies, about me and ugly perversions you imagine I'm enjoying with my music. And about committing a murder . . ." She pulled a long breath. "No."

"The girl reminded me of one of the California victims."

"*There!* You see it's connected with that crime in the *past*. Next, you'll want to make another false confession . . . pure fantasy."

"You, of course, always reminded me of Virgie."

"Virgie?"

"She was called that. In mockery of her purity, her virginity. She suffered the most. She welcomed death. The last to go . . ."

His voice softened, lowering gradually until the words trailed away into silence and for a while there was an enveloping hush in the room.

"That *mournful* tone in your voice, you must have loved her."

A statement of the obvious; to confirm it would be superfluous.

"Are you giving me the silent treatment? Are we back to *that?*"

He gazed blankly at her.

"*Or* . . ." She caught her breath. "Or is it that you don't want me intruding on your dreamy mood remembering her. . . ."

He smiled vaguely.

He watched her shift her weight from one leg to the other, the blue velvet gown swaying gracefully. He could see the strong, quick pulse in the soft hollow at the base of her exquisite throat. He could feel a nervous excitement emanating from her, an invisible trembling through the atmosphere. She was in a controlled state just short of hysteria, still capable of thought. She sneaked her hand to the drape cord and pulled . . . on the wrong one.

She made an exasperated sound and yanked

the other one, opening the drapes.

"Why, it *is* snowing."

In the instant she glanced out at the window pretending to see snow that wasn't there, he closed the distance between them.

She winced at his touch and protested thinly when he snapped off the light.

"Don't . . . it's creepy . . . turn it on."

He simultaneously closed the drapes and relighted the room. She blinked and looked at him with stunned eyes. She remained motionless, totally irresponsive when he kissed her neck and shoulders. He felt her body with feverish hands.

"Undress."

"I don't feel like—"

"I have to see you naked."

"*Naked?* When I'm ice cold?"

She struggled, turned her face when he tried to kiss her mouth. She resisted, writhing her body against his tightening embrace. He had a pantsbuster. She freed herself, kept circling, backstepping, sidestepping, staying out of reach. She looked stark, her flower face showing pink splotches. She saw an opening, rushed to the door, and had the chainlock off, knob in hand, when he caught her. She whimpered when he clapped a hand over her mouth.

"Panic," he said softly.

She kicked his shin, drove an elbow back into his gut, and even made a grab at his groin. He laughed, uncovered her mouth but held on to her.

"I want out of here, let me *go*."

"We're finally getting some intensity. That's good. Necessary. Soon the stimulus of pain—"

"*Stimulus?* You *are* a torturer, threatening me with pain."

"Not *threatening* . . . promising . . ."

"I *will* scream!"

"You'll *start* to scream," he warned.

"Don't talk about pain that crazy way, Joel, use your head, you're not a sadist, or . . . or . . . any of those things. . . ."

She twisted around, stared into his face desperately.

"You wouldn't hurt a fly."

He was off-guard a moment, getting out a cigarette. In a flash she had got to the door and opened it. He grabbed her violin case, started to open it. She saw him and watched from the doorway.

He got the instrument, held its neck in his fist, stared grimly at her.

She swayed.

"You wouldn't. You're bluffing. I know you wouldn't do *that*."

She made a really convincing and truly poignant case.

In the beginning there was a shrill note to her voice that scraped his nerves. She spoke in a rush and jumbled her syntax but she was coherent and her meaning came through. She reminded him that he had heard and loved the music of her violin before he ever saw her. And had he not said, yes, he had, that he knew her immediately the first time he set eyes on her because she was the physical embodiment, the spirit made flesh, of the aural beauty of that violin. To destroy *it* was unthinkable because—the logic was irrefutable—it symbolized and was inextricably fused with—he wasn't sure of her exact words, they were unimportant—his love. And he had reasserted his love, strongly, not half an hour ago, could he deny that? No, he could not deny that.

She sensed hesitation in him. A relaxing of his features. Her voice mellowed.

She granted that this was not, in *fact*, the same violin, but in truth it was, because the principle, the meaning, was the same. He accepted that, didn't he? At least he didn't reject it.

Her soprano voice began to flow and soothe and charm with the sweetness of song and there was the natural eloquence of her flower face and gorgeous eyes and the innocent voluptuousness of her young, supple, essentially virginal figure, and above all she had the clear perception that her very life might be at stake and it gave an impact to her performance which moved him deeply.

There was no moment when she did not monitor his slightest reaction, his overall mood. Her hyperalertness gave her a luster, an exciting high-pitched tremulous tone. She closely observed her effect on him. She duly noted the fact he had not yet smashed the violin. Probably, unconsciously, she added up the number of seconds he remained calm and tried to judge whether enough calm time had accumulated for her to risk taking a step.

He judged that there was a limit to the length of time anyone could wait in a cold, drafty doorway. At last she came into the room. But after one step she stopped. She stood there, mute. He relaxed his grip on the neck of the violin. She read that as a good sign. Yet she did not move closer or shut the door. Just watched him steadily.

He held his breath. He gave her another reassurance, a tiny retreat, shifting his eyes away from her scrutiny. Without taking her eyes off him, she reached back and swung the door shut. He let his breath out, suppressed a smile.

She stayed over there. She cleared her throat.

"Wouldn't you like to lay it down?"

"No," he muttered. He gave her a toned-down look of anger, a mere sulk.

"Admit it, you're completely over that rage. You don't have any irrational desire at all to break that violin anymore, do you? I can read you like a book, Joel."

Still she didn't come an inch closer.

"I had a funny insight driving up here. Oscar Wilde said each man kills the thing he loves. I thought like this: If a man kills what he loves, he destroys his own motivation, his will to live. So it would be a bungled suicide."

That did it. He had a giddy comic image like he'd seen in movies when a photographer's film is reversed and a high diver comes back up out of the water and stands poised on the board. Shattered Humpty Dumpty flew upward, reassembling himself, and instantly sat on the wall intact again. Just so, Pam's known, safe world was restored, and she soared with high hope and came to him, projecting beauty, the word song flowing sweetly from her throat, soothing the charmed harmless beast. She understood her power. She knew herself to be irresistible. *Sis* had always known she could do anything with anybody, too. Till one of those rough lovers she had a taste for put her in a casket wearing a high ruffled collar up to her chin to hide the bruises on her throat.

He gave Pam the violin. He put his forefinger under her chin and said, "Ah-h-h-h, God, how really defenseless you are, how beautiful you are."

Perhaps there was too much emotion in his gaze. She edged away from him.

"Let yourself *know* it, thrillingly, know you're in the presence of a killer. Pain and the fright are powerful stimulants, aphrodisiacs. Don't do anything sudden. Don't trigger off violence prematurely. Just let yourself anticipate it all."

The new shock staggered her.

"Pull a big breath. Or you'll faint."

"I *want* to . . ."

He grabbed her shoulders and shook her, jolting her head.

"Stay alert! *That's* better. You don't understand! Just as you can't distinguish at the mundane level the difference between shallow sexy little thrills and fun-scary chills, at the higher level of intensity beyond passion and in another dimension, there is no distinction between unbearable joy and unendurable pain. It's difficult to achieve such heights, such altered states of consciousness, but—"

She whimpered.

"Don't do that. It sets me on fire. I won't be able to hold back and develop things gradually and bring you up to a pitch where you can absorb and enjoy pain's unique pleasures."

"You love me, you *know* you do in your heart. You *can't* do this to—"

"You *won't* grasp it, Pam, sweetheart. There's no contradiction between love and hurting. They intensify each other. They're indispensible to each other. What's love without suffering? Shallow. Trivial. Transient. Listen, fright and pain call up the most profound, powerful life instinct, sex itself, to fight against the threat. The intense struggle fuses everything together. Another dimension is achieved to fight against the threat. The experience will have meaning, as a *triumph* . . . *above* life, beyond it. Death is not horrible. But we must earn its blissful beauty."

He expected constant interruptions. When none came he began speaking more and more slowly, then broke off entirely.

He gave her an opening. Time to assemble her thoughts and shape her arguments and appeals to reason, or to plead or protest in some way. But she didn't speak.

At this stage she would be incapable of accepting or agreeing with what he said. Her mind *must* be rejecting it all.

Her face became expressionless. Unreadable. There was a vagueness about her eyes as though she were looking into distances. Or sleepwalking.

Maybe she was simply tuning him out. Refusing to hear what she did not want to hear. Worse—his fists clenched-unclenched-clenched spasmodically . . . she could be ignoring mere words as if they were childish bluff-bluster and she did not believe he was man enough for violent action.

"You're not convinced! You want details, gory details. I'll tell you about Virgie!"

He began. He stopped at once, because he realized that he was *there*. Nothing more was needed to terrify her out of her senses. Her mind was already gone.

He felt a surge of power, a rushing joy through his whole body, a giddying sense of total mastery. His mind, his will prevailed. Her submission was total. Her arms hung limp, passive. A thought flashed excitingly. If only her eyes were closed, her beauty would reach another dimension. He visualized her luscious naked body writhing frenziedly beneath him. It overstimulated him so much that he imagined himself clamping a hand over her mouth to stop the scalded sound of her scream. Above the stifling mask of his hand her wide-open eyes stared, bulged, suffered. . . .

Overwhelming lust threatened his control. He yanked himself back to the immediate moment. Pam, in reality, was on her feet. And except for an expanse of pale delicate skin above the blue velvet gown's scooped neckline, her exquisite body was still concealed. There was something repulsive about her as a mindless zombie that chilled his desire one moment and intensified it fiercely the next.

And there was the threat. What if her condition was temporary, a shock from which she might recover long enough to ruin everything, or at least disrupt the momentum? He passed a hand before her eyes. He detected no shifting, no response of any kind.

But the apparent glazed immobility could be cunningly willed. Her expressionlessness might be a mask to conceal devious workings back there somewhere in the animal depths of her mind. Was she concocting survival strategies? Behind even the blankest eyes—he'd seen them on back wards—were flickers of awareness, instinctive senses which roused and recognized the border between life and death. . . .

He was prepared for anything she might

do—a desperate run for the door, a futile attempt to reach the phone, sudden wild screaming . . .

Abruptly, her eyes rolled up and her body went down.

She lay collapsed at his feet.

He stood looking down at her warily. He began to tremble with excitement. He remained controlled, on guard. He held his breath. The beat of his heart quickened.

Her final strength seemed to escape her in a long sigh. Her lids closed.

He bent down.

For a split second he was off-balance.

Her hands flew upward, her fingers clawing into the material of his jacket, and jerked violently downward and at the same time pulled herself into a half-sitting position. While he flung one arm out to brace himself on the counter to keep from toppling, she went into a twisting, driving frenzy of motion, and was out from under him and gone like quicksilver down a crack.

She'd bumped his leg and his turn was wobbly, and his belated awkward grab missed her arm. She was at the door, twisting the knob and gasping but wasting no breath on screams, when he got oriented and lunged at her with an enraged curse. The sound alerted her. She spun, braced her back on the jamb, and aimed a straight-legged kick at his gut that grazed his shoulder instead because he was in a crouch. He grabbed her leg and dumped her flat on her back. He slammed and chainlocked the door. She squeezed her eyes shut and opened her mouth wide for a scream that never came because he pounced, mashing his hand over her mouth. She tried to bite.

She gouged her nails into his hand and wrist. She pried at his fingers. She shook her head violently from side to side and arched her head back straining the cords of her neck, trying to break his hold and making strangled sounds in her throat, her eyes glitteringly overbright and bulging. He could feel the breath from her nostrils on his hand. Once or twice she got an opening to gulp air through her mouth and time enough for a brief, muffled yelp.

She lurched and heaved and pitched her body incessantly and convulsively and writhed and rolled from side to side and kicked the air till she lost both shoes and tried to batter his ribs with her knees and raked her nails savagely in the direction of his eyes with one hand and the other and alternately she doubled her fists and punched at his face and throat. Some of the blows made harmless glancing contact.

She was a handful. Within minutes the overall intensity of the situation had risen to exhilarating heights. He dodged, ducked, blocked her blows and squelched her passionate and multiple resistances with increasing pleasure. He smiled at her. After a little while he used one hand to stroke her bare kicking thighs. He merely touched her panties without the slightest pressure into the soft mound of lusciousness. Instantly her eyes froze with hatred and her whole body stiffened.

Ah-h-h! What a powerful reaction! He allowed himself a moment of bliss so rich that he closed his eyes to contain it.

It was at that point, within those few seconds of clock time, that a phase ended and a phase began and everything changed.

Because . . . because . . . he wasn't completely sure. But when his eyelids shut out the light, he somehow tasted the darkness and it was like ambrosia and nectar of the gods, so immeasurably potent and irresistibly delicious that the merest sip set off an unslakable craving in him to be drunk on it. Again. Or it was because Pam used the time of his temporary blindness—and her hard little fist!—to mash his lips into his front teeth. The reasons blurred together, lending flavor to each other and both were indispensable. Still, the most immediately important one was Pam's escalating everything.

He suppressed his impulse to laugh exultantly. He calmly explored the inside of his upper lip with his tongue. He didn't know whether or not he actually detected the salty tang of blood. Unmistakably, though, she'd intended to hurt him. She couldn't help feeling satisfaction in landing a good solid blow. She'd delivered it with remarkable force considering the unfavorable conditions and the limitations of her swing. And she continued with all limbs and her whole body in an all-out, admirable, but inefficient effort to inflict damage on him.

He reflected with affectionate sympathy that she had a further handicap: Nice girls never went for the balls.

He simply watched her. Presently she was watching him watch her. All her energy began to concentrate in her eyes; the movement through her body and limbs slowed. That punch in the mouth she had given him, he knew from the depth of his guts, had begun to dominate her. Given a second chance to think about it, she would not have had the courage to do it, to give him that authentic message that she was now participating fully. She knew very well that her hard blow invited—required— retaliation.

Soon enough her anticipation, her mingled dread and craving, stopped her physical resistance entirely. She simply existed, waiting, waiting, a paralysis in her mind. There was an insidious action below, in the pelvic area, and she was beginning to feel an incomparable combination of sensations: the cold hollow fear in the lower gut and tingling in the genitals.

He shared the sensations while they hung there together in that suspended period of waiting and dreading and anticipation. There was a timelessness about it, a hovering pause on the brink that tended to stop the breath. In fact, there did seem to be a diminution of the exhalations from her nostrils to the merest tickling against the side of his hand. Had he freed her mouth, he was sure she would be mute. The eerie force of that time-stopped eternity of anticipation formed an indissoluble bond. . . .

He touched his lips. What small pain there had been had been transcended. He smiled wistfully. When he'd been knee-high to Sis and she performed dental work with her knuckles, free, he would make a noisy ungrateful spectacle of himself, howling and bawling like a snot-nosed sissy. Afterward she petted and loved him and made wonderful promises. It made her feel good to make promises and she always believed, when she was in that mood, that she'd keep them. When he'd stood belly-high to her and she'd get rolling in one of those high-luster moods of hers and choose him to participate in her excitement, he would sometimes have the guts to do something. Like slug her. The minute he did it there would be a stop. A dead stop, a paralyzing stare from those eyes, and he'd feel a prestorm barometric drop in the atmosphere and in his gut just before she turned into a tornado. Sometimes it was bad, and she was unleashed hell, but the worse the better. When she got it out of her system, she was an angel, a weeping angel, and in the end he would be more hurt by her tears of remorse than by his own physical pain and he would hate his own contemptible weak inability to absorb mere blows, and he would know he'd failed her.

He was mistaken about Pam. Because far

from being mute when he freed her mouth, she set up a horrendous din of yelling for help and stupidly threatening him and in general made herself unrecognizable. She became a mindless wild creature, incapable of learning from experience. He had to hush and overpower her repeatedly to convince her of the obvious, that she could not win. She butted him with her head when he pulled her to her feet, and enroute to the bed, while he was holding her around the waist from behind with one arm and stifling her noise with the other hand, she grabbed a cold cream jar and smashed it in a display of futile destruction.

The minute he dumped her on the bed, she grabbed the phone and tried to bash his skull. The pillow over her head allowed her to breathe while muffling the noise. Although she continued thrashing about totally refusing to cooperate in the removal of her panties and gown and bra, he used minimal force and inflicted no pain of an acute form. He spoke soothingly, whether or not she heard, and caressed her body and now and then directly stimulated her erotically. She appeared to respond negatively; he didn't allow it to disturb him; eventually there would be an avalanche of sexual joy.

Basically her resistance was a form of incitement, a growing pressure on him to retaliate, to take her out of the waiting period and into the real and totally unique experience, the final fulfillment.

She did not cry out as Virgie had, *get it over,*

get it over, or anything of that sort.

Her energy was exhausted. She could express herself only in muffled sobs of hopeless rage and despair.

He switched off the lights. He tasted the darkness. To deepen it and transcend the imprisonment of this particular time and space, he closed his eyes. Once he sat in the front seat of a roller-coaster car with Sis. It climbed and climbed to the sky and went over the hump at the top of the first and highest and steepest downpitching stretch of track. They could feel the forward glide approaching the brink and there was a dread in his gut and Sis yelled, *Shut your eyes, don't look, don't look, the track is gone.* And she laughed and their car plunged and they screamed and wild sexual sensations burned his pants, and at the bottom of the grade, beginning the swift neck-jerking new climb, he realized he was alive.

He opened his eyes and they were at the top of another climb and then they were there, he and Pam, on the glide toward the brink and he was throbbing with a pantsbuster.

The darkness was imperfect, a deep grayness that bled the color from her hair and eyes. The contour of her exquisitely balanced top-heavy oval face emerged, an almost ghostly luminosity.

He was peering down at her when she spoke, quietly. Very quietly. Too quietly to hear.

"What did you say?" he said.

She repeated. He bent closer, straining.

"What?"

She talked in a dull monotone and her voice hovered at the very edge of silence and even her lips seemed fearful of disturbing that silence because they did not seem in the shadowiness to move at all.

The third time she spoke, he barely managed to make out the words. After an uneasy hesitation he catered to her senseless whim, obeying it as if it were a command. He went over and looked at himself in the wall mirror above the counter. He stared at his murky reflection and awaited further instructions from her.

She issued them at once. Not just obedience, but creative obedience was called for. He was expected to catch the almost inaudible words, decipher their meaning, and take the initiative in carrying out her orders. She ignored the fact she was conquered, at his mercy. It was as if her power were so absolute and irresistible that she didn't even need it to control him. Her tone was unassertive, unemphatic, her voice very soft, and she didn't stir. If he was going to hear, he had to move to her will. He went back to the bed.

Her words flowed together, swift as thought. It tensed him to keep up. Everything was mystifying, incomprehensible. It was not his to reason why but to do or die. Moving again to her command he found himself returning to that mirror.

He was peering at her ghostly image when he had an eerie sense that she was receding deeper into the shadows and he was slipping backward away from her and there was no floor under him.

There was an immeasurable period of nothingness. He came out of limbo. He reoriented himself. They were just where they had been. He stood facing the mirror. She lay on the bed behind him. Everything seemed to be the same as it had been.

Still, the darkness had another atmosphere that was no part of this placelss place, this motel room in Keystone. It belonged to another night, another room, a bedroom in a special place, a lost dream world, the high tower where dwelt the shimmeringly beautiful golden princess and where the night was filled with music. . . .

Absurd! A trick. He had been alert for sudden moves or stealthy movement of her hand to the phone or the sound of dialing. Her strategy was infinitely subtler. She had evoked the mood of that night before she had come on this tour, and hynotically she had enmeshed him in it.

She was truly an artist. No wonder she had been able to create—to *co*create with him—that powerful fantasy in which he had been able to truly believe in his own innocence. That perfect goodness in her made possible all beautiful things. He had not been wrong in attributing to her the meaning of Easter and of resurrection from the dead into a new and superior life that obliterated past evils. The fantasy had not begun to disintegrate till that night when he'd felt her going away as imminent death.

His love had come to seem truly exalted. Lustless. Spiritual. He'd told her that he recognized her as the physical embodiment of the beauty of her violin's music the first time he saw her. She'd cherished that lover's version and so had he. Poetry. Better than truth. The grubbier truth was that he'd seen her from shrubbery outside her dorm at bedtime on several unforgettably stimulating occasions.

Instinctively Pam was now trying to restore their shattered fantasy by making him reexperience that night before she had come on this tour.

She'd conveyed a fact he had not guessed. She had not been asleep while he had been in the bedroom fondling the panties in her drawer. She had been aware of his powerful lust. She had not understood at all that those dead California girls had resurfaced in his mind. But she'd seen him fold his arms across his chest, clamp his hands to his sides, putting himself into an imaginary straitjacket.

At first she had supposed he was chilly and was hugging himself the way she sometimes did.

Just the idea of chilliness affected him insidiously. His upper body felt cold right now.

Without thinking he started to hug himself. He stopped instantly.

His eyes skittered nervously, then settled

and narrowed. He stared suspiciously at her in the mirror.

There was a fierce, dancing heat in his groin. They were physically in the same relative position to one another as they had been that night. Bedclothes had covered her then, containing the warmth and heady scent of her soft body. Now, it was maddeningly naked. So was her strategy.

She intended to ease him into the exact emotional condition he had been in that night. So that he would put himself into another mental straitjacket, immobilized.

Goddamnittohell, it couldn't be done without *his* consent, *his* will to believe. The only power she had ever had over him was what he had invested in her. An illusory power, a fantasy, *his* fantasy. It was done. There was no way to reverse time and get back into that fantasy.

He'd still been in it and fighting to stay there, that night. So he had not been able to break free of the imaginary straitjacket. He had not let himself know what he wanted to do.

She had not known, either, sensing only that his conflict was intense. Dangerous. Just how dangerous she now knew.

She had succeeded in slowing his momentum, weakening his craving for the ultimate joy to a painful throbbing.

He brought himself back up to high pitch with a cat-and-mouse ploy.

He slowly assumed the straitjacketed position.

For quite some time he just stood there and she just lay there. At last he began a mock struggle to break out of his self-imprisonment.

She became convinced that he could not break free, that this was the test of the truth about himself. He laughed inwardly, exultantly, throughout the preposterous dialogue they engaged in.

She told him he would not do her further harm and could not go beyond terrorizing her and inflicting verbal abuse and moderate physical pain. She informed him with sweet solemnity that he was incapable of carrying out any sustained pattern of torture. His jabbing an ember into Mona's buttock had been unintended, and he had not inflicted any more agonies. She told him to remember he'd failed to kill Darleen. She reminded him that even while he still intended to do it, he decided to crush her skull and get it done with fast. In order to spare her unnecessary fright and pain.

He was amazed at Pam's omniscience. How could she know all those things she could not have known about in detail? She couldn't.

He realized everything she'd seemed to say must have actually been his own mind's working, as if in a dream.

Gradually he felt the dream thinning out and consciousness returning.

Pam was saying his name over and over and

desperately shaking him and telling him to wake up, wake up, he was walking in his sleep and dreaming terrible things and scaring her. . . .

And then, gloriously, he recognized his surroundings. He knew where he was and when it was, their own bedroom, the night before she was going on tour. He embraced her passionately. It was all right, all right. She had not gone yet. He had not done any such thing as get drunk in an unlucky thirteen kind of bar or kill somebody named Mona. None of it had happened, the nightmarish days and nights had not yet been lived.

Best of all he had not gone on any wild trip to overtake Pam on tour and do terrible things to her that would have wrecked their marriage . . . or worse. . . .

The sobering light of dawn deflected from the closed drapes to whiten the ceiling and spill out over the carpet and beds. He sat in an armchair gazing across at her sleeping beautifully.

Light climbed the sky. The phone rang frequently. Now and then he heard some of her friends calling her name and knocking at the door. Soon enough she would be getting up and would have to leave on the tour. Meantime he gazed on her tenderly.

The voices outside were louder and insistent and the knocking more urgent and the door was unlocked and pushed noisily to the end of the chain and aggressive male voices threatened and people saw him.

He looked down at his lap. There was a residue from that bad dream. A dangle of strings and shattered red-gold wood. He patted her smashed violin and after a while some policemen smashed through the door.

"Hi, fellas," he said cheerily, and later, getting into the police car, he asked, "Are we going for a ride?"

He expected they were thinking something, and sure enough one of them said it, nastily.

"Crazy as a loon!"

He smiled.

MAKE THE MOST OF YOUR *LEISURE* TIME WITH THESE TIMELY LEISURE NOVELS

MORE BLOOD-CHILLERS FROM LEISURE BOOKS

Make the Most of Your Leisure Time with
LEISURE BOOKS

Please send me the following titles:

Quantity	Book Number	Price
_____	_____	_____
_____	_____	_____
_____	_____	_____
_____	_____	_____
_____	_____	_____

If out of stock on any of the above titles, please send me the alternate title(s) listed below:

_____	_____	_____
_____	_____	_____
_____	_____	_____
_____	_____	_____

Postage & Handling _____

Total Enclosed $ _____

☐ Please send me a free catalog.

NAME _____
(please print)

ADDRESS _____

CITY _____ STATE _____ ZIP_____

Please include $1.00 shipping and handling for the first book ordered and 25¢ for each book thereafter in the same order. All orders are shipped within approximately 4 weeks via postal service book rate. PAYMENT MUST ACCOMPANY ALL ORDERS.*

*Canadian orders must be paid in US dollars payable through a New York banking facility.

Mail coupon to: **Dorchester Publishing Co., Inc.**
6 East 39 Street, Suite 900
New York, NY 10016
Att: ORDER DEPT.